DIAMONDS AREN'T FOREVER

DIAMONDS AREN'T FOREVER

CONNIE SHELTON

W⊕RLDWIDE

TORONTO • NEW YORK • LONDON
AMSTERDAM • PARIS • SYDNEY • HAMBURG
STOCKHOLM • ATHENS • TOKYO • MILAN
MADRID • WARSAW • BUDAPEST • AUCKLAND

W⊕RLDWIDE™

Recycling programs
for this product may
not exist in your area.

ISBN-13: 978-1-335-90143-9

Diamonds Aren't Forever

First published in 2017 by Secret Staircase Books,
an imprint of Columbine Publishing Group, LLC.
This edition published in 2024.

Harlequin Enterprises ULC
22 Adelaide St. West, 41st Floor
Toronto, Ontario M5H 4E3, Canada
www.ReaderService.com

Printed in U.S.A.

AUTHOR'S NOTE

As always, I have a huge amount of gratitude for everyone who helped shape this book into its final version. Dan Shelton, my husband and helpmate of twenty-seven years, puts up with less-than-regular meals and a less-than-clean house during my weeks of the initial first-draft stage. Editors Susan Slater and Shirley Shaw spot the plot and character flaws and help smooth the rough bits in the prose. And topping off the effort are my beta readers, who drop everything in their own lives to read and find the typos that inevitably sneak past me. Thank you for your help with this book: Judi Shaw, Debra Bolling, Paula Webb, Marcia Koopmann, Elaine Pool, Sandy Fields, Becky Johnson, Richard Butler, Christine Johnson, Ginger Griffin, Sandra Anderson, Dot Wichert, Katherine Munro, Lisa Train, Maria Edrozo, Debbie Wilson, Jeanie Jackson, Carol Blacklock, Gail Wolf, Joanne Horak, Jan Evans, Susan Gross, Jane Parker, Isobel Tamney and Ginger Weinstein. You guys are the best!

ONE

MORE THAN FIFTY carats of diamonds, twenty-eight of emeralds—the stones sparkled with a brilliance Penelope Fitzpatrick had forgotten. She held the necklace with both hands, once again taken with its beauty. Strands of platinum formed a winding ribbon studded with diamonds, the ribbon looping into five simple bows with an oval-cut emerald at the knot of each. When worn, two of the bows touched collarbones, while the other three tracked enticingly downward toward cleavage. Before Penelope, her mother had occasionally worn the necklace—the masterpiece design flattered any woman who put it on.

"Safe and sound," said the private investigator.

"Yes." She finally raised her eyes to look at the man. It was the first time she'd noticed touches of gray in his hair. "Thank you. I can't tell you what this means to me."

"Just doing my job, ma'am." Dick Stone accepted the check she handed him, beamed a most sincere smile and turned to leave.

Penelope walked him to her carved front door and watched him cross the flagstone veranda to his late-model sedan. Even for Scottsdale, her spacious, mountainside home was a showpiece with its tiled roundabout and winding drive. She watched the car begin its descent to the valley below.

Already, the April day had begun to warm into the eighties. How lucky she'd been to find this special property, perched on the side of Camelback Mountain, with sweeping views of the city and yet far above the fray of freeway traffic, noise and heat generated by the millions of people below in the Valley of the Sun. And how extremely lucky that the advance for her last three books had afforded her this luxury. She stepped back into the cool foyer with its travertine floors and the thick walls which protected her insular little world.

She picked up the necklace and ran her fingers along the ribbon of diamonds, coming to the clasp and unclipping it with more difficulty than she remembered. The arthritis was minor, only an unwanted reminder of her age. And, really—wasn't seventy the new forty? She refastened the clasp behind her neck, stepping in front of the mirror above her hall table.

Spreading the collar of her green silk blouse, she made a couple of minor adjustments and smiled at her own reflection. An image of her father's face came to her, stern and commanding. He had admonished her to take great care with the few remaining pieces from her grandfather, one of several jewelers to the last tsar of Russia. She sighed. How close she had come to losing this, the most elegant of all.

TWO

Stopped at the traffic light on Shea Boulevard, Frank Morrell leaned toward his rearview mirror and checked his hair. The touches of gray had fooled the old lady. She had that Lauren Bacall sophistication—classy, surely into her seventies—but who knew how good her eyesight was? The main thing was, could he pull off the disguise with a younger person when he got to the airport?

He decided he could—after all, the hair color had come from the supplier used by the best Hollywood makeup artists. If it stood up to high-def photography, it could surely pass inspection in what he hoped would be no more than a fifteen-minute transaction.

The light changed. He pulled through the intersection and made a quick right turn into the parking lot of a busy tire store. From his inner jacket pocket he pulled the wallet containing his Richard Stone identity. A fake driver's license and three credit cards—handy for the rental car and airline ticket. None of them would stand up to an actual credit check, but by the time anyone might go that far he would have discarded this persona completely.

Dick Stone. He laughed aloud. Stone, Dick. Did the old lady not see the complete joke about a guy who called himself Stone Dick? Frank loved his work, especially his ability to be anyone he wanted and to have a sense of humor about it.

Frank Morrell, Junior had learned from the best. Frank Senior had settled the family near Evansville, Indiana, where nearby communities of gypsies had brought the finest of con games and swindling techniques to America four generations earlier. The elder Morrell soaked up their knowledge like a sponge and by the time his young son could walk and talk, the two had worked up a series of routines such as the "My kid's desperate—can he use your bathroom?" ploy. While Pop chatted up the lady of the house, Frankie's instructions were to head straight for her bedroom and find her jewelry box. With his pockets full of swag, a flush of the toilet for authenticity, the two were out of the house and the lady never knew what hit her.

Frankie had watched the sweetheart con play out so often that he'd seduced his first wealthy older woman when he was fourteen. The forty-something mark honestly believed her handsome suitor was twenty-five, and she practically glowed every time she showed him off at one of her snobby society functions. Even after her late husband's insurance, retirement funds and real estate were completely gone, the poor delusional thing didn't realize Frankie had planned and carried out the con well in advance. If she knew what had happened, she was probably too humiliated to admit it.

The current mark, Penelope Fitzpatrick, was no rube. He'd tested the waters, only to learn that Fitzpatrick had a gentleman friend already and the guy's background was in law enforcement. A past district attorney or some such. Frank's motto was never to associate with someone on the right side of the law unless he knew he had that person firmly in his pocket. He'd steered completely clear of Fitzpatrick's friend.

He took another look now in the rented Toyota's rearview mirror. From a small black case on the passenger seat he pulled a bottle and small brush, adding a few more touches of gray to his dark brown hair. A stick of purplish makeup gave him a pretty realistic scar across his nose. It rarely failed—a prominent scar drew attention so well that the person would rarely remember enough other details about him to make a positive ID. As added insurance, he daubed a tiny stroke of black across the corner of one front tooth, making it appear chipped.

If the police should get far enough along to ask questions about the man who'd cashed one very large check, neither the teller's memory nor the bank security cameras would be able to pinpoint the real Frank Morrell. Not that his mugshot existed anywhere around here. Frankie always managed to vanish just ahead of the lawmen who sought to question him for his little infractions. He stuck with big cities, east coast and Midwest mostly, where the caseloads discouraged overworked police departments from pursuing the small stuff. This was his first trip to Phoenix and would be the last for a good, long time. For the big stuff— hell, he'd never even been suspected by the police, and the marks were always too embarrassed to admit how stupid they'd been.

He stashed the makeup items, dropped the black case over into the backseat, gave himself a final glance in the mirror, and started the rented Corolla. While the air conditioning took effect, he admired the number of zeros on the check the old lady had just handed him. With a smile he folded the paper and put it into his wallet. Now, off to the bank.

THREE

Penelope straightened her collar with a crisp tug, concealing all but the centermost of the diamond bows with its stunning emerald center. No more museum displays for the historic piece. She was taking it straight to her safe deposit box, right this minute. Quickly checking the doors, picking up her purse and phone, she walked through her fully equipped chef-worthy kitchen and out the connecting door to the garage.

Her Mercedes sat alone in one of the three slots in the cavernous room, which was cleaner and more organized than most people's houses. Occasionally, Benton's SUV stayed a night in the bay next to her trim convertible. She smiled. Twenty years ago, after Joseph Fitzpatrick's heart attack left her a widow, she and Benton struck up a friendship, eventually became lovers, and had settled in recent years back into companionship of the steady, comforting sort. They shared confidences and meals, plus she had to admit they made a stunning couple at Phoenix's variety of society events and charity fundraisers. He, a good four inches taller than she, sported still-thick silver hair. There was a time—she flushed at the memory—when not a single boy in school wanted to date the girl who was nearly six feet tall. Time, and a better selection of dates, had eased her into the present where she was comfortable in her skin.

The garage door glided upward and she started the little car, the favorite of all she'd ever owned. Down the winding drive, through the stone portal at the end, turning right at the bottom of the hill, Penelope negotiated her way through traffic and steered into the parking lot at Desert Trust Bank. She glanced affectionately at her car as she clicked the remote lock. It would be fun to put the top down on the way home.

Inside the bank she scanned the lobby. While several of the tellers could help her, Penelope preferred to deal directly with Sandy Werner, the branch manager who'd been with Desert Trust since Pen opened her accounts there. Sure enough, in the glass-enclosed corner office, she spotted Sandy at her desk talking on the phone. A moment later, the manager hung up the receiver and gave a wave of recognition. The bright smile, friendly blue eyes and neatly coiffed blonde hair were a few of the things Pen liked about the slightly plump woman in her tidy sapphire business suit.

"Mrs. Fitzpatrick, how nice to see you today," Sandy said, meeting Penelope at her office door. "How are you?"

"I'm especially well. It's been a wonderful day."

Sandy started to lead the way into her office but the older woman stopped, explaining that she needed to get into her safe deposit box. The manager pulled a small ring of keys from her pocket and led the way toward the vault. Pen signed the log and produced her own key, standing by while Sandy inserted them both and opened the door concealing the metal box behind it.

"Let me just get you settled into one of the private rooms," she said over her shoulder as she opened a door and flipped a light switch.

She set the metal box on the built-in desk and turned to face Pen again.

"Let me know when you're finished." Her glance went

to Penelope's throat. "Oh, I *love* your necklace. The style looks Russian."

"You have a very good eye. That's where it was made." She reached up and unhooked the clasp behind her neck.

"Well, I've always loved jewelry of every type," Sandy said, "but I've recently been studying a book on the Russian crown jewels. My gosh, they spared no expense in those days, did they?"

Pen chuckled. "That's true. My grandfather made this one. It was to be for the tsar but, unfortunately, the royal family was deposed only days before he planned to deliver it."

Sandy's face went a shade lighter than her natural ivory, her expression shocked. "Oh my gosh."

"Of course, I only know this story as family lore. My father was an infant and the family escaped within moments of grandfather's shop and home being raided and burned. Apparently they grabbed everything they could and ran for the hills, so to speak. Although a few wars took their toll, they escaped to England where my father grew up and met my mother. I was actually born in London."

"I wondered. You still have a slight trace of an accent. So you've been in America a long time?"

"Oh, yes. This country has always been home to me."

Sandy's eyes went to the necklace, which Penelope had removed.

"May I look closely?"

"Of course." Penelope placed the historic piece in the banker's hands. "Grandfather made my ring too. For my grandmother. Three generations of us have worn it."

Sandy turned her attention to the ring on Penelope's left hand. Diamonds formed the loops of a bow, very similar to the design on the necklace.

"Are they a set?"

"That's what I was told. Father told me there was a third piece, a crown made for the tsarina, which is styled very much like the necklace. I have a photograph of her wearing it. Apparently, she loved it so much that she commissioned the necklace. Had things—history—gone differently, she would have also owned the ring and they say grandfather had designs drawn and ready to make a matching bracelet."

Sandy touched the ring, staring at the setting with its perfectly proportioned stones and the emerald in the center of the bow knot. Penelope opened her safe deposit box and pulled out an envelope, from which she drew a small sheaf of photographs. A sepia-toned one did, indeed, show the famous tsarina wearing a crown of diamonds formed into the shapes of ribbon-tied bows encircling her head.

"It's fantastic," Sandy said, handing back the necklace. At the last second she paused. "May I just take one more look?"

She adjusted her glasses and ran a fingernail over the clasp. "Did you have this replaced at some point?" she murmured.

Penelope shook her head. "No, it's mostly been either in storage or on display with the royal jewels collection. No one has ever worked on it."

Sandy took Pen's hand and held the ring finger closely to the desk lamp, then did the same with the necklace. She handed it back to its owner.

"Mrs. Fitzpatrick, I don't quite know how to tell you this. These two pieces weren't made by the same jeweler. I really believe the necklace is a fake."

"My dear, how would you know that?" Pen's voice sounded cool but her heart was pounding and she could hear the pulse rushing in her ears.

"Well, I mentioned that I've always loved jewelry… I've

taken classes and made a few pieces myself. Nothing at all like this, of course," she said, apology brimming in her voice. "It's just that in studying various artisan's techniques and skills, we practiced identifying the work of various masters. I'm no professional—and I certainly suggest you see one—but even to my eye I seriously doubt these pieces were made by the same person. The ring has the patina of wear, of course, which the necklace does not, plus there are other little differences such as the way the prongs were constructed and the stones mounted. If you know the ring is genuine, then the necklace came from someone else."

The robbery. The stolen item's recovery. Pen felt her legs start to give way. She pulled out the chair at the desk and quickly lowered herself to it, clutching the heirloom necklace until her hands ached.

FOUR

PEN CARRIED THE velveteen bag she'd removed from her bank box, experiencing an otherworldly feeling as she stepped through the open door Sandy Werner held for her.

"Are you sure you're all right to drive?" the banker asked.

The older woman blinked, shaking off the feeling. "Yes, fine, thanks. The glass of water did help."

"Good." Werner met Pen's gaze with her own steady blue eyes. "And I'm sorry to be the bearer of bad news. I really do hope your friend says I'm wrong about the necklace."

Penelope nodded, unable to think of a good response. Surely, Sandy Werner had to be wrong. Certainly. After all, she was a banker, not a jewelry expert. Penelope zipped the velveteen pouch inside her leather handbag and walked to her car. She could think of only one place to go—to the jeweler with whom she had worked for two decades, the certified gemologist who had appraised her collection for insurance purposes, the man who'd made several of Pen's favorite pieces. His shop sat on North Street in the heart of Scottsdale's most exclusive shopping district. She took it as a positive sign when she was able to get a parking spot a short walk from the front door.

Regis Potts came from the back room immediately when Penelope identified herself to the young woman at the counter. His perfectly capped teeth and neat, receding gray hair went well with the thousand-dollar business suit and five-carat diamond pinky ring, the dazzler all of his clients wanted to emulate in their own collections.

"Pen, how lovely to see you again!" Regis was nothing if not a consummate host.

He started to ask how he might help her, but it took a fraction of a second for him to notice how distraught she was.

"Come, come. Let's sit in my office and visit a moment." He raised his eyes to his clerk. "Juliane, a pot of tea please."

The young woman nodded and scurried away while Regis steered Penelope gently toward the room where they'd transacted most of their business. Furnished more like a living room than a business office, the lighting nonetheless was aimed toward the antique coffee table and designed to give gold, silver and gemstones the best possible effect to please the customer and ensure a tidy sale.

Regis indicated the grouping of sofa and two comfortable armchairs, and Penelope chose one of the striped brocade chairs.

"Pen, we've known each other a very long time. I would ask if you're doing well, but at a glance I can tell something has greatly upset you."

She reached into her purse and brought out the cloth bag, starting to undo the drawstring top, when Juliane arrived with a fully laden tea tray. Pen dropped the jewelry bag into her lap until Regis had taken the tray, centered it in the middle of the table and indicated he would pour. Both waited until Juliane had closed the door behind her. Wisely, Regis continued to hold back and let Penelope make the next move.

She thrust the bag into his hands. "Please tell me what this is."

"What do you think it is?" he said after lifting the exquisite necklace and holding it up in the light. The diamonds and emeralds sparkled with such intensity Pen felt somewhat reassured. Sandy Werner had been wrong. But he was holding it overly long.

"You're familiar with my collection," she said nervously. "You know these pieces intimately and have appraised them for insurance companies who are extremely particular about such things."

Something in his face closed ever so slightly.

"Are you…?"

"Oh, Regis, I'm not doubting you at all. I'm doubting the necklace. Please tell me it's mine, that it's real."

In a flash, he pulled a loupe from his jacket pocket and concentrated upon the individual stones. Each place he focused his attention caused his head to shake a bit more firmly.

"It's not. I'm so sorry but this isn't the same piece I've seen before. I can tell you that without even consulting my measurements and diagrams. The stones are decent copies but they are of the variety created in the laboratory. Cubic zirconia, lab emeralds. The platinum may be real but, if so, it's a very thin veneer of plating over something far more base. More likely, it's not even that."

"Someone said it's the workmanship that gives it away."

He nodded. Did she detect moisture in his eyes. "I'm afraid it's not even close to your grandfather's work. To put it crudely, if his work competed in the World Series, this is high school softball." He dropped the necklace with a thump on the black velvet display board he always kept on hand. "My dear, how did this happen?"

FIVE

THE WHOLE STORY spilled out. The necklace going on loan to the Philpont Museum for a show on the royal jewels of Europe, the robbery six months ago where three armed men took the night guards by surprise and were able to bypass the museum's supposedly state-of-the-art security system. The police working the case for a few months but leads petering out quickly. Penelope's desperate hope that the private investigator might have better luck, not being constrained by the complexities of a bureaucracy. Dick Stone's call yesterday that he had located her piece and would deliver it today.

"I was so thrilled to see it again, I didn't even look closely. Regis, I feel like such a fool, a bloody *old* fool. Why didn't I bring it to you before I paid him for his services?"

"Darling, it's not your fault. You are the victim in all this."

Penelope felt herself bristle. "One thing I am not, my friend, is a *victim* sort of person. I shall figure out what to do."

Her mind raced. "I need to place a phone call."

He excused himself, leaving her alone in the office. She pulled out her phone and immediately dialed the bank.

"Sandy, I need you to stop payment on a check for me." She gave the information, having to take a deep breath when she got to the amount, $104,000 which represented the detective's hourly rate plus a finder's fee. Why she had ever agreed to that, she had no idea. Desperation—it had caused her to act rashly.

The bank's catchy theme music played, interrupted by perky-sounding ads for brokerage services and the best rates on CDs. Pen's exasperation rose as a full eight minutes ticked by before Sandy Werner came back on the line.

"I'm afraid it's not good news," she said.

Pen felt her spine stiffen.

"The check has already been cashed."

"Cashed? My god, I thought at the worst it would be sitting in his account."

"He walked into the Paradise Valley branch and convinced someone it was your wish that he have access to the cash immediately. Of course since there was no question of there being sufficient funds in your account…the assistant manager told me he verified your signature and, well, apparently the man was very persuasive. He left there not more than fifteen minutes ago."

Silence from Penelope as her mind churned.

"Mrs. Fitzpatrick?" Sandy had tears in her voice. "I'm so sorry. I wish I knew what to do."

"I'll call the police right now. Maybe there's still something…"

"I feel personally responsible somehow."

"Nonsense, Sandy. If nothing else, it was your sharp eye that led me to question the necklace's authenticity immediately. Perhaps there's a chance the police can retrieve the money yet."

"Please let me know what they say. If there's anything at all I can do—"

SIX

FRANK MORRELL BREEZED out of the Paradise Valley branch of Desert Trust Bank twenty minutes after he walked in. There had been one brief moment of anxiety, when the female teller decided to call on a male assistant manager to okay the cashing of such a large check. Frankie wowed them with his best smile and sent the teller a secret wink. *Sure, I understand*, the gesture said, *must make sure the customer has enough in her account to clear this.*

He made inane small talk with the cute little teller, kept his gaze averted from the security cameras, while inwardly holding his breath. This was one area where it could all go wrong. As a rule he stayed away from technology. No GPS in a car, no cell phone registered under his own name or that of his many aliases. Pop had coached him well. *Don't make their job easier, son. Make them work hard to find you.*

Yeah, that was the golden age of grifting, back in Pop's day. No internet. None of that Facebook crap where people looked up all their old high school buddies (not that Frank had buddies back in school). Movies today showed the government with eyes everywhere and ways of tracking a guy to the ends of the earth. Frank knew the reality wasn't quite so weighted in favor of the law. He tested the limits and still managed to get away every single time. His offshore accounts were divided into small enough amounts Uncle wouldn't be interested, not to mention the money was in many banks under many names.

Still, times were changing. He had plenty of cash to live in fine style for the rest of his life, even if he made it to a hundred, double his father's age. Maybe he ought to think about retiring after this one. Break down the real necklace, have the big stones recut, the smaller ones sold off as needed… Yeah, he could live a long time on what he already had.

The assistant manager had returned with apologies for the delay, along with twenty paper-banded packs of hundred-dollar bills. They fit easily into Frank's briefcase. Obviously, Penelope Fitzpatrick's account was well funded.

He practiced nonchalance as he closed the case and walked out of the bank. He'd parked the Toyota at the edge of the parking lot, out of sight of the people he'd just dealt with. Ten minutes later he was on the ramp to the 101 freeway. He let out a whoop. How could he even consider giving up this life?

From the moment he'd closed his fingers around that check for more than a hundred thousand dollars, Frank had debated the split with his partners. A long con like this one required the help of insiders. The agreement had been a small fee up front with a 30-30-40 split at the end, Frankie taking the larger share because he'd come up with the idea and had fronted all expenses.

Okay, the others had done their parts. But c'mon, they weren't the pros here. Frankie planned and executed the job and took the risk. Those guys had earned their fees but, he decided on the spot, that was it. He'd remained vague about exactly when and where they would meet up. Good thing. Because Frankie Morrell was on his way to the airport.

SEVEN

PENELOPE ASSURED SANDY WERNER she would stay in touch, ended the call and dialed the number for Detective William Caplin, the head of the Major Crimes unit, the man who had led the initial investigation of the museum robbery and the one who'd given her the name of retired detective Richard Stone who was now a private investigator.

"Of course, Mrs. Fitzpatrick, I remember you. I'm afraid we have nothing new on the museum case. As I told you back in February, we followed all the leads we had. Nothing's changed."

"I take it you haven't talked with your friend, Mr. Stone." She could hear the chill in her own voice.

"Well, not since our First Fridays gathering a couple weeks ago. Bunch of us meet up for lunch at a pub we like, once a month."

"Did he say anything about my missing necklace?"

"Why would he? I'd asked him awhile back if he'd taken your case and he said he never heard from you. I assumed you'd given up on recovering the piece and just decided to file with your insurance company."

"That's not at all true," she said, sitting straighter in her seat in hopes it gave her voice more authority. "Your so-called *friend* has lied to you. I've been in contact with him regularly and he came to my home this morning. He brought the recovered necklace—except that it's a fake. I want the man arrested."

She could hear papers rustling at his end of the call.

"Describe him to me," Caplin said in a terse voice.

"You know him!"

"I know the Richard Stone I recommended, retired police officer, one of the most honest men on the planet."

"He's in his late forties, I suppose…slender, average height, dark hair with a little gray at the temples. I didn't notice his eye color."

"Rich Stone is sixty-two with a gut like a basketball. Pretty much bald on top, and his remaining hair is completely gray. How did you first meet the man you hired?"

"Called him, of course. At your reference." Of course, now that she thought about it, she'd left a message on a machine and waited for the investigator to return her call.

"Somehow, someone intercepted you." Caplin gave a large sigh. "I'm afraid you've been taken in by a con man."

"Can't you put out a warrant, catch him and arrest him? I'll be happy to pick him from a lineup or whatever it is you do in these cases."

"You said he came to your home. What was he driving? Did you get a license plate number?"

"It was an average sedan—I don't know what make. And no, I didn't memorize the license. Why would I have thought to do that?"

"Ma'am, with the description you just gave me I'd have to bring in at least forty-thousand men in this city alone." He let a moment go by. "Did he touch anything at your house, surfaces we might take prints from?"

She thought about it. Stone had worn white gloves when he handed over the necklace. At the time she thought keeping the stones clean showed professionalism on his part. Now it looked as if he was a pro of a different sort.

"Our bunco division has mug shot books of known con artists in the area. You're certainly welcome to come downtown and go through them. Maybe you'll spot him. It would at least give us a starting place."

Her hopes rose a bit. Surely she would know Dick Stone's face if she saw the right photo.

"I'll warn you though, it's very likely this is a guy from somewhere else. Chances are, he left your house this morning, abandoned that plain vanilla car and picked up his real one. He could be halfway to California, Utah or New Mexico by now."

"But—"

"The story of the museum robbery made national headlines six months ago. That's ages in the life of a master criminal—plenty of time for him to commission a copy of your necklace and show up, promising he could find it with his superior detecting skills. It might have been pure luck that he chose the name of the same retired detective I recommended, but more likely he found some way to listen around, put out feelers and figure out that I would give you Rich Stone's name. These con guys have uncanny good instincts."

"So, there's nothing we can do?"

"I'll review the case file, put the word out and see if I get any hits. It's possible the museum people may have some ideas, although we pretty well beat that horse to death months ago. I'd suggest you file an insurance claim on the necklace and get on with your life. The odds you'll ever see your real one again are slim to none. Lower than that— minuscule to non-existent."

EIGHT

AT THE RENTAL car return office, Frank went into the men's room and removed the fake scar and scraped the touch of black off his tooth. The gray in his hair would have to be washed out, but he decided that wasn't such a problem. The fact that his hair was dark on his ID and a bit gray in reality would only muddy the process if the police began questioning people, asking them to describe him. The answers would be so jumbled they would have no real idea who they were after. He grinned at himself in the mirror.

With the locked briefcase gripped tightly in one hand and a wheeled carry-on bag in the other, he entered the airport. The new kiosk check-in method suited him perfectly—no chatty ticket agent to see his face up close. He'd already planned his route and chosen the airline most amenable to last-minute changes. In under five minutes his existing ticket for San Diego was changed to an earlier flight to Miami.

He wheeled his bag to the security area, pleased to see the lines were long and the TSA agents harried. A shift change was due to take place in twenty minutes so none of them would want to get into a lengthy examination of a passenger. As long as you gave them no reason to suspect you.

Of course Frank had a huge piece of bling and a hundred thousand reasons in his briefcase.

"Is that cash in your briefcase?" asked the agent who'd done a double-take at the monitoring screen.

"Yes, it is. I need for you to hold this case up where I can see it while I walk through the scanner. I'm not allowed to have it out of my sight."

Frank reached into his jacket and produced a business card. Richard Stone, Certified Gemologist, Tiffany and Co. He'd duplicated the famous logo exactly and used the exact font and card stock as the sample card he'd picked up at the store in Scottsdale. The laptop computer and small wireless printer in his carry-on bag were the sort any businessman might take on a trip.

The young agent didn't question a thing. He politely walked alongside Frank, carrying the cash and the real necklace until he placed the case back in Frank's hands. How stupid Frank's partners had been not to insist that one of them hold the real necklace while Dick Stone delivered the fake to Penelope Fitzpatrick. The difference between a rube and a pro, he thought with satisfaction.

"Thank you very much," Frank said to the TSA man, turning and smiling as he walked toward the gates.

The secret to a successful con is to become the role you are playing, Frank Senior had always told him. Right now, Frank was a Tiffany representative on his way from a meeting with a wealthy client to another meeting on the east coast. The Miami flight was being called for boarding as he approached. Feeling flush at the moment, he'd upgraded his ticket to first class so he walked right onto the plane.

In Miami he would visit the airport locker where he'd stashed his passport and a ticket he'd purchased for Cartagena, Columbia. A guy he knew there had a boat. Within forty-eight hours there would be no paper trail connected to either Dick Stone or Frank Morrell.

NINE

PENELOPE CLICKED OFF the call, feeling her hopes plummet. The detective was the second person to suggest an insurance claim. Maybe she should do it. But this was her grandfather's legacy. She couldn't simply let it go.

She dropped the phone into her purse and stood up, almost at the same moment Regis Potts opened the door. Had he been eavesdropping?

"Everything all right?" he asked.

Not at all. But she forced a smile to her lips. "I'll manage."

He carefully placed the necklace of fake stones back into the velveteen bag she'd carried in. "The tea's gone cold, I'm sure, but I can have Juliane brew another pot if that would help."

"Thank you, Regis, but no. I need to be on my way."

She drove the familiar route up the mountain to her home. As she was getting out of her Mercedes, her cell phone rang. Detective Caplin wasted no words.

"I've been back in touch with Todd Wainwright, one of the assistants to the director of the Philpont."

"Yes—did he have any ideas about all of this?"

"He's now claiming their expert spotted the necklace as a fake a long time ago. Says they assumed you substituted a copy for their display to keep the real one out of danger."

"That's absurd! Detective, you don't actually believe

him, do you? They signed a receipt when they accepted the loan, stating they understood the piece's true value. I countersigned, acknowledging I had the loaned item insured under my own policy. To say, all these months later, that they never had the real necklace—" She sputtered, practically speechless.

"If you can produce that receipt, it would contradict what they're saying now, Mrs. Fitzpatrick, but it doesn't make them any more liable for the loss than they were before."

Pen felt her blood pressure rise, her heart thumping in her chest. She wanted to scream at him—something she'd never done, *ever*, in her life. English decorum had been bred in her and taught from her earliest days. The rudest move she could make was to hang up on him. She did so.

With shaking hands she unlocked her front door. Normally, Naomi would still be here, finishing her housekeeping duties for the day, preparing Penelope a simple dinner before going home to her own family. But Thursday was her day off and Pen faced an empty house. A good thing, she decided, still feeling as if she could bite the detective's head off.

Her phone rang again as she deposited her things on the hall table.

"What?" she answered with uncharacteristic abruptness.

"Mrs. Fitzpatrick, sorry to bother you again. It's Sandy, from the bank. I just thought I would check back with you, see if you're all right."

To her utter surprise, Penelope broke down in sobs. "I'm…fine."

"It doesn't sound that way," Sandy said, a tender note in her voice. "Can I do something for you? Meet you somewhere? I get off work in fifteen minutes. I could…"

Pen felt tears drip off her chin.

"Do you have anyone with you?" Sandy asked. "How about food—do you have anything for dinner? I could bring you something to eat."

A smile crossed Penelope's face. Sandy clearly wanted to take care of her. As if she were needy or poor. The offer was surprisingly touching, something no one had done for her in a very long time. She caught herself nodding, then remembered to speak.

"Dinner would be lovely, dear. But don't you have a family to get home to?"

"I don't. Aside from my cats, Heckle and Jeckle, I am as free as the proverbial bird. Shall we meet somewhere?"

Pen glanced around with a moment's hesitation. She'd already been burned by someone she thought she could trust, someone she had allowed into her home. On the other hand, she had no desire to go back out tonight and she'd known Sandy Werner for years.

"Come to my place. Bring whatever you're in the mood for. No, wait. Do you like pizza? I so rarely get a good slice of pizza—bring that."

Sandy laughed at the other end of the line. "Absolutely. I know an excellent pizza place. I'll phone in the order and be there…well, I guess you'd better give me your address."

Pen found it reassuring that Sandy had not gone into the bank's records to find out where she lived—she appreciated the privacy. She gave directions and Sandy said she could be there in thirty minutes.

Company for the evening would be nice, would help take her mind off today's shocking events. She went to her bedroom, changing from her silk blouse and narrow skirt to soft, loose pants and a fitted T-shirt. She gathered up her chin-length, pale blonde hair with a clip and added a touch of tinted lip balm to bring a hint of color back to her face.

Say what you will about aging, she thought as she stood by the cheval mirror in her room, I still look damn fine for seventy-two. She gave herself a little smile of encouragement. She'd escaped war-torn Britain as a child and outlived two husbands, the second trying his best to make off with what little she had inherited from the first. She'd dealt with crooks and criminals, snobs and socialites, and more than one man who thought he could or should control her life—and she had survived them all. Somehow she would get through this anguish, as well.

She firmed up the smile, thrust her shoulders back and went to the kitchen, where she located a bottle of red wine. Pairing wines with meats and seafood was something she felt comfortable with; choosing the right one to go with pizza was a bit new. The one she opened might be overkill for the occasion, but as any good American would say— what the heck.

TEN

HEADLIGHTS SKIMMED THE far wall of her living room as Sandy Werner pulled into the roundabout and parked. Penelope watched through the side glass as Sandy got out of her car and stared in wonder at the house. After a moment, though, she gathered her poise and picked up a cardboard pizza box from the backseat of her Mazda. She started slightly when she realized Penelope was standing in the open doorway, watching.

"Sorry, Mrs. Fitzpatrick, I can't help but say it—this place is awesome."

"First off, it's Penelope—Pen, if you wish—I can't manage to share wine and a pizza if we have a lot of formalities standing in the way. About the property, thanks. I chose it after my first decent advance on a book. My first husband and I lived in Chicago most of our twenty years together. I became weary of the cold, so I visited Phoenix for a month to get away and decide where my life would go. I never left."

She ushered her guest toward the kitchen.

"I hope this wine is the right thing," she said.

Sandy smiled, immediately at ease, and Pen realized the banker was no stranger to clients of great wealth, although it was likely she seldom visited their homes.

"I doubt you could go wrong when it comes to a wine for pizza." She set the box on the granite countertop and lifted the lid. "I got half pepperoni and half veggies. I should have asked what you wanted."

Penelope breathed deeply. "It all smells heavenly. Here are the glasses. Would you pour while I get plates?"

She switched on quiet background music and they sat at the breakfast table with its view of the glittering lights of the city spread out below.

"Sorry it was such a rough day for you," Sandy said. She raised her glass. "Here's to better tomorrows."

Pen flexed her eyebrows and nodded. Half a slice later, she began to recount her visit with the jeweler followed by the call to the police department. "And then the museum's absurd claim that they knew the necklace was a fake all along? Ridiculous! I'll have to fight them on that, most certainly. Otherwise, I don't really know what to do next."

"It was insured, I assume?"

"Yes, but how does one replace a family heirloom? My real necklace is worth more than a million dollars, the value of the stones alone. Its real value, as a piece designed for the tsarina, is priceless. A check from a corporation isn't going to replace it, I'm afraid."

"An insurance company will have investigators. With a payout that large, they'll go to great lengths to get the necklace back."

"For themselves—not for me. If I accept their check, I'm afraid I may never get the necklace back. It will belong to them and they'll sell it for a fortune, and that's just not right." She stopped, downed the last of her wine and refilled both glasses.

Sandy took another slice of the pepperoni. "So, what will you do?"

Pen shook her head sadly. "I don't know. I can't seem to think rationally today."

"You know what we should do?" Sandy said. "We should find out who this stupid fake investigator is and then steal the necklace back."

"Steal it back?"

"Sure."

"The two of us?"

Sandy chewed slowly, her eyes rolling upward as she thought. "We'll need a team. I'm pretty good with computer searches, but there's got to be someone who is truly a whiz at it. We'll get her to… I don't know…hack into some big database of criminals and get his name."

"And we'll automatically know where to find him, based on that?"

"Well, let's take this a step at a time. We can do it."

Pen drained her glass and realized they were halfway through a second bottle. A tiny voice inside told her she should not be making such a major decision right now. Could she trust Sandy? The voice chided: *what have I got to lose?*

"Okay, I'm switching to water," Sandy said, setting her wine glass down and rubbing her temples. "It's not a long drive for me, but I need to get home safely and then I have to wake up functional at seven in the morning."

Sandy folded the empty pizza box and asked where the trash basket was, then helped herself to a tumbler of water at the dispenser on the refrigerator door.

"I meant what I said about helping, Pen. I told you how I feel about very special pieces of jewelry. Now that I know a bit more about the history of this one, I can't stand to think of this shyster getting away with it. Not to mention, if he's this smooth about it then I'm sure it's not his first crime. Or his last. If the police aren't going to chase him down, then we will." She set the tumbler down with a clack against the counter. "So, I'll get out of your hair now, but I'm going to give this some thought. I'll let you know what I find out."

Pen still felt slightly giddy as she closed the door behind Sandy. Was it possible? Could she and a few friends actually solve this crime?

ELEVEN

EVEN AT MIDNIGHT, there probably wasn't a completely dark spot in the city. Street lights, traffic headlights, security lighting were everywhere, but here beneath the 202 overpass in east Mesa was as close to total darkness as a person could find.

Todd Wainwright pulled his Corvette into the deepest shadow, nervously peering every direction, wary of every slight movement. The idea of drug addicts or homeless people lurking around squeaky-clean Mesa was almost ludicrous. *Almost.* One never knew.

He spotted the other car and knew by the license tag it was one of the men he was supposed to meet. He steered toward it and stopped, the driver's side window of his low-slung car placing him a few inches below the corresponding side of the other vehicle. It felt like a disadvantage, as if he was the shortest guy at a cocktail party. Which shouldn't bother him—frequently, he was.

Both windows slid down. The men's eyes met. Todd looked for any sign of his own nervousness reflected in the other expression. There was none.

"So, where's Dick?" he said to the man across the way.

"Told you on the phone, I haven't heard from him all day. He told me yesterday he'd be here." The man glanced at his watch. "Any minute now."

Todd's stomach had been in knots for weeks, beginning the day he agreed to switch those documents in the Director's file cabinet. It all came down to this, tonight, the moment he would receive his share. Until he had that money in his hands he wouldn't relax. He looked at his dashboard clock. 12:17. Two minutes late.

Nothing to worry about. Except he noticed the other man's eyes darting every direction, watching rear and side mirrors, ahead, behind.

A car passed along Power Road, slowing. Both men became extra alert but it was soon obvious the car had slowed only to make the turn to the on-ramp. It entered the freeway and disappeared.

I'm not a bad person. Todd thought of his own culpability in this affair. When questioned by police he'd apologized profusely for the fact he'd *accidentally* forgotten to arm the security system that night six months ago.

12:38. Todd wriggled in his seat, impatient but wary of showing it. He was the youngest of the three men and they'd unabashedly treated him as the junior member.

"Can you call him?" he asked the guy across from him.

The man gave an irritated glare, but picked up his phone and pressed a number. He gnawed his lower lip while it rang. After a few seconds, he held the phone out and stared at the display, checking the signal strength. Listened again.

"No answer."

"How long should we wait?"

"We wait. Until he comes."

As particular as Dick Stone had been through the whole operation, the way each move was timed to the minute, Todd couldn't believe he'd simply allowed himself to run late now. Maybe there'd been an accident. These freeways were notorious for bumper-to-bumper crazy drivers.

At midnight?

Maybe Dick had gotten a ticket or something, or was stopped by a cop. Todd glanced at the other car. Nah. That wouldn't have happened. He thought once more of the precision timing of the museum robbery.

Todd's bosses had mildly questioned his need to work late that night, but he'd been smart enough to do it another time or two before, so the important occasion didn't stand out. The Assistant Director had put Todd in charge of checking the descriptive placards for a new exhibit on the mining history of Arizona to be set up Monday morning. Plus, no one else wanted to work late on a Sunday night.

Exactly as instructed, he'd 'remembered' the alarm twenty minutes later on his way home and rushed back to remedy his mistake. No, he didn't check the contents of the museum. He'd merely set the code and gone on home. Except that wasn't quite the whole story.

He'd gotten away with it. Only one other person besides the man sitting in the other car right now could reveal the truth and send him to prison.

TWELVE

PEN WOKE WITH a headache, a reminder she'd not consumed more than two glasses of wine in an evening for quite a number of years. Her entire head resonated with an insistent din. When it did not stop and she opened her eyes tentatively, she realized the noise came from her bedside telephone.

"Penelope, it's Sandy. I've already found someone and she's got a recommendation for our computer whiz."

What on earth? Pen felt like mumbling instructions that Sandy must wait until she'd at least risen from bed, put on her robe and brushed her teeth, but her mother's teachings on decorum forbade admitting one was still in bed at— heavens!—nine-thirty in the morning, much less responding in anything less than an entirely composed tone of voice.

She ran the fingers of her left hand through her hair, as if that might be a suitable substitute for combing it. Sandy continued to talk.

"It's a good friend. I absolutely trust her, although I'll leave it up to you to decide how much to tell about the necklace. Anyway, Gracie can tell you her own reasons for joining us."

Fragments of last night's loosely conceived plan came back to Pen as Sandy kept talking. The police were unhelpful, an insurance claim was out—the women would steal her necklace back from the crook who'd swindled her.

"Can you make it?" Sandy said.

Pen had to admit to letting her thoughts drift and asked Sandy to repeat.

"Lunch today, one o'clock at Brimmer's. I figured by going a little later we'd pretty much have the place to ourselves, and Gracie's husband is available to pick up their daughter and take her to ballet."

A child and a husband? School and ballet? How is this ever going to work? Pen squashed her doubts and agreed to the meeting. It couldn't hurt to talk about it.

In the bathroom, she swallowed two aspirin with a large glass of water and stepped into the shower. Twenty minutes later she felt like a new woman. Last night's excitement began to return, the idea she could have a hand in retrieving her lost treasure and she didn't need the police to do so. Well, it sounded good in theory anyway.

She thought about the place they were meeting for lunch, a casual sandwich shop in nearby Mesa, popular with college kids and young mothers. Pen knew of it only by its reputation. She chose tan slacks and a light peach cotton sweater for the occasion.

Breakfast consisted of a bowl of fruit and Greek yogurt, drizzled with honey and sprinkled with slivered almonds. Pen was glad she'd given Naomi an extra day off. Now she could concentrate on the plan she and Sandy had discussed only in the broadest terms last night.

She remembered Detective Caplin's offer for her to look at their collection of mug shots and, although the idea of paging through books in some cubicle of a room downtown didn't hold much appeal, she supposed she should do it. A vestigial twinge from her headache pinged her forehead. She decided she could visit Caplin tomorrow.

She spent the morning watering the bright, potted ge-

raniums on her back terrace and jotting notes pertaining
to the necklace—any little thing that might help locate it.
Unfortunately, there wasn't much. She had a hard time
thinking beyond her anger at the police for not handling
this more efficiently in the first place.

She arrived at Brimmer's a little early—the trip was
quicker than she'd anticipated—and sat in her car until she
saw Sandy Werner's blue Mazda pull into the lot at pre-
cisely 12:57. They walked inside together.

A woman with long, brunette hair waved from a far corner table. She stood and smiled. Dark eyes, dimples bracket-
ing perfectly aligned teeth, slender athletic build, probably
five-six or so. Penelope guessed she was in her mid-thirties.

"Penelope Fitzpatrick," the woman gushed. "I couldn't
believe it when Sandy said I would get to meet you today.
I'm a huge fan—*huge*. I mean, your book jackets say you
live in the Southwest but I assumed somewhere artsy...well,
like, Sedona or Taos or someplace."

Penelope smiled and wished they would hurry and sit
down.

Sandy spoke up. "Obviously, Pen, you need no introduc-
tion. This is my friend, Gracie Nelson."

Pen extended her hand and Gracie looked a tiny bit flus-
tered as she shook it. They weren't going to get far in a working relationship if the young woman kept up this star-struck
business, Pen thought.

"Let's just sit and relax," she suggested, noticing Gracie
had brought one of her books.

An autograph seeker, to boot. Suddenly, a glass of wine
with lunch sounded appealing. But she'd gotten herself
wrapped up in Sandy's enthusiasm for stealing the necklace, all because of a bottle of wine last night. Better to

keep a clear head and tread slowly here. She ordered iced tea from the server who approached their table.

They spent the next twenty minutes on their sandwiches—hers an excellent chicken salad, Pen noted—and getting to know each other.

Gracie was a suburban wife and mother of two ("Scott is a dear and he totally won't mind shuttling the kids around if I have to be somewhere else."). She pulled out her wallet and showed pictures. The husband's good looks went right along with his wife's. School photos showed a girl of eight with awkward teeth in need of braces and a teenage boy who, judging by the outfit he'd chosen for picture day, was somewhat on the nerdy side.

"So, what makes you want to get involved with my situation?" Penelope finally asked. So far, Gracie's main contribution seemed her claim to bake the most fabulous brownies on the planet.

"Sandy told me a little about what happened. No details, really, just that you'd been taken in by a con man who'd stolen something valuable and you two have decided to catch him and get it back."

She glanced back and forth between Sandy and Pen. "Frankly, I want to learn how to do it. My sister was swindled out of her entire life savings—this was about a year ago. She probably won't ever recover financially. Well, Sandy's heard this story before, but what I want to do is learn how to go about catching these types of bad people. Once I know what to do, I'm going to help my sis get her money back. That's all."

Penelope felt as if she were walking through the plot of one of her own books—romantic notions like saving the family fortune were easy enough to come up with on paper, but how well would they succeed when the whole thing was for real? She merely smiled and turned to Sandy.

"Have you any idea how we might accomplish this?"

"Actually, I do." The banker reached into her wide shoulder bag, which she'd set on the floor near her feet, and pulled out a notebook. "I've outlined a starter plan."

A starter plan. Pen felt her eyebrows arch upward.

"Item one: Identify and locate the man who presented himself as Richard Stone, private investigator."

Since Detective Caplin had already verified that the man who'd come to Pen's house was not the same man he'd recommended, this seemed only logical. They had to know what audacious soul had come around pretending to be friendly with the chief of detectives and had pulled off the charade.

"Item two: Find out what he did with the real necklace. Item three: Steal the real necklace." Sandy set the notebook down on the table.

"Um, that's as far as you've gotten?"

"So far. Well, those are the basics. I've got more ideas."

Gracie spoke up. "As I see it, the easiest way to find anything these days is on the Internet, right? We'll probably need access to records that aren't entirely public, if you know what I mean." She turned to Penelope. "You had a scene like that in *For Love Or Money*, right? So you know how to hack into police files and stuff."

"Oh—well, I have no idea how to actually do it. I wrote the scene the way I thought it might happen, but my editors called some experts and added things to make the whole thing plausible. I mean, who among my readers is going to actually *know* how to do what Brett did in that story?"

Gracie got quiet. Had Pen just burst her bubble about the invincibility of fiction writers?

"Gracie, you told me you knew someone?"

"Oh. Well, yeah. I think she could help us out." Gracie

leaned forward in her chair. "She's twenty-one years old, so bright she dropped out of college because she was smarter than half the professors and more energetic than the other half. When my sister's, um, situation came up, Amber's the one who helped me get a look at the bank records proving the money really was gone."

"Bank records? At Desert Trust?" Sandy's face registered shock.

"Yeaaahhh. It was." Gracie realized what she'd just admitted to the bank's branch manager.

"I'll need to talk to her about that later," Sandy said. "We would insist on interviewing the young woman anyway, and we should also do a background check. You know, seeing as how..." She didn't say it but the idea was clear—one crook had already worked his way into Penelope's confidence.

THIRTEEN

TODD WAINWRIGHT FIDGETED beside his mother. While "Onward Christian Soldiers" poured from the big pipe organ and from the vocal cords of the congregation, he groused inwardly about his lot in life. He had felt like that cartoon character with the black cloud over his head ever since Thursday night when Dick Stone never showed up.

I'm not a bad person. It's this damn city—no, the whole damn world—everything just wants to crap on me. Nothing ever goes my way.

Aggie Wainwright glanced up from her hymnal as the song went into a second verse, her eyes edging toward Todd's face. He automatically picked up the words and threw his voice into the hymn.

"Marching as to war..."

She smiled and turned her eyes forward again.

The song ended, replaced by the rustle and groans of a hundred people taking their seats. Todd leaned back and heard the crackle of paper in his suit jacket.

Dunning notices on those dumb student loans, barely making the rent. God, don't make me move back in with Mom. She's the one who pushed me back to college, that useless degree in history.

The other voice took over, his argumentative side: *You love history. You chose your major.*

Yeah, but who knew they'd already filled all the archae-ology spots.

And now he had no better prospects than Assistant to the Assistant Director at the Philpont Museum. To move much higher, or to teach, he'd have to go back to school—again—and get his master's. And what school would accept him, seeing he'd been six months delinquent on his last loan?

At the front of the sanctuary, the pastor thanked the choir director and adjusted the microphone at the podium to his own lanky height. The man took a long, deep breath and the congregation tensed in preparation.

"*'Thou shalt not steal,' sayeth the Lord!*" The words thundered forth. This guy began every sermon with a bang.

"My friends, ye lambs of God…" His voice became ominously quiet now. "Take heed of Exodus 20, verse 15, for to ignore these words of Truth is to assure yourself of the peril of eternal damnation."

Todd tuned out everything after that. The archaic language was more than he could handle right now. Today was his first time in church in months. He always forgot what a downer it was, listening to this guy promise eternity in flames. It didn't matter whether you actually committed the sin of the day or only thought about it—you were doomed either way. He'd created his own mini-hell by coming, lured by the free lunch afterward. Aggie couldn't get him there any other way but to treat him to his favorite, the all-you-can-eat extravaganza at Big Country Buffet.

He glanced around the congregation. A pretty blonde sat across the aisle to his right, two pews ahead. Her pert nose faced directly toward the preacher, giving Todd a nice view of her attractive profile. She was probably close to his age, and there wasn't a man with her.

He created a little fantasy where she would leave the

church slightly behind him and see him get into his red Corvette out in the parking lot. Aside from approaching middle age—with the fear he would die in his fifties, as his father had—the whole reason for the flashy car had been to attract women. Certainly, he hadn't needed to attract the hefty payments.

Once he had her attention, he could suggest the blonde join them for lunch. Maybe even upgrade the restaurant a bit, say, Red Lobster instead of the buffet? The vision began to dim a little when he remembered his mother. They'd have to take two cars, and no doubt Aggie would make a show of paying the bill. She always did. Couldn't give a guy a little shred of dignity, could she? He'd have to think of a different approach.

The blonde turned her head his direction, a warm smile playing over her lips. He started to smile back but a moment later he saw her reason. Two little identical blonde heads popped up, looking sleepy. Her smile conveyed all the love in the world. Only not for him. Todd's little vision-bubble burst.

He had to stop thinking about women. It was Dick Stone's promise of a date with his extremely attractive sister that roped Todd in the first place, made him agree to switching the documents. The photo Dick showed him was—wow. She would be easy to seduce; her brother said she'd just endured a breakup. Then the sister just happened to be away for three weeks? And now Dick was unreachable. Todd wondered now whether a sister even existed.

So, forget women. There was still the money. His thirty-percent take would have completely paid off the damn loans. Why couldn't he catch a break these days?

"Thief! Larcenous villain!" came the preacher's loud

voice again. "Do not let the Lord greet you at the gates of heaven with that stain on your soul. Shall we pray?"

Todd felt his face redden. Thief. It hadn't started out that way. He only had to get into the Director's files and switch one piece of paper for another—that was it. No one would ever know and the cash Dick Stone gave him was enough to get him off the hundred-twenty-days past due list. That's all he meant for it to be.

Before things changed. Before the money became irresistible.

Suddenly he felt glad everyone else in the room had their eyes closed.

FOURTEEN

SUNDAY AFTERNOON, Penelope approached Sandy Werner's house with a little trepidation. She wanted her heirloom necklace back—no doubt about that—but what sort of plan was she getting herself into with these women? She knew Sandy on a professional level; the others were complete strangers. But then, what was it her mother used to say? A stranger is a friend you haven't met yet. Mum and her outgoing ways.

She parked her Mercedes at the curb in front of a tract home in a tract neighborhood. Most of the Phoenix suburbs were built this way, she'd noticed. Developers with four or five floorplans and two exterior themes—entire neighborhoods existed in tones of beige-on-brown or brown-on-beige. Tiled pitched roofs, aluminum window frames, heavy screens over the glass to ward off the intense heat of summer. An air conditioning unit that ran eight months of the year.

Sandy's neighborhood was probably twenty years old. Acacia and palo verde trees had grown well above the rooftops, and most of the standard stucco colors had been repainted to suit individual tastes. Sandy's home, in shades of coral and peach, had a brilliant blue front door and a seating arrangement of wicker chairs under a covered front porch. Beside the door sat a painted flowerpot with a small signpost "Welcome" that bordered on being way too cutesy.

Pen reached for the doorbell but the door opened before she could press the button. Gracie Nelson smiled, her dark hair up in a long ponytail today. She wore black capris and a magenta T-shirt, with dangling beaded earrings in pink and purple hues.

"Come in, come in!" She waved an arm toward a mauve-carpeted living room where white sateen-upholstered chairs testified to the fact that Sandy had no children. "I just got here about a minute ago myself. Sandy's making tea."

Gracie seemed a little out of place as she considered the white chairs and took a seat on a deep rose-colored couch instead, dropping a three-ring binder on an end table next to her. Before Pen could sit, the doorbell rang again.

Sandy's voice came from another room, presumably the kitchen. "Can someone answer that? I'm almost ready."

Pen complied, opening the door to a tiny waif of a girl wearing black skinny jeans and a turquoise halter top. A tiny purse hung by a thin strap running diagonally across her torso. She stood barely over five feet tall, with springy curls to her jawline, dark chocolate eyes, and skin the color of milky cocoa. She couldn't have weighed much more than a hundred pounds. She clutched a small computer in one arm.

When Penelope said hello, the girl smiled with perfectly even, perfectly white teeth.

"Hi, I'm Amber," she said. "You must be Penelope."

Without waiting for an answer Amber stepped inside, edging past Pen, greeting Gracie with a happy shriek. Gracie had already crossed the living room and the two quickly embraced.

"How are Dylan and Kylie?" Amber asked.

Gracie made little head-wag gestures that must have meant something like, *You know—kids will be kids.*

Pen sensed motion behind her.

"Tea is served," announced Sandy, coming forward with a huge tray bearing an ornate china teapot and matching sugar bowl and cream pitcher. Two slender black cats followed, tails pertly in the air, obviously knowing they were invited to the party.

The others cleared a path and Sandy set the tray on the table in front of the sofa.

"I hope I did this right," she said with a glance at Pen. "I'm sure you learned the art of making tea the proper way. I had to read about it in an article I found online."

Pen felt honored Sandy would go to so much trouble. Truthfully, at home she usually just dunked a tea bag in boiling water, American style.

"You went to a lot of trouble, Sandy. This is beautiful."

The table already held four delicate china cups and saucers and two tiered serving plates, one with tiny sandwiches and the other with sweets.

"Let's have our tea while it's hot. We can talk as we nibble. Take a plate and get started," Sandy told them.

The cats settled into curled bundles, both on the back of the upholstered chair where Sandy sat. Penelope remembered her calling them Heckle and Jeckle, apt names, since both were black as crows. She noticed Sandy breaking off tiny bits of her sandwiches, feeding morsels to each of the pets in turn.

Sandy spoke up, filling in Amber on what had been discussed over lunch with Gracie two days earlier. "Each of us has specific skills we bring to the table and each element will be crucial if we hope to succeed in getting the real necklace back," she said.

"I have financial expertise and know how the banking system works, Amber is our computer whiz, Gracie is a fantastic organizer, and Penelope has the social connections."

Amber had already opened the lid of the small laptop and was tapping keys while the others sipped tea and ate sandwiches.

No wonder she's a size zero, Pen thought. *She hasn't eaten a thing.*

"First task on our list is to identify the criminal," Gracie said, consulting the notebook she'd now picked up.

"I spent all yesterday afternoon at the police station," Pen said. "I'm afraid it was a daunting task. Even with computerized mug shots to look at, all the faces begin to blur after awhile. I pointed out one that seemed familiar, but I felt so uncertain. I'm worried that we can't really move forward as a group until we know who it is we're chasing."

"Too much data," Amber mumbled. "Let me see if I can narrow it down." She kept typing.

"Meanwhile," said Gracie, "I've created some lists."

Sandy turned to Pen. "Gracie and her lists."

"Hey, if I can keep a husband, two kids, three pets, and the PTA going, I can create schedules and calendars to keep this group on track."

"True," Sandy said with a chuckle. She accepted the stapled pages Gracie handed her. There were four sheets, one set per team member. She took one and passed the rest along.

Pen found herself impressed with the notes Gracie had already made. She looked around at the group.

"Is it permissible to make a toast with tea cups?" Pen asked. "Because I would like to toast all of you for volunteering to help with our little caper. It's a mission which serves none of you and yet you are willing to pitch in."

"You betcha. We'll heist that little gem right back for you," Amber said.

Pen raised her cup. "All right, then. Here's to the Heist Ladies!"

FIFTEEN

GRACIE'S HANDOUTS WERE amazingly detailed, considering their initial meeting had lasted only an hour. She began by listing the facts as they knew them. Necklace taken from the Philpont Museum; Police have no luck recovering stolen items; Private detective named Richard Stone returns necklace; Returned necklace is spotted as a fake by Sandy Werner, verified by Regis Potts, certified gemologist; "Richard Stone" revealed as a fake, as well.

"Add to that, I've had no luck recognizing the man from mug shots," Pen said, her voice sounding discouraged.

Sandy and Gracie seemed at a loss. Amber was still typing.

"Okay, I'm into the bank's security camera footage," Amber said without looking up.

"You what—?" Sandy sputtered.

"Don't ask. If you can take a look, Penelope?" Amber turned the screen to face the older woman. "This shows customers who entered the front door from the time this man was at your house until you called the bank and learned your check had been cashed."

Pen looked at the screen. "Not that one."

Amber ran her finger over the pad to forward the tape. A woman's figure appeared. She went past it.

"Not that one, not that one," Pen said, skipping through them quickly.

"Remember, he may have changed some item of clothing or added a cap or something to disguise himself."

"Go through them a little slower." Pen watched, studying the faces more carefully. "That one. That's definitely him, although I'm certain he didn't have that scar on his nose. He's wearing the same suit, though."

"Okay, good." By now Sandy and Gracie had also gathered behind Pen to watch.

Amber opened another screen which showed the interior of the bank from different angles. The man stood still a moment, looking toward the tellers. He chose one who was young and pretty and headed to her window. The camera behind the tellers picked up his face but since it was set to sweep a row of four teller windows, it only returned to him every few seconds. Amber isolated him, leaving out the other customers, and the women saw a series of photos where Dick Stone gave the female teller a charming smile while presenting the check and a driver's license. He kept his gaze lowered while she typed at her computer terminal.

"He's absolutely aware of the camera," Amber said. "See how he's making sure not to look directly at it? He turns slightly each time it comes toward him, so we're mostly seeing his shoulder and the back of his head."

The teller apparently asked him to wait a moment and soon a man appeared.

"That will be the branch's assistant manager," Sandy said.

The next shot showed the male banker taking the check and going away. From the young woman's body language, apparently Stone was flirting with her. He seemed completely at ease. The time stamp indicated passage of less than ten minutes before the assistant manager returned with stacks of bills.

"He got the money. Barely a question asked," Pen said.

"They would have verified that the check was genuine, had all the proper watermarks and magnetic ink. Then they would have checked your account to be sure it would clear. As long as the man presented identification showing him to be the person the check was made out to, there was no real reason not to give him the money," Sandy said.

Pen felt a little sick inside. Some part of her had held hope the bank could admit to making a mistake and return the money to her account. Obviously not.

"Okay, now he leaves the bank," Amber said. "Let's see where he goes."

She skimmed ahead through the video, following the back of the business suit as the man passed out of range of one camera and into another across the parking lot. He got into a plain white sedan.

"Looks like a rental car to me," Gracie said.

Amber watched footage of the car backing out of a parking space, halted the motion, then zoomed in on the bumper where she magnified a tiny sticker to show the Alamo rental logo.

"That's amazing," Penelope said.

"Give me another minute," Amber said. "Have an extra cookie or something."

She looked a little irritated at being hovered over, so they all complied. Pen fully expected she would be pacing the floor before an answer came but it literally took the time to finish a delectable butter cookie before Amber gave a grunt of triumph.

"Ha! Alamo Rental shows a white Toyota rented by Richard Stone being returned at 1:19 on the twenty-third. They don't have cameras at their counters or I'd have that little sucker's face on file again. But...since normal procedure is to bus the customers over to the airport terminal, he'll turn up there and I can pick him up again."

For some reason, airport cameras in the main halls near the ticket counters didn't show the same man with graying hair and a business suit.

"He's done a little disguise work," Amber said, sounding a little more knowledgeable than she should have. "I'll check the airline flight manifests next. But I'll need a little more time for that."

The tea was gone and the cookies had been reduced to mere crumbs on the serving plate. Gracie ticked off a couple of items on her checklist.

"We've made great progress so far," she said in the tone of a Little League mom giving a pep talk. "Here are your assignment sheets. I suggest we meet again in a few days so everyone can report her progress. What do you think, Pen? This really is your call."

Penelope nodded, feeling a little dazed. So accustomed to writing her own plot, weaving the details together, she'd not worked at a team effort in a very long time. The idea that each member would take some of the burden was a new concept—and a huge relief.

"I don't need a few days," Amber said. "No one by the name of Richard Stone checked in for any flight that day. It's like he walked into the airport and vanished."

SIXTEEN

PEN THOUGHT OF Amber's comment all the way home. The man she knew as Richard Stone had gone to the airport, then vanished. Sandy was probably correct—he must have changed identities at that point. Possibly, he'd had a different persona all set up in advance. All he would have needed to do was walk into the terminal and check in under another name. Changes in clothing, perhaps wearing a hat, sticking to crowded areas—whatever he'd done, the women had not been able to spot him on camera.

Her initial unease about Amber was mitigated by the amount of data the young woman had been able to find in such a short time. Pen smiled at the memory of Sandy's startled expression when she saw how quickly the bank's security footage became available. Despite Amber's assurances that she had no access to customer accounts or bank financial records, Pen had the feeling Sandy was going to drop the hint that her employer might want to double check their online security levels. At any rate, Pen was happy to have Amber on her team now.

She parked her car in the garage, entered the house, and walked into her office. She laid the papers from Gracie on her desk and stared at the clutter, unable to concentrate well enough to pick up the pages of plot notes she'd made three days ago. Her writing routine was certainly suffering as a result of this whole mess with the missing necklace.

She picked up Gracie's notes once again. Gracie had taken Sandy's initial simple plan and expanded upon it.

Identify Richard Stone. Amber was working on that.

Find out what he did with the real necklace. No idea how they would do that.

For now, she couldn't even contemplate the last step: *Steal the necklace back.* Other than the time in seventh grade when she'd been lured by a tube of Passion Pink lipstick at the neighborhood variety store, Pen had never stolen a thing in her life. Given the repercussion—Mum forcing her to return the lipstick and apologize to the store's manager—it had never again been a temptation. She put on her reading glasses and looked at Gracie's rounded handwriting.

Penelope will request copies of police reports regarding the original theft and ask what the police did to track the stolen goods. I can do that much, Pen thought. Detective Caplin might be embarrassed by the fact they never solved the case but surely he can't deny me access to the information.

Sandy and Gracie will investigate at the museum. Break in if necessary.

Pen blanched a little at the thought. Now Amber, there was a girl who would likely have no qualms about it. She'd been a little testy when the meeting adjourned; the fact that she'd not come up with all the answers in one afternoon clearly gnawed at her. Amber would surely find more answers to get them on track in their mission. Once again, Pen felt glad to have the Heist Ladies on her side.

Pen picked up the phone, intending to call Detective Caplin, then remembered it was Sunday afternoon. Let the man at least have his weekend, she thought. Before she set the receiver down it rang in her hand.

"Pen, it's Sandy." Her friend sounded keyed up. "I've just learned there's a gala fundraiser at the museum tomorrow night. It could be our way in. We just need tickets, and I figure you've got the connections to pull it off."

Penelope thought about it. She'd heard about the fundraiser but the event had been sold out for weeks. She'd declined complimentary tickets for herself and Benton. The museum allowed her million-dollar necklace to vanish. She'd felt a certain righteous indignation that they still wanted her support. But now—

"How many tickets?" she asked Sandy.

SEVENTEEN

ANNIE STRAW HANDED Todd Wainwright a sheaf of papers.

"What's this? Filing?" he asked. "Isn't that your job?"

The saucy intern looked him in the eye. "It will be. But Mr. Higgins wants you to look over everything before I file them. It's just a bunch of bills of lading, receiving papers on the Grand Canyon artifacts exhibit for next month."

Todd snatched the pages from her.

"In a mood, are we?" she asked. "Everyone else is looking forward to the gala tomorrow night."

He turned away, stalking back toward the cubicle that served as his office. Sure, all the interns thought it was great fun to dress up and hobnob with the society folks who were invited annually for the museum's biggest fundraiser. He hated squeezing into a tuxedo. Those monkey suits only looked good on tall, slim James Bond types.

The main exhibit hall had been rearranged, display islands pushed to other areas, and round tables with eight chairs each had been rolling in all morning. The plain gray walls were now festooned with gold, copper and silver bunting, in keeping with the theme: Strike it Rich in Arizona! A play on the state's mining history, going along with the big exhibit running this month. Balloons in metallic colors were being formed into a huge entry arch this morning. Flowers and plants had been gilded and arranged as table centerpieces, while on the more rustic side of it an old mining cart and a few picks and shovels added to the glorified mining theme.

Live and silent auctions were planned, each item fitting the same subject. He knew of several pieces of valuable jewelry that would no doubt attract sizeable bids. Everyone had carefully avoided talking about the events of last autumn, especially the missing emerald-and-diamond necklace. Of course, no one here knew that the necklace and its status had been so recently under investigation again. Which reminded him, why had he still not heard from Dick Stone?

Annie startled him, peering around the corner of his cubicle with a cardboard box in her hands. "It's something more for the gala, I suppose."

Todd nodded toward the corner of his desk and she set the package there. He recognized the return address of the company where museum flyers were printed.

"Annie!" The female voice belonged to another of the spring interns. "I wanted to ask you if you've bought your dress yet."

Annie gave Todd a wary look and steered the other young woman away. "I found the most gorgeous..." Their voices trailed off.

Employees had been told to wear the colors of precious metals—Todd's only nod to the theme was a gold bow tie. He'd heard the ladies talking about how much fun they'd had shopping for glittering new dresses. Personally, he thought the whole thing was a bit much, considering mining was dirty, dust-covered work.

After you'd done these events a few times, it became more a matter of dreading the stiff, rented tuxedo and spending hours with a smile on your face in response to the b.s. chatter from men who compared their brokerage accounts and bragged to each other about their yachts down in Mexico.

Meanwhile, he was nothing but a glorified paperwork shuffler. Todd flopped into his swivel chair. See? There was a new memo someone had dropped on his desk in the few minutes he'd walked to the copy machine and back. He set aside the pages Annie had given him and glanced at the printout. It was the final guest list for the gala.

As third in command at the museum he was expected to memorize the names, know their credentials, and be ready to chat and smile with any of them. He scanned the list. Most were the city's elite, already familiar to him since they attended every year. At the bottom of the second page, he came to a sudden stop. A few last-minute guests had been added: Penelope Fitzpatrick plus one, and Sandra Werner plus one.

He didn't know this Sandra Werner but he sure as hell knew who Penelope Fitzpatrick was. They'd never met but her name had been on his mind for more than six months.

Surely she'd been sent an invitation early on, so why was she only now added to the list? This week, of all times. Could she be suspicious of the museum staff? Worse, could she have any idea of his own involvement? He thought frantically. What would he say to the woman when they met?

EIGHTEEN

PENELOPE SQUARED HER SHOULDERS, steeling herself for a confrontation. Her persistence was wearing Detective Caplin's nerves thin, and she knew it. Considering herself something of an amateur psychologist—a matter of pride when it came to creating solid characters for her novels—she loved to figure out the motivations and reasoning behind the actions of people she dealt with. In her opinion, Caplin was simply fed up with her. He knew he and his department appeared inept when they failed to find her stolen necklace, worse so when his recommendation of a private investigator went completely wrong. Now he wished Penelope and every reminder of this case would simply go away. That was her take on it, anyhow.

She pulled open the door at police headquarters and walked through a noisy, crowded room full of the very sorts of people she almost never had to associate with—poorly dressed women with dirty-faced, dirty-diapered babies, sullen teens with earbuds plugged into their heads, gaunt females in tacky sequined tight dresses. Pen felt a tug of empathy for their circumstances; they wouldn't be here if they didn't have to be. It was visiting hour at the jail.

Feeling decidedly out of place in white linen slacks and a purple Thai silk blouse, she edged her way through the throng and presented Caplin's business card to the tired-looking officer behind his bulletproof glass enclosure. He gave the card a bored glance, picked up a phone and punched a couple of numbers. In a moment, the door to her right buzzed and the lock clicked open. She escaped into a long hallway painted shiny gray.

On her last visit, Caplin had been almost cordial, nearly accommodating. She'd been here at his suggestion to look at mug shots. This time, she had phoned ahead to see if she could take a look at the case file on the museum robbery. He'd refused. When she'd tossed out the fact that she knew his superior officer quite well, he'd grudgingly agreed that she could come down here this morning. She took a deep breath and put on a smile.

A female officer stepped into the hall and greeted her.

"Mrs. Fitzpatrick, this way please." With a sweep of her arm, the officer showed Pen into a small room containing a metal table with four chairs. "Detective Caplin sent this file. He said you may make notes but cannot take the file with you."

"Is there a copy machine?"

"I'm sorry. I'm not supposed to allow you to make copies. Just your own handwritten notes, please."

Pen glanced at the brown folder the woman set on the table. The contents looked very skimpy. A few years ago, as research for a book, a police officer she'd befriended in Chicago allowed her to browse a murder case file. The thing was huge, nearly a foot thick, with pages and pages of witness testimony, transcripts from interrogation of suspects, photos and diagrams of the scene of the crime. This file, covering the police investigation of the theft of a million dollar necklace, probably contained no more than twenty pages. The difference, she supposed, in the value of *things* versus a human life. She looked up at the officer.

"This is it?"

"Everything we have, I'm told. Detective Caplin did mention that the case was handed off to the feds at some point. It could be they took the most pertinent information."

He'd never told Pen that. Most likely, the local police had spent very little time on it. Either way, it was rotten luck.

Pen sat in one of the chairs and flipped open the folder's cover. The female officer closed the door and stood just inside, her hands behind her back. *Really. I need to be watched?* She pulled her reading glasses from her Gucci bag and settled in, lifting the file's cover.

The page on top was a printed form, apparently the final requirement for the police to close the case. In the space for "Resolution of Case" it simply said "Unsolved." She paged quickly through to the sheet on the bottom, the original police report filed the night of the robbery. It contained the responding officers' observations and the basic facts: date, time, location, circumstances.

The following pages were transcripts of interviews, first with the museum employees. The robbery had been discovered by a Helen McGraw when she showed up for work Tuesday morning. It was noted that the museum was open Tuesday through Sunday each week, closed Mondays. So the last time any employees were on site was Sunday evening. The museum had closed to the public at five o'clock.

Past five, only two interns and a cleaning crew of three, supervised by the Assistant Director's assistant, Todd Wainwright, remained. The interns both left around six p.m., although not together. The cleaning crew finished around eight o'clock. Wainwright said he had additional paperwork to do and had stayed until nearly ten, when he was simply too tired to finish.

He locked up and started home, but halfway there began

to question himself. Had he remembered to set the alarm system? He turned around and went back. Finding the doors securely locked, he set the alarm and went home. No, he had not walked through the building to examine the displays. No, he had not checked the safe where the rare jewels were put at night. He was certain he had done all those tasks earlier.

But he was tired? The interrogating officer asked it several times.

Yes, said Wainwright, he was tired. But he'd been with the museum many years now. He always followed protocol and could do the shut-down procedures in his sleep. He was 99.9 percent certain—no, make that 100 percent certain—he had locked away the gemstone collection, had set the infrared sensors in the exhibition halls, and had securely locked the building.

And yet, he had forgotten to set the main alarm system. Even in print, the detective's tone sounded stern.

For no more than twenty minutes, probably more like fifteen, was Wainwright's response.

The detective noted that Wainwright was in severe distress while answering the questions. Pen felt sure the recorded tapes would substantiate that claim.

Stanley Higgins, the Philpont's director, verified Wainwright's employment history and thought the young man to be very good at his job. Dan Stevens, assistant to Mr. Higgins, said much the same. Todd Wainwright was his assistant, third in command in the organization. The young man might have his personal quirks but his work was impeccable. Normally, either Higgins or Stevens stayed until the cleaning crew left but there had been a number of times Todd Wainwright did it. There truly was no reason for suspicion, they swore.

Statements from the secretaries, docents and interns all

seemed to bear out the same opinion. All in all, it was a very congenial workplace.

The cleaning crew came from a well-regarded agency, licensed and bonded, who normally sent the same trio each week to the Philpont. That week was no exception. According to testimony of the three individuals, they rarely even looked at the old junk in the displays. Their job was to dust the cases, clean grubby-kid fingerprints off the glass, and see that the floors and restrooms were spotless. That particular Sunday evening in no way stood out from any other in their recollection.

And yet, Pen wondered as she wrote her notes, how did the robbery happen without inside help?

NINETEEN

GOLDEN CHAMPAGNE SENT trails of delicate bubbles rising to the top of the crystal flute Benton Case handed Penelope. She smiled. They were a handsome couple, she had to admit it. She in her favorite black sheath with a silver guipure lace jacket, Benton in his best designer tuxedo, to which he'd added a silver satin tie and cummerbund. This was one occasion where being silver-haired was an asset, definitely.

She turned to survey the museum's main exhibit hall, which had been transformed for the evening. Strategically placed lighting glimmered off each gold, silver and copper decoration while leaving the dining tables in enough shadow so the candlelit arrangements glowed.

"Penelope and Benton, welcome!" Stanley Higgins walked toward Pen, arms stretched expansively. "So glad the two of you were able to join us."

"Thank you, Stan," Pen said. "One of those things…we were able to get out of our other obligation." The story she'd concocted when requesting four last-minute tickets.

Benton smiled—that lovely natural smile of his—and shook the other man's hand. As a former prosecutor, later a successful attorney in private practice, he'd learned the fine art of conversation without really saying anything. Pen had already cautioned him that the entire reason she wanted to be here tonight was to spy on the museum staff, to see if their versions of the robbery all those months ago seemed to hold up.

What she hadn't confided was the plan devised by the Heist Ladies.

There they were…across the room. Sandy studied the items on the silent auction table, while Gracie mused over a collection of photographs of an 1890s mine camp down near Bisbee in southern Arizona.

Stanley Higgins noticed where Pen was looking. "Ah, Penelope. Be certain to take a look at our lovely collection of auction items. And, Benton, you be certain she bids on them."

He gave a wink, as if her being here tonight indicated her forgiveness for this organization's part in the loss of her most valued personal possession. She wanted to send her black Ferragamo-clad toe right into his shin. But she had something better in mind. She merely offered an enigmatic smile.

"Here's Todd now," Higgins said.

He beckoned subtly to a short, chubby man in his early forties who straightened his gold bow tie as he approached. Introductions all around. Pen pretended she didn't know of Todd's position here or the fact he'd been the one who left the alarm system off for a short time that fateful night.

"Todd can show you around, point out the best of the auction items…" With a hand on Todd's shoulder, Stan steered the participants together. He excused himself, his eye already on his next target.

Too blatant, Pen thought. But since Wainwright was here… She gave a quick glance toward Sandy Werner, who met her eye and gave an imperceptible nod.

"Benton, could you be a dear and see about refilling my glass?" she said.

He headed toward the bar in the farthest corner, taking the hint, leaving her alone with Wainwright for a few minutes.

Pen stepped to one side, forcing Todd to turn his back to the door that said Staff Only at the far side of the room. Sandy, meanwhile, had her eye on Stanley Higgins. When he became engaged in conversation with a lovely young woman in a very low-cut dress, Gracie neatly glided over beside Sandy and the two slipped through the forbidden doorway to the offices. Pen smiled and turned her attention back to Todd.

"So, let's see some of those wonderful auction items," she said.

MINIMAL NIGHT LIGHTING covered the office section of the museum, Sandy quickly discovered. Amber had graciously located floor plans of the building for them, but they had no way of knowing in advance which office they wanted. All they knew was they had very little time—and no safety—in being here. Almost any employee could walk in at any moment.

We want every document the museum has pertaining to that robbery, Sandy had told the Ladies at their meeting earlier this afternoon. Pen had filled them in on what she'd learned at the police station. Now, if they could only find some type of proof to refute what the police had been told.

"Here!" Sandy murmured. She pointed to the black and white plate beside a closed door. "Stanley Higgins, Director."

They'd guessed that the safe and the most important files would probably be located here. Slipping inside, Sandy closed the door.

"Lock it," Gracie whispered.

"But what if he—"

"Better he questions whether he really locked it than to have him popping in here with no warning. At least he has to rattle the doorknob this way." Gracie switched on a small desk lamp.

With an extra fifteen seconds security, they took opposite sides of the room. Sandy sat in Higgins' desk chair and pulled open his file drawers. Gracie began looking behind pictures on the walls, hoping to find the safe.

"It's not going to be sitting there unlocked," Sandy said, keeping her voice low. Her fingers played over the tabs on the files but nothing seemed related to the European crown jewels collection or the robbery.

"I know. I just… I don't know."

Gracie had peered behind four large paintings, the only ones large enough to conceal much of anything. She stepped to a narrow doorway, assuming it would lead to an executive washroom or such.

"Ha! Look here." The closet contained a fairly large safe, about three feet wide by five feet tall.

Sandy stood up. "Great, a Lexington Five. Nobody without the combination can get into that thing. Except maybe an expert safecracker who has a couple hours to work on it."

"The night of the robbery… Pen said…"

"The guy who was supposed to lock up was back within twenty minutes. Not even the best safecracker could get in and out of it that fast." Sandy stared at the complicated buttons on the front of the safe. "I think this model even has a timer feature. Properly armed, no one would get into this until the museum opened for business on Tuesday."

"So, we have nothing? There wasn't exactly anything in the files."

"Not so," Sandy said, pointing out a manila folder on the desk. "Look at that."

Before Gracie could step over to the desk for a peek, the doorknob rattled. On the other side, a mild curse in a male voice.

TWENTY

ACROSS THE ROOM, Penelope spotted a familiar figure. Detective Caplin. Drat—he was walking in her direction. Benton had become involved in conversation near the bar with some men from his club. She was on her own.

"Ms. Fitzpatrick, how are you this evening?"

She wanted to ask how a man of his station came to be at a two-thousand-dollar a plate dinner, but that would be rude and condescending.

"I'm well, detective. And yourself?"

She scanned the room, wondering how Sandy and Gracie were coming along with their mission, but the police officer's glance began trailing hers. She brought her attention back to his face.

"Sorry I wasn't there when you came by the station this morning," he said. "I hope you found what you wanted?"

Hardly. What I want is my necklace returned to me.

"Nice shindig, eh?" He ran his index finger along the inside of his shirt collar, looking ill at ease in a tux. She noticed he didn't have a drink.

"Is the museum one of your personal causes," she asked, "or are you here to represent the fine city of Phoenix?"

"Strictly business, I'm afraid. With all the gold and silver floating around here tonight, the directors thought it would be a good idea to have a police presence, even though we are somewhat incognito." He patted the side of his jacket, just enough to indicate he was armed.

"Ah, I see." She covered her distress by taking a sip of her champagne.

Where were Sandy and Gracie? She'd seen them slip through that Staff Only door, but no sign of them since. If they happened to set off an alarm, there would be no way to avoid involvement with the police. Their mission would be—as Amber might say—toast.

Above the rim of her glass she caught sight of Stan Higgins walking purposefully toward the offices. Oh, no. Her body tensed.

"Everything all right, Ms. Fitzpatrick?" Caplin asked.

"I, um, just had a bit of a light-headed spell. I should probably switch this champagne for water. Would you be a dear?"

Without waiting for an answer she handed her glass to him. Thank goodness, he walked toward the bar.

Higgins had passed through the Staff Only door. Pen held her breath. All she could do at this point was hope Gracie's naturally quick thinking would come up with the right excuse at the right moment.

Less than a minute elapsed before Higgins came back. He looked frustrated, striding quickly over to the woman she'd seen him with earlier, most likely his wife. There was a quick exchange between them and the woman reached into her evening bag and pulled out something that looked like a keyring. He took it and headed back toward his office.

TWENTY-ONE

SANDY CLAMPED HER hand over her mouth, stifling the tiny shriek that wanted to escape when the doorknob rattled. She felt certain her eyes were every bit as wide as Gracie's. Both women stood frozen in place.

On the other side of the thin door, the man cursed. After an interminably long fifteen seconds his footsteps sounded crisply in the hall. Walking away. Thank god.

"Do you think he came to this door by mistake?" Gracie said breathlessly.

"We won't be that lucky."

"Okay, then. Quick! Let's get pictures of what we found." Gracie pulled her phone from her tiny evening bag and snapped a photo of the closet safe and its control panel.

Sandy opened the folder from the tsarist collection exhibit and paged through until she found a contract, an appraisal and a receipt for Pen's necklace. Gracie quickly snapped photos of each document and dropped the phone back into her purse. Sandy tamped the pages together and jammed the folder back in the drawer.

"Let's go!" Gracie was at the door.

"Check the hallway first. We can't let anyone see we were in here."

Gracie peered out and waved Sandy forward. She pulled the door closed.

"Lock it," Sandy whispered.

Good thinking. The same man returning would most certainly know something was up if he found the door unlocked now. Gracie twisted the thumb-turn on the knob and prayed they could get out without a sound. They'd nearly made it to the outer door when it began to open.

PEN EDGED HER way through the crowd, as unobtrusively as possible, toward Stan Higgins, searching for a topic to distract him. But she was still a good ten yards away. Her eyes darted between that Staff Only door and Detective Caplin, who had procured a glass of water for her and was on his way back. No sign yet of Sandy and Gracie, and Higgins had his hand on the doorknob now.

She couldn't think what to do. A glance in her purse revealed few choices. Her fingertips touched a tube of lipstick. With a flick of her wrist she flipped it out and sent it rolling along the floor.

"Watch out for that!" she called out to Higgins, rushing toward him at the same time.

The tube rolled into his path. Pen followed.

"Oh, heavens," she gasped. "It just got away from me. Wouldn't want you to step on that thing and take a tumble."

Higgins bent to pick it up.

The Staff door opened and Sandy peered out. Quick assessment, seeing Higgins handing something to Pen. She grabbed Gracie's elbow and steered her toward the busy roomful of people.

"Ladies?" Higgins gave them an intense stare.

"Oh, sorry. We thought this might be the way to the ladies room," Sandy said.

He pointed to the sign on the door. "You're mistaken."

Gracie came up with a high-pitched giggle. "Silly me. I could have sworn—"

"Go back to the vestibule and you'll see the sign on your right," he said.

"Sorry," Sandy said. "She's had a little too much…"

His head dipped politely but there was a twitch beside his eye. "No problem."

Diplomacy of the non-profit director, Pen thought. She wanted to feel sorry for his having to cater to this crowd, but truthfully she found his position at the moment a little humorous. She stood still while Sandy steered Gracie toward the lobby and Higgins proceeded toward the offices. Detective Caplin arrived at her side, extending a glass of water to her, his sharp eyes taking in everything.

As much as Pen was dying to know what the other Ladies had discovered, she knew they dare not talk until later. She thanked Caplin for the water and drank it down. He excused himself, murmuring something about his duties.

She meandered toward the vestibule on the pretense of wanting to check out the items in the silent auction. Sandy emerged first from the ladies room and headed toward the same table Pen was browsing.

"We can't be seen in conversation," Pen said, not taking her eyes from the auction sheets on the table. "Ladies room, right before the dessert course?"

Sandy nodded, pointing at a copper vase with an intricate inlay as if she were interested in bidding on it.

Pen moved on. It was going to be a very long dinner.

TWENTY-TWO

Todd Wainwright strode toward the kitchen where the caterer's staff was busily assembling salads in preparation for serving the first course. He had no interest in the food—basically, he was only working off some of his pent-up energy.

Hobnobbing with this class of people left him nervous, afraid he would say the wrong thing at the wrong time. Thank goodness Stan would act as master of ceremonies and would give the after-dinner speech with the usual money-beg for generous auction bids and open wallets when it came to donations. A local celebrity, one of the television morning show hosts, would act as auctioneer. The man was known for his flirtatious personality and winning ways at these charity events. *So, really*, Todd told himself, *I have nothing to be nervous about.*

Yeah, right. Tell yourself that. The old lady whose necklace had consumed so much of his attention in recent months was here. He felt as if her eagle eye watched his every move in the main hall, one reason he'd escaped temporarily to the kitchen.

"May I help you, sir?" It was the caterer. "Something we've forgotten?"

"Uh…no. Just taking a peek to see how things are coming along," he said.

"We can start with the salads any time now."

"Let me check with Mr. Higgins. I believe he'll want to make an announcement."

The woman nodded, her hands clasped properly at her waist.

He turned away before she could come up with some other question. He paused in the corridor leading back to the exhibit hall, trying to slow his racing thoughts. What this was really all about was his nagging feeling that he'd been screwed royally by his two partners. He'd had no word from either of them in days—well, no word from Dick Stone in a couple of weeks. Todd reached into his pocket for another antacid, took two from the packet and chewed them, letting the soothing cherry flavor trickle down his throat. He pushed through the swinging doors where the chatter of the crowd had risen above the volume of the background music.

Across the room he saw Stan Higgins emerge from the wing where the offices were, the pages of his speech in hand. The boss headed for the dais where a small podium and microphone waited. At the edge of the crowd, Todd spotted a familiar figure, one he'd never seen in formal dress clothing before. Just the man he wanted to see. He pushed through.

His quarry spun, startled, when Todd touched his arm. "Oh, hello, Todd. Nice party you guys have thrown here."

"We need to talk. What have you heard from Stone?"

"Not here. Too many eyes and ears. Just smile and assure me that I'm having a great time. When everyone else is eating, meet me outside by the fountain." He turned and left Todd standing there, feeling foolish.

"Todd, there you are." It was one of the interns. She'd surely seen who he was talking to just now. "Mr. Higgins wants us to get the guests to take their seats. He says there's a gong or a chime or something around here."

"Yes, right there." He pointed to an antique Chinese gong, a gaudy round thing with the tone rivaling a cathedral bell. "Go easy with it."

She hurried away. A few seconds later a soft, musical *bom* sounded. Conversation lagged. Another tone from the gong, and a third. The museum staff began passing the word, "Please take your seats."

Todd ushered a couple of ladies who seemed a bit lost, pulling out their chairs for them. The entire room filled with the swish of fabric and the soft scuff of dress shoes on the marble floor. Conversation dwindled as the guests settled, made introductions among tablemates amid the flutter of printed folders describing the auction items.

Mr. Higgins took the podium, blew lightly into the microphone to assure it was on; it was, and his breath came through a bit too loudly. Slight laugh.

"Welcome, ladies and gentlemen, to our 'Strike It Rich' night. The staff and volunteers of the Philpont Museum welcome you to our annual gala. We hope you enjoy our glittering theme this year, along with the glittering company of your fellow diners and philanthropists."

Todd stood to the side, watching the catering staff waiters set salads at each place, while Higgins went on—perhaps a tad too long—about how the purpose of the fundraiser, as everyone knew, was to assure the Philpont had enough funds to keep the doors open and to provide the city with… blah, blah, blah. Todd tuned out most of it. Eventually, Higgins apologized for going on so long, promising to be back at the end of the meal with more information and to introduce their celebrity auctioneer for the evening.

The man Todd so urgently wanted to speak with was

seated at a full table, apparently charming the ladies with some story. Todd decided he might as well take his own seat. His stomach felt better now. He was the only single man at the eight-place table, and the others all seemed to know each other already. He stabbed at the curly lettuce on his plate, letting the conversation flow around him.

Salads were cleared. Filet mignon arrived. Drinks were refilled. The chatter around him continued while Todd chewed the tender steak. He had opted for beef rather than chicken but the filet might as well have been hamburger for all the enjoyment he received. He kept an eye on the other man and saw him rise from his chair. Before the waiter could take his plate, he folded his napkin and excused himself.

The stone fountain in front of the museum added a nice ambiance to the warm spring evening. Todd spotted one man standing there, alone. As he approached, the man pulled a pack of cigarettes from his pocket and offered Todd one.

"I don't smo—"

"Take it. Having something to do makes our meeting look entirely coincidental."

Todd took the cigarette and accepted a light. He couldn't force himself to inhale the hot smoke, but he could fake the motions well enough.

"So," said the man, "you think you're calling the shots now?"

TWENTY-THREE

PENELOPE HID A yawn behind her dinner napkin as Stan Higgins droned on about the museum and all the great things it did for the city. Salad arrived and she picked at it. At her side, Benton—bless him!—made conversation with the other couples at their table, entertaining them with stories from the golf course. His best stories, of course, came from his days in the prosecutor's office but he rarely talked about those. She merely put on a smile, hiding her thoughts.

Had Sandy and Gracie been able to glean any new information on the robbery from the museum director's office? Had they actually gotten in before he came along? How long could this bloody dinner go on?

Pen glanced around the room. Three tables away, Sandy and Gracie sat with two couples and two single men. Gracie was laughing at something one of the men said, gesturing as she added something to the conversation. Sandy appeared much the way Pen must—a false smile, a distracted darting of the eyes, complete boredom with the surroundings.

As a banker with frequent duties toward customer service, she must have had her fill of client dinners and community banquets. Gracie, on the other hand, was no doubt enjoying a dressy night out without her kids.

Perhaps Pen could make use of something here for a character or situation in a future book. She began to take note of little things—the way a particular dress fit its wearer, the melodic tone of another diner's giggle, the coquettish glances between two of the wait staff who were no doubt romantically involved. To fill her mind with something interesting, she began to concoct an intriguing little plot around them as she cut into the filet before her. The meal was not extraordinary but the sauce was interesting.

SANDY KEPT AN eye on Gracie's evening purse, sitting there so precariously on her friend's lap. The phone inside held all the evidence they were ever likely to get for Pen. She forked the tender-crisp broccoli from her plate. The sauce on her chicken smelled good but she was dieting again and tried to eat her fill of the lower-calorie foods first. Well, maybe just a bite… She was glad Pen suggested meeting before the dessert arrived.

Thinking of Pen, Sandy glanced toward the other table. Pen's gentleman friend was talking animatedly with another man. Pen herself had a serene smile. Hard to believe she was in the midst of tonight's plot. Sandy's own thoughts didn't seem to go anywhere except to the close call she and Gracie had awhile ago in Higgins' office.

A handsome young waiter who looked about eighteen years old came around and asked if she was finished with her plate. She nodded. He might have been her grandson… if only… She turned her thoughts in another direction, a habit so ingrained she hardly had to think about it.

Another glance toward Pen. Dinner plates had been cleared and desserts—something in short parfait glasses— were being set before each diner. Sandy raised her eyebrows and Pen gave a quick tilt of her chin toward the vestibule.

Sandy cleared her throat and turned toward Gracie. "I'm heading for the ladies room…"

"Oh. Oh! I think I'll come along." Gracie excused herself to the group who seemed a little perplexed that she'd cut short the punchline of her joke.

At the far side of the vestibule, it became apparent the visit to the restroom was not a good plan. A lineup waited outside the door.

Sandy turned toward Gracie and Pen. "I think I could use a smoke."

Pen looked startled. "I didn't think—"

"I could go for some fresh air," Gracie piped up. She started for the large double exit doors.

The others followed along. Outside, the air felt balmy and the scent of orange blossoms somehow managed to reach the center of the city from the acres of outlying orchards. Or perhaps they came from the few trees on the museum grounds. A fountain bubbled quietly in the roundabout where cars would later arrive to pick up the benefit attendees. To one side an arbor draped with trumpet vines looked like a secluded place for conversation but two men already stood there, their conversation seeming rather intense.

"How about this pathway?" Pen suggested, heading the opposite direction.

Flowering trees, their trunks entwined with fairy lights, made the isolated area feel safe and well-lit as the three walked along, as if for a cordial stroll. Sandy related what little she knew about the safe inside the director's office—that it was a good one, tough to get into—and Gracie pulled out her phone with the pictures.

Pen peered at the photographed documents. "I don't think I can make out much detail here."

"I'll send them to you. On your computer you can enlarge them quite a lot."

If I know how, Pen thought. She needed to move ahead

in her knowledge of technology if she meant to associate with this group. She watched as Gracie tapped a few lighted buttons on her phone.

"Okay, they're on the way to your email," she said.

Pen had a feeling their little computer whiz, Amber, would be called back to action on this one.

"We need to decide our next step," Sandy said, as if she'd read Pen's mind. "Amber is working on some things. Let me contact her in the morning and I'll let everyone know."

"Meanwhile, we should get back inside," Pen said.

"Separately, I'd suggest, since we don't know who among the museum staff might have been involved with the robbery," said Sandy. "Pen, you go first. We'll take this other side path so we don't end up going inside at the same time."

Pen doubled back, taking enough time so it appeared she was there to admire the landscaping. She passed the arbor where the two men had been talking a few minutes ago. One had left, and she thought she recognized the gait of the man she'd met earlier, Todd Wainwright, who was either Dan Stevens' or Stan Higgins' assistant—she'd forgotten. The other man was stubbing out a cigarette in an urn of sand. She definitely knew him. It was Detective Caplin.

TWENTY-FOUR

DETECTIVE CAPLIN AND that young man who works for the museum—do they know each other well?" Pen asked Benton on the way home.

They were in his car, and she was feeling the adrenaline letdown after the evening's previous rush of nerves. She nestled into her seat and closed her eyes against the glare of oncoming traffic on Interstate 10.

"I have no idea," Benton said, watching his mirrors for an opportune lane change. "I assume you're thinking in terms of the robbery and your missing necklace?"

He didn't have to ask. Pen had told him about the disappointing news from Caplin and her subsequent debacle with the private investigator.

"I imagine they must have had contact," Benton said. "After all, Caplin surely questioned everyone at the museum right after it happened."

"True. He did. It's just that I saw the two of them talking tonight, off in the shadows, away from the party. It just seemed odd."

"And I bet you'll soon find out. In all our years together, Pen, I've never known you to let many questions remain unanswered."

He reached for her hand and gave it an affectionate squeeze. They had exited the freeway and he was following the familiar route to her hillside home. She glanced at his handsome profile, reminded of the day they met. Hard to believe it was more than twenty years ago.

She'd been working on her first novel, in retrospect a pitiful thing that never made it to a publisher's desk. Part of her plot revolved around the prosecution of a felony murder case and she had no idea, aside from television stories, how such a thing worked. She'd called the district attorney's office and asked to speak with someone who could answer her questions. A community relations person was supposed to return her call but when four days went by with no call from the woman, Pen simply drove downtown and marched in.

The CR was out with the flu. The district attorney himself walked through the room, turned to an attorney who was standing there and asked if he could take care of the lovely lady. It was Benton Case. With his salt-and-pepper hair and blue eyes, the man in the perfectly tailored suit charmed her immediately.

Penelope and Benton had discussed her questions for the novel over lunch. It turned out to be pure luck that put them together. Benton had retired from his position as District Attorney several years earlier to start his own private practice. It was coincidence that he'd stopped at the office that morning. He, of course, didn't have to follow the new DA's request. He admitted he did so merely to get to know Pen better.

Within two months they were lovers, a carefree arrangement both of them accepted for what it was. Pen, with two previous marriages behind her, had no desire to push for another. Benton, widowed years earlier, had a busy law practice to fill his days. They traveled together and saw a lot of the world. Eventually, he received an offer to sell the practice and he happily retired to golf. Sex became infrequent and the relationship settled into one of pleasant companionship shared by two dear friends. They were each other's choice for social occasions which required one to bring a date. He still answered her questions about the law; she still loved having him along as a traveling companion when she went on her ever-less-frequent book tours.

He steered his Lexus up the hillside and parked at her front door.

"Come in for a nightcap?" she asked.

It was tradition with them and would have been rude not to ask but, truthfully, she had her mind on the photos Gracie had emailed to her earlier. She hoped the picture quality would be good enough to read details on the documents her friends had found in Stan Higgins' office.

Benton walked around to the passenger door and opened it. An old-fashioned tradition, one most women would either refuse or had never experienced these days. But Pen enjoyed the small acts of gentlemanly kindness and she waited to take his hand.

Inside, she poured his favorite, Drambuie on the rocks, and brewed herself a cup of tea. Conversation dwindled but it was all right. They sat on the back patio staring at her incomparable view of the city lights. When he left, a half hour later, she hoped her goodbye didn't seem too eager.

As his taillights vanished down the driveway, Pen rushed to her office and entered her computer password. Emails from both Gracie and Amber awaited. She opened Gracie's first.

The first photo showed the front of a safe with a heavy handle and a keypad of numbers, along with a little panel with lights that presumably showed its status as locked. Not sure what I'm supposed to do with this, she thought.

The other photos showed documents with very tiny print.

It appeared the ladies had found items of interest, but Pen's eyes were tired and she wasn't sure how to enlarge the pictures enough to make them readable. She set that message aside and went to Amber's. Copies had gone out to the whole group.

We need to meet. Found very interesting info on Richard Stone.

TWENTY-FIVE

A FLURRY OF emails and texts brought the group together the following afternoon at Amber Zeckis' apartment a few blocks from Arizona State University in Tempe. Pen took the 101 freeway and found it easily, a tan stucco two-story building typical of off-campus student housing. Apartment 27 was at the east end of the second floor. To her knock, Amber's voice shouted a casual, "Come in!"

It had been so many years since Pen had seen the inside of a twenty-one year old's apartment, she'd forgotten the sheer chaos of it. The one-room efficiency had a galley kitchen at the far end with two wooden stools at the counter. Aside from an open door to a tiny bathroom, it was all right here. A garage-sale end table beside a crooked futon was scattered with colorful hair ties and bottles of blue and purple nail enamel. Magazines littered the futon's cushion, most of them following themes of computers or travel rather than the celebrity slicks favored by most young women these days. Framed memorabilia on the walls consisted of science fair awards, a few extra unexplained blue ribbons, and a framed photo of Amber (it had to be, the curly hair was the same on the twelve-year-old version) standing beside Bill Gates.

Amber looked up from the oversized computer screen at the desk which dominated the room and caught Pen looking at the picture.

"I had the wildest older-man crush on him back then," she said. "I nagged my mom into taking me to the electronics show that year."

Pen smiled. Her own girlhood crush had been for cowboy star Roy Rogers, not exactly the logical choice for an English-born girl who lived in Chicago. Her reflections were interrupted by the arrival of Sandy and Gracie at the same time. Amber gave them the same verbal invitation to enter then turned back to her computer.

For the first time, Pen noticed what was on the screen. A spread of pages, the documents Gracie and Sandy had photographed in the museum, enlarged to a readable size.

"Some interesting stuff here," Amber said. "Can you all see the screen?"

Sandy had moved toward the futon, picking up the magazines and stacking them. While she straightened the end-table mess into neat piles, Gracie ignored the clutter and walked to the kitchen counter bar, picking up the two light-weight wooden stools, placing them slightly behind Amber's chair—one for herself and one for Pen.

Pen glanced toward Sandy.

"I'm fine over here." Sandy brushed some kind of crumbs from the futon cushion and sank down, the seat obviously giving way a little more than she'd expected.

"These are the documents you sent me from the museum file," Amber said to Gracie.

With a dizzying flick of the mouse pointer she rolled through them. "The copy of the police report is interesting because it shows the robbery as petty theft."

"What!" Pen practically shrieked. She couldn't believe she hadn't caught that notation when she looked through Detective Caplin's file.

"What does that mean?" Gracie asked.

Sandy spoke up. "Grand theft, in Arizona, is theft of something worth more than one thousand dollars. Anything less is considered petty theft. The big difference is in the jail or prison time that can be given. And, of course, how much time the police devote to solving the crime." She shrugged. "Just saying, because of a few things down at the bank."

Pen considered that. This could be what was behind the Philpont staff insistence that her necklace was a reproduction. Lesser value, lesser criminal implication, lesser penalties. They all seemed to believe she would never miss the money. But money was the least of her attachments to the family heirloom. No one seemed to understand that.

"Here are copies of two appraisals," Amber said, dragging the two documents side by side on her large monitor.

The pages looked identical, exactly like the one Pen had provided when she loaned the necklace for the exhibit. The letterhead from Potts Fine Jewelry was a perfect duplicate. Regis Potts's signature was the same on both. But the sheet on the left gave precision measurements of each stone and valued the necklace at 1.3 million dollars; the one on the right described the stones as lab-created emeralds and cubic zirconia diamonds, value $950.

"Conveniently below the thousand-dollar threshold," murmured Gracie.

"Are there photos with the appraisals?" Pen asked.

"There should have been, but we didn't find them in the file," Sandy said.

"I can show you exactly what the cheap one looks like," Pen said.

She reached for her handbag and pulled out the familiar velvet pouch. When she undid the cord at the top and tipped it over, a cascade of brilliance landed in her other hand.

She let the strands trickle between her fingers. "There

you go, ladies. Less than a thousand dollars worth. Not enough to send a man to jail for ninety days."

"Oh, Pen, that's awful," said Gracie, reaching to place her arm around her friend's shoulders.

"I don't understand why the museum's leadership would risk its reputation with this," Sandy said. "Forging appraisal documents is very serious."

"Perhaps that's the very reason someone created the forgery. Someone on the inside must have switched the necklaces, so they needed documentation to back it up."

"Hell of a mistake, not destroying the original," Amber said.

"Why would they think this would fly, anyhow?" Gracie said. "The jeweler surely kept a copy. They had to know Pen most surely had another copy. Who would think they could get away with the switch?"

"Some dweeb," Amber said, shaking her head.

"Or someone who knew he would never, ever be questioned." Pen voiced her thoughts aloud. "Not a museum insider. Someone else set up the museum to be suspected of switching the necklaces, to be caught as responsible for the theft *and* for the false paperwork. Such a thing would be the death of a non-profit organization."

She thought of Stan Higgins and the near-desperate pleas for donations last night. Maybe the director knew the museum was either culpable or had been expertly framed. But who could pull off such a thing?

TWENTY-SIX

TODD WAINWRIGHT FELT certain he would throw up if he saw another pair of blue shoes. His mother picked up a low-heeled thing in sky blue, turned it in her hands to examine all sides, set it back. She caught the eye of a clerk and asked if they didn't have the same shoe in a darker shade. While the girl went to ask her manager, Todd pretended his phone had buzzed, pulled it from his pocket and excused himself.

Longing to flee the department store, the mall and the city itself, he walked out of Aggie's earshot and stared at the display. Wishful thinking had not caused it to ring. Where the hell was Caplin?

Todd knew Penelope Fitzpatrick had spotted the two of them talking outside the museum last night at the gala. If she'd caught even a portion of their conversation, Todd fully expected the bomb to drop at any time. He stuck the phone back in his pocket and picked another antacid from the foil-wrapped roll he always carried nowadays.

The conversation had begun on Todd's terms: *Where's Dick Stone and where's my money?*

Listen, kid, you think you're the only one wants Stone's head in a noose? At least you got paid a little bit up front.

You did too, right?

Ha—if you only knew.

What?

Caplin had fidgeted a moment, embarrassed.

What?

He was short on cash that first time you met him. Talked me into coming up with the thousand dollars. Said he'd be at the bank the next day and would pay me right back. Worse, I got stuck for the cost of the forger and the grand for the fake necklace. I don't even know those guys, and I'm the one paying for their work? Shit, if I get my hands on Stone...

Todd had wanted to laugh. A cop being taken in by a classic I'll-repay-you-later scam. But he didn't dare. The lady had been all over Caplin's case since she figured out the necklace was bogus. Now she knew of their connection... she was likely to start pestering him as well. And that old guy—the one who'd been her date that night—Caplin said the man used to be a prosecutor, still knew everyone in that end of things. If they got caught now, the lady's friend had the power to make all their lives pretty miserable.

The thing about the conversation that still haunted Todd, and the reason he really needed to get this thing done and finished, was what Caplin told him right at the end.

You screwed up royally, buddy. You put the fake appraisal in the museum's records, yes. But you forgot to take out the real one.

I didn't! I swear, I destroyed the real one.

Well, they've got another copy of it somehow. The detective's look had been so skeptical, Todd began to question himself. Maybe he had messed up. He'd been so nervous that night. Maybe the sheet of paper he'd fed into the shredder was something else. Oh, god, maybe he really had botched it.

If so, he'd be lucky if they didn't haul him to a dark alley somewhere, let alone never pay the rest of the money he was so desperately counting on.

Caplin's voice nagged at him: *Yeah, see, you're doubting yourself. Well, my department was only given copies of those appraisals. Your boss has the originals in a file somewhere in there, and if he ever really sits down with that file and reads everything...well, your ass is grass. Because, believe me, I'm not taking the fall for this. I'm already out a bunch of my retirement fund, but I'm not admitting to anything illegal. That's a hundred percent on you.*

Even now, standing in a mall department store, Todd swallowed hard. Caplin would cut him no slack at all. So much for being partners.

He glanced back toward the ladies shoe department where his mother was seated while the young clerk knelt beside a tall stack of shoeboxes. Good. She'd be there awhile. This damn shopping trip had turned into another nightmare when Aggie informed him she was buying a new outfit and shoes for his cousin's wedding, and he was going with her.

No wangling out of it. He'd be stuck as the single, eligible bachelor who had to dance with the homeliest of the girls and the eldest of his mother's generation, every female who couldn't scrounge up a date. And Iris—sheesh, she was the cousin no one ever believed would find a guy, much less a man who wanted to live with her forever. It made Todd feel even more like a loser, the last of his generation to find a partner, the failure in life.

He paused by the jewelry counter, his eye drawn by a display of gold watches. Maybe if he showed up at the wedding sporting one of those and dressed in a terrific suit. He saw the price tag on the coolest watch and it kind of took his breath away.

Money. Another sore subject in his life right now. Which

brought his thoughts full circle to the memory of what he'd done with the thousand dollars Dick Stone had given him.

His damn student loan had been two thousand in arrears at the time. A stupid, stupid visit to Laughing Rock Casino—one of those tribal places with terrible payout rates—hoping to double the grand and get himself caught up.

He turned away from the watches as an eager clerk approached. At this moment, he wanted to hide in a corner and cry.

TWENTY-SEVEN

PEN VOICED HER question aloud. "Who could manage to set up this whole thing—the fraudulent paperwork and the theft—while making the museum look culpable?"

"Would a master con man do?" Amber answered without a blink.

She closed the pages of documents on her computer screen and opened a new tab.

"I found quite a few Richard Stones, but most of them checked out as regular, law-abiding guys."

A little graph appeared, obviously designed to impress the group with Amber's abilities to ferret out information on the computer.

"When I cross-checked them with what we knew of our Mr. Stone's travel plans and the rental car data, that's when it turned interesting. There was no such man. The address he provided was a fake. The driver's license he presented agreed with the address all right. It's just that it's a vacant lot in Muncie, Indiana."

The screen flashed to a Google Earth view of—yes—a vacant lot. Thorough, Pen had to admit, although she found herself becoming a little impatient. Did Amber find their man or not?

"Here's the photo from the license." She made the picture stretch until it nearly filled her screen.

"It's…" Pen hesitated. "It's close. The shape of his face is right, the hairline, hair color. But his mouth is different and the nose isn't right either. It's not him."

"Close enough to pass muster with a busy rental agent or airport security, those guys who barely give a glance to be sure the names match with the rest of their documentation," Gracie said.

"Exactly." Amber switched to another screen. "So, I did another type of search. The security photos from the bank are next to useless but I patched them together, along with the one from the driver's license, and I came up with this."

She showed another photo. Pen had to admit this one was closer to the real man's face but it wasn't quite right yet.

"I ran this picture through facial recognition software." Amber glanced around the room. "No, it's not commercially available and, no, I didn't really steal it from a government agency. It's better if you don't ask about that."

Pen closed her mouth. Yes, in this case it was better that she didn't know too many details.

"With the search parameters and the picture…" Amber's voice trailed off as she moved images around on her screen and brought up a sort of spreadsheet. "…I narrowed it down to two possible Richard Stones."

Amazing, thought Pen when Amber showed the photos she'd found. The two looked very similar. She felt hard-pressed to say which was her phony private investigator. If she could see them in action, hear their voices—something like that would help.

"One of these men lives in California, the other in Indiana. Assuming our guy would want to stick somewhat close to home—familiarity with the local places, maybe his accent, you know—I dug a little deeper into the background of the one from Indiana. Who, it just happens, reported his identity stolen about three years ago."

Pen felt her heartbeat quicken. It made perfect sense.

"Did the authorities catch whoever stole the identity?" Sandy asked.

"Well, this also gets interesting. There's a community of gypsies in Indiana."

A chuckle popped forth from Gracie.

"I know, right? How weird is that? But it's true. Apparently a few generations back, a bunch of them came to the U.S. from eastern Europe and managed to end up in the Midwest. They tended to hang around together, I guess."

Pen was having a hard time wrapping her head around all this new information.

"The gypsy community is adept at stealing—take pride in it, in fact. There are so many scams you wouldn't believe it, even among the children. Stealing wallets is like first grade work for them. They get hold of credit cards and licenses and then sell them, barter them, sometimes even... use them." The dramatic pause gave everyone time to figure out what Amber was telling them.

"Our Richard Stone is a gypsy?" Pen asked.

"It looks that way."

"My god," said Sandy. "How will we ever track him down?"

"Well—there's good news and bad news," Amber said. "The bad news is that Richard Stone is far from the only alias this man uses. I've found about a dozen so far."

"And the good news?"

"I discovered his real name." She did a couple more clicks of the mouse. "This, ladies, is Frank Morrell, Junior."

This time the photo was definitely her private investigator.

"I'm impressed," said Pen, genuinely meaning it. In a few days, Amber had got much further with her searches than the police even hoped to do.

Gracie and Sandy seconded the kudos.

"Of course, the question now," said Pen, "is where on this planet is he?"

TWENTY-EIGHT

WATER, TURQUOISE CLEAR to the horizon, sand that looked like sugar, and a lounge chair in the shade of a couple palm trees. Life didn't get a whole lot better than this, mused Frank Morrell. A slender twenty-something girl flounced her hot-pink bikini through his field of view and a slow smile spread across his face. She could have been the blonde twin of the brunette who'd come to his room last night. Nope, life couldn't possibly get much better than this.

He debated asking the blonde to put some lotion on his shoulders—always a good ploy—but she was already twenty yards down the beach. Ah well, the view was nice from this angle. He took a deep breath and enjoyed it until another girl, this one in a set of vivid yellow strings that hardly covered anything, came toward him and passed the other direction. His head followed her trail, the way a dog is distracted from one rabbit to the next.

He thought of the money, snuggled safely in a numbered account. The million-dollar necklace he kept close. It was in a money belt under his tropical shirt. He patted the surface of it. God, he loved the Caymans. Here, you could be anyone you wanted to be. And while his Romani cousins and uncles stayed in the effing-cold Midwest and pulled insurance scams of the slip-and-fall variety, Frankie congratulated himself for graduating to a whole lot better neighborhood.

A cloud passed in front of the sun and his mood changed. He could be happy here for another few weeks but he knew his nature. He'd become antsy pretty soon, ready for another play on some other dumb mooch. In fact, he'd already caught himself sizing up a few of them right from his lounge chair.

The Arizona con had involved partners. Frankie didn't much care for that, especially involving a cop, which had probably been dumb, although the guy played right in as he was supposed to, more worried about padding his retirement fund than actually catching Dick Stone. He chuckled at the recollection. How convenient one of Frankie's seldom-used aliases fit right in with the real name of the retired cop old Caplin knew. Simple matter to have him suggest his legitimate friend's name to the mark, that rich-bitch socialite. Neither of the partners nor the mark herself had seen old Frankie swoop in and take the whole bundle.

But this next time he wanted something simpler, a grift he could work on his own. A chubby guy wearing oversized swim shorts in a horrendous geometric pattern walked by. Frankie noted the posture (slumpy), the gait (lackadaisical) and the expression (lost). This guy was so basic, even the Nigerian prince con would work on him. But he also probably had nothing to give away.

This was the guy who'd taken out a second mortgage to pay for his middle-aged wife's dream vacation. Yeah, a grifter with Frankie's talent could probably get another mortgage out of him, no doubt raid the kids' college fund. But Frankie wanted more than that and it wasn't because of some stupid notion of giving the man a break. He didn't do that shit. He'd just scored a million dollar deal; he was in the big leagues now. A rich, older lady would work for a sweetheart scam...or a businessman made a great target for The Wire or the Stock Market scam. He was looking for a certain type.

And here he came, fifty yards away and closing. Less than handsome but not bad looking, trim physique but not muscular, short enough and nerdy enough to have insecurity issues. A real honey of a younger woman clung to his arm. She wore a diamond the size of an apple on her left hand and a half-dozen gold chains draped over her tanned, ample cleavage. Oh yeah, definite insecurity issues for this guy.

Frankie gave a yawn and began gathering his things. Time to call it a day and go inside for a shower. The end of another sunny afternoon at the beach. In his peripheral vision, the couple came closer. He timed it perfectly to back into them as he left his lounger.

"Hey, watch it!" the mark said. An American. Perfect.

"Oh, sir, terribly sorry," Frankie said effusively in his best London west-end accent. "Madam, are you all right?"

He fussed over them, apologizing twice more for his clumsiness.

"Well, just look where you're going," the man said. The woman was already smiling.

"Let me buy you both a drink later, make up for my rudeness," Frankie said. "Are you guests here at the hotel?"

The mark might look a little slow but he wasn't giving out information that easily.

"Oh. Right. Well, I am a guest here. Woodsworth Coddington, the fourth." It was the name he'd used to register here, although not the same one he'd given the bank. "My friends call me Woody."

Frankie's smile was genuine. Last time he was Stone Dick and now he was Woody. He sometimes amazed himself with his own cleverness. "At any rate, I'll be in the pub—er, the bar or whatever they call it here—in about an hour. If you come in, I'm good for those drinks, I assure you."

The mark mirrored Frankie's smile, while the woman showed a dimple. She'd picked up on the innuendo but probably assumed such a proper British gentlemen didn't realize what he'd just said.

Frankie preceded them to the lobby, where he made a show of digging his key card from the pocket of his shorts and pressing the elevator button for the upper, restricted floors. He smiled at them as the elevator door closed. The wife was whispering something into her sweetie's ear as they watched him leave. Frankie placed a little private bet with himself. A lobster dinner if they showed at the bar. They would.

TWENTY-NINE

Where is Frank Morrell? More importantly, where is my necklace? Pen pondered the questions while Amber left her computer momentarily to get herself and Gracie sodas from the fridge. She returned to her chair, took a long swig of the cola and reached for her computer mouse again.

"Where he is, that's a question I haven't figured out yet. I've got tons of background now, though."

"So, let's sift through that information and put our heads together to figure out what he would do next," Sandy suggested. She'd given up the saggy futon for a straight-backed chair she pulled closer to the rest of the group.

"I've printed a few things," Amber said, reaching for pages near the big monitor. "Figured it would be good for each of us to memorize some of this data."

She handed them around. The list consisted of names:

Known aliases of Frank Morrell:
- Frank Martin
- Martin Frank
- Richard "Dick" Stone
- Stone Barrington (this one borrowed from a fictional character)
- Stone Martin
- Woodrow Frank
- Franklin Woodrow

"I'm seeing a pattern," Gracie commented with a wry grin.

"I read a book once," Amber said, catching Gracie's chuckle. "Yes, I've read books—a lot. This one was about a family of con artists. Anyway, one thing this group did was change names all the time, and they frequently switched first and last names around. For them, it's easier to remember the name they're using at the moment. For us, maybe we'll spot a pattern. I haven't had time yet but when I get into them and search airline records, I'll see if tickets show up issued under any combination of these names."

"Well, I think you've done a marvelous job here, Amber." Pen had to admit she'd been skeptical about bringing such a young person into their group. Now she was glad they did.

A second page was attached and Amber flipped to her copy now. "These are the things I've found from police records. He's worked the Midwest a lot, Florida and the northeast some. Apparently, your case was the first time he came to the southwest."

Lucky me, thought Pen. She looked at page two.

Known cons of Frank Morrell:
• The Wire
• The Sweetheart
• The Market

There were more but Pen stopped. "What are all these?"

Amber sent a quirky smile toward Gracie. "From that same book… The Wire is an old one that goes back to the days when horse race results were sent by telegraph across country. Con men figured out how to interrupt the signal just long enough to place bets on a race that had already been run, ensuring they always won their bets. It becomes a real con when he convinces the mark to bet big. First they let him get a few wins, and as he increases his bets the con makes sure he loses. Modern day versions might not be about horses and they certainly aren't about telegraph lines, but they always involve convincing someone they are privy to inside information and can make big money by betting on it."

Pen thought of the Robert Redford movie, *The Sting*. She'd loved that film.

"The Market is similar—some kind of so-called inside information about the stock market," Amber said. "The Sweetheart is just what it sounds like. The con artist—most often female, sometimes a male—targets an older, lonely person. Widowed men are prime targets but con men will go after older women too."

"Oh my gosh," Sandy said. "It happened to one of our clients at the bank. A successful gentleman with a tidy account. This woman came into his life. She wasn't even especially a pretty one, but she convinced him she loved him more than anything in the world. Of course she didn't start out asking for money—it never works that way. She just wanted to spend time with him, take up his hobbies, adapt to his interests. He was flattered beyond belief.

"Pretty soon her extended family came into it. Her granddaughter just lost her apartment—could he help her find a place? Could he make the repairs and cover just a couple months rent? A son out of state got into a bit of a jam—could Mr., um, Smith loan him a thousand dollars? After awhile, it's bigger things. A new wardrobe for a trip, proper jewelry to go with the new clothes—all expenses, of course, paid by our client. After awhile he 'gifted' her some real estate and wrote her into the will. This went on for years, until his money was completely gone."

Gracie's eyes were wide. "How does a successful—

presumably smart—man fall for that? Can't he see what's going on?"

"The heart never sees those things. Our client even went through with a marriage of sorts, although no one from his immediate family was invited so they don't know if it was real. And he'd never admit to having been duped. He's too smart to have been scammed, in his mind."

"It's called a long con," Amber said. "When the payout is big enough, these people will spend years working it. The con artist often goes off during the day—either to a fictitious job or 'doing her own thing' when she's really consulting with the rest of her cohorts—while the old guy just blissfully waits for her to come home and hop in bed with him."

"Okay, that part of it I don't even want to imagine," Gracie said.

"Back to Frank Morrell," Pen said. "He doesn't seem the sort to hang around with someone for years, working to clean out her bank accounts."

Sandy spoke up. "It could be he has a woman somewhere, just comes and goes from her place?"

"The only time he was questioned by police in a sweetheart scam," Amber said, "was a quick-and-dirty sort of deal. Met this lady on a cruise ship and they really hit it off. She bought him a ton of expensive gifts in the shops, visited the branch of her bank on a shore excursion for cash to 'help him out'… He promised to come see her in Fort Lauderdale as soon as he'd run home to Atlanta to take care of some business. Of course he never showed and it took a lot of nagging by the woman's friends to convince her he didn't live in Atlanta and wouldn't be coming back. A friend actually dragged her to the police station to file a report, in hopes the cruise line would somehow prevent him from doing the same routine on some other passenger."

"I'm glad he didn't come on to me romantically, not that I couldn't have handled such an advance," Pen said. "But then I guess he did get away with what he really wanted."

THIRTY

FRESHLY SHOWERED AND wearing a crisp linen suit he'd picked up a half hour earlier in the hotel gift shop, Frank took the elevators at the west end of the building. He knew the credit card he'd used to secure his room, one of the fanciest penthouse suites, would soon come into question and he didn't want to pass directly by the front desk where someone might have an eye out for him. Although he could use another one, the game became chancier as time went on.

Two thousand in cash, the diamond necklace and a passport in the name of Franklin Woodrow lay securely tucked next to his belly in the money belt. Things could get dicey in a hurry and he was prepared to hop into a taxi and be on the next plane or boat if necessary.

But the evening was young—no sense in borrowing trouble that didn't yet exist. He didn't even know the names of his marks, but he was pretty confident about earning that lobster dinner. The elevator halted and Frankie put on his most carefree smile as the door opened.

The bar at the end of the corridor opened onto the beach, with those grassy roof overhangs and some kind of twisty tropical wood pillars supporting them. Lava rocks cemented together formed a low wall and flowering bushes added spots of brilliant color. A good choice to put his quarry in a nice, relaxed mood.

The place was still nearly empty, Frank noticed as he scanned the tables. Perfect. He ordered at the bar, a glass of water with a sprig of mint. He took one of the tables beside the lava wall, stretched out his legs and leaned back as if he hadn't a care in the world, and stared out toward the sea. Less than ten minutes later, he sensed motion nearby.

"Mr. Coddington?" His mark, right on schedule.

Frank stood quickly, extending his hand, remembering at the last second that he was English. He put on the accent just in time.

"Right-o. I'm afraid I was terribly remiss in not getting your name, sir?"

"Tom Anderson." The man shook Frank's hand. "And my wife, Danielle."

She wore a strapless dress in a bright tropical print and Frank had to work to keep his eyes above her shoulders. The tanned skin held great appeal but the necklace of heavy gold strands was almost equally enticing. He took her hand and noticed she wore an exquisite sapphire ring, in addition to the monster diamond engagement ring. He wondered if she remembered to lock their in-room safe each time she went out. He stopped the speculation—back to current business.

"My pleasure," he said truthfully. "Join me? We'll get those drinks on order."

Frank signaled a young black man with a tray and the Andersons placed their orders. Before he'd quite settled in his chair, his cell phone rang inside his jacket pocket, startling him. He plucked it out and looked at the readout. A Phoenix area code. Shit! He'd meant to toss this phone days ago. He must have left his real one back in the room. He declined the call and put the phone away.

"Problems?" Anderson asked.

"Business. The New York office," Frank said.

Anderson was nodding. "I know. Employees. You tell them you're on vacation, not to disturb you…"

"Exactly." He shook his head dolefully. "What line are you in?"

"Auto parts. You?"

"Jewelry. In fact, I couldn't help but admire your wife's rings." He lowered his voice, even though he hadn't been speaking loudly at all. "I'd guess that little beauty runs upwards of five carats."

Danielle held her hand at arm's length, admiring her own stone.

"Four-point-eight," Tom Anderson said.

"May I?" Frank reached toward Danielle. She placed her hand in his.

"Oh my. A princess cut, and even without my loupe I'd say it's nearly flawless. You are definitely a couple with *very* discriminating taste."

Their drinks arrived just then and Frank offered a toast. "To excellent taste, and to an entire holiday without a call from the office."

He sipped his water, as if it were vodka, letting the couple down their fruity drinks quickly, ordering them another round. The Market would be the con, he decided after thirty minutes' conversation. Anderson had already boasted of his gains in stocks last year and bragged how he did it all himself. No sense in paying a broker, he said.

"Absolutely," said Frank in his posher-by-the-moment accent. "I place all my own trades. I do, however, follow the tips I get from my one friend. Was with the London Exchange for a number of years, you know, but he's broken away from the establishment now. Does a bit of, shall we say, his own research."

He waggled his eyebrows, letting Tom know he was referring to things slightly outside the strict rules of the law.

"You've done well with this advisor?" Tom asked.

"His advice bought me the jet I flew in on. My girlfriend, back in London, loves it. She took the plane when I located a forty-carat Burmese ruby awhile back and she wanted to go pick it up herself."

Danielle's lovely blue eyes went a little wider. A private plane and a forty-carat ruby! She looked toward her husband. He lifted his chin and gave her a smug smile.

"Tell me more about this guy you invest with, Mr. Coddington."

"Oh, enough about business for now," Frank said, carefully timing his moves. You didn't dare reel them in too quickly. "Let me treat you to a lobster dinner. I know this wonderful place just up the beach."

This guy was the type; the ones who felt they knew a bit about investing were ripe for Frank's insider tips. And Tom was clearly a man who thought he was smarter than he really was. This could shape up nicely.

THIRTY-ONE

THEY WERE DEALING with a master manipulator and accomplished con man, Penelope realized as she drove home from Amber's apartment. Their young computer genius had said she would need more time to check out Frank Morrell's various aliases, and the Heist Ladies had agreed to meet again in a week to see how she was coming along.

Already, Pen had to admit she was impressed with their progress. The police had spent six months investigating the robbery with no success, and they'd shown no interest in going after the con man once they believed the necklace wasn't worth much. The Ladies had managed to identify their suspect and find the discrepancy in the museum's paperwork. With luck, they could put the two together and get someone convicted of this crime.

The crime. Pen steeled herself for the worst. Well, the very worst was the way things stood now—no resolution at all. But next worst would be if they caught Frank Morrell too late, if the beautiful necklace made by her grandfather had already been handed off. It could be in the hands of some unscrupulous collector who would never let it go or, heaven forbid, have made it to those in the business of moving stolen goods. It might have been torn apart, the stones sold individually or even recut. She couldn't bear to think of it.

She resolved to focus ahead, one step at a time.

Naomi had gone for the day but left Pen a light supper in the fridge, a salad and a nice white wine to go with it. Pen carried her plate out to the veranda with its sweeping view of the city below, thinking all the while about what she'd heard today. Such a terrible thing, those who were out to cheat and steal from others. It broke her heart to think of the elderly people who fell prey to those sweetheart scams and were almost always too embarrassed to admit it, even to their families, much less the authorities. She had to remind herself that she, too, was over seventy and could well be considered a prime target for one of those men.

Who am I kidding, she thought in disgust. I've already been a target. And the horrid man got away with my most prized possession. Her fork clattered to the plate. She couldn't take another bite.

The telephone was ringing when she walked back into the kitchen.

"Pen, it's Amber. I've got some news."

"Already?"

"Frank Morrell traveled from Phoenix to Grand Cayman using the name Franklin Woodward. He was on a plane within two hours after he left your house that day."

"No wonder the police couldn't track him."

"I have this on a conference call with Sandy and Gracie standing by. Shall I open their lines?"

"Oh, by all means. This is exciting! We have to share it."

The other two voices joined the conversation. "Aren't the Cayman Islands a prime spot for untraceable offshore accounts?" asked Gracie.

"Used to be," Sandy said. "It's become trickier in recent years, but Morrell may have found a way."

"Do you think he went straight there to deposit the cash from my check? He must have."

"Most likely."

"And what about my necklace? He could put it into a safe deposit box there as well?"

Gracie spoke up. "If that's what happened, how can we get to it—the cash and the necklace, I mean?"

"Amber, can you somehow hack into his account there and just bring the money back to mine?" Pen asked.

"Well, I don't..."

Pen had to keep in mind there was a banker in the group. If Amber had ever been involved in such shady—and illegal—dealings, it wouldn't be wise for her to admit it.

"There would be passwords and several identity safeguards in place," Sandy said. "Without the user name, passwords and answers to security questions I don't see how it could be done. Plus, we don't know which of his many names he used to set up the bank account. I'd venture to say it would not be the one he used to travel there."

That made sense, they all agreed.

"And we don't know which bank. If you begin trying various accounts in various banks, it's quite possible they'll pick up your server identity and you'll be shut out. Or caught and apprehended."

"True," Amber said.

Why was it the bad guys got away with these shenanigans while those trying to right a wrong stood the chance of arrest? Pen pondered that thought but a better idea came to her.

"So, let's go there. It's the weekend coming up. Can everyone take a couple of days to get on a plane?"

Her voice held so much excitement it generated a buzz of approval from the others.

"We can figure out where he's staying, can't we? We'll spy on him and see which bank he goes to." This from Gracie.

"It's not a large place. We're likely to spot him walking down a street, right?" Amber's idea.

"Hold on a minute," said Sandy. "Even in a very small place we could spend days just hoping to spot him. We need a better plan going in."

"I've already checked the hotel guest registers on the island and there's no one under any of the aliases we know about," Amber said.

"Okay, then it's going to come down to some old-fashioned lying," suggested Gracie. "Let's see… I'll call each place—Amber, email me that list—and I'll say that I need to reach my, um, my aunt who is visiting the island. It's a family emergency. But she's—she's staying with a friend and I don't know the man's name. I'll describe him—"

"Ooh, better yet," said Amber, "say you can fax or email a photo and ask if they have that guest staying with them."

"A mug shot or driver's license picture?"

"No, no. I can make a photo," Amber assured them. "Mom won't mind. Okay, gotta go."

"Mom won't mind?" said Gracie and Sandy when they heard the click on the line.

Pen decided she didn't need all the details. "All right, then. Gracie, you start with your calls to the hotels. We'll see what Amber comes up with. Meanwhile, I have an idea."

The four-way call ended and Pen went to her desk and booted up her computer. A quick check showed eleven p.m. flights tomorrow night that would put them on the island by noon the next day. She put four seats on hold.

Fifteen minutes later an email with a photo attachment arrived from Amber, subject line: What do you think?

The woman is my mom, she'd written. *Think they look like a fun vacationing couple?*

The photo showed Frank Morrell standing beside a lovely woman with caramel skin and Amber's unwieldy hair smoothed back and held with a clip. Granted, Frank's expression was less than exuberant—they'd only had his driver's license to borrow from, after all—but the setting was tropical, the body attached to the face was of roughly the same build as his and the flowered shirts gave the whole thing an air of authenticity. Coming through electronically, it just might work.

Already replies from Gracie and Sandy cheered the effort. Gracie added that she'd called four hotels so far, another six to go. She assured them she would be sending the photo out to the manager at each place. If she found the right hotel, she said, she would personally put on a maid's uniform and get into his room. Pen would have her necklace back!!

Pen liked the addition of the exclamation points. Their chance of success was beginning to feel real.

THIRTY-TWO

FRANK SLEPT LATE the next morning and woke with a vague unease about his latest marks, the Andersons. Had he managed to keep his British accent firmly in place all evening? The lobster dinner had gone well. Somewhere around ten o'clock, he'd tired of pretending to be drunk from his water martinis and had switched to the real thing. Tom Anderson, of course, was well in his cups by then, and Danielle had begun rubbing Frank's leg with her bare foot under the table.

He'd managed to slip her hotel key card from her purse when she left it behind on a trip to the ladies room. Not that he intended to use it for what she had in mind—it would come in handy for his own plans later.

The three had hung out in the bar until well after midnight, Frank playing it cagey about his investment advisor. Anderson persisted—what would it take for him to get in? Well, I don't know, Frank responded, it was a pretty exclusive group and the really hot deals didn't come up very often. The whole thing became almost hilarious, with Tom practically drooling into his late-night Drambuie and Danielle sending seductive glances which became more pathetic since the woman could barely hold her head up.

If either of the marks had noticed Frank's accent slipping, they wouldn't remember it this morning. He tossed the sheets aside and stared out his balcony window at the peaceful blue water. The beach curved around the small lagoon where the hotel sat, a few miles away from town. Palm trees waved in the gentle breeze and already the bikini set were beginning to spread towels on lounge chairs and rub oil into their already-bronzed skin.

Yeah, he thought with a sigh, I could stay awhile and really get into this lifestyle. Except he never settled very long anywhere. If everything fell into place today, he would be taking his leave sooner rather than later.

He took a quick shower and dressed in tropical-weight pants and a flowered shirt, the all-important money belt with the necklace in it strapped securely to his waist. The room phone rang as he picked up his sunglasses and cell phone. He ignored the noise. Damned front desk, no doubt, wanting to pester him again about that credit card situation. He walked out.

At ground level, he paused beside the stone wall where he'd begun the play yesterday with Tom and Danielle Anderson. He surveyed the beach, ignoring the relentless swoosh of the waves—too boring to keep his attention—and focusing on the people. He spotted them almost right away, Danielle's upright posture and proud bosom next to Tom's shuffling gait, about a quarter mile in the distance and heading his direction. Frank smiled and stepped out into the sunshine.

He raised his cell phone to his ear, walking along to a spot where there were no loungers nearby, gesticulating and talking as if he were on the most important call of his life. From the corner of his eye, he saw that Tom Anderson had spotted him. He turned his back to the couple and paced a few steps the other direction, turned again, paced toward the waterline, still gesturing, still ignoring Anderson.

When the mark moved within earshot, Frank went into the play.

"Archie, I'm on an island, for god's sake!" Pause. "Yeah, yeah, well sure there are...let me think..." Pause. Definite interest from Anderson, although the man had half-turned away in a gesture of offering privacy. "What time is it there? Okay, I'm on it. I'll get to the bank immediately. You watch for my transfer and make *sure* you get me into this thing today!"

He snapped the phone shut and pretended a startled re-action as if he noticed the Andersons for the first time.

"Oh! Tom, Danielle, I was hoping to run into you. Have you had your breakfast? I've been considering the brunch buffet inside..." He waved vaguely toward the hotel. "Then it turns out I can't. Just got a call...listen, must rush."

He started to turn away.

"That was your advisor guy, wasn't it?" asked Tom. "Sorry, I heard you call him Archie. That's the one, right?"

"Well, yes. I'm afraid he's just given me the most brilliant tip. You've heard the copper market has been in the crapper for months now? At any rate, the market closes in London in about an hour. It's Friday, you know." He punctuated his words with quick little gestures. "If I don't get to the bank in town this very minute, I completely lose out."

"Wait—can I get in on this one too?" Tom asked. The hunger on his face was a sweet thing.

"Oh, Tom, I don't know. It's such a limited offering..." He counted three silent beats. "Look, ride along and we can discuss it in the car."

"What about brunch, honey?" Danielle whined.

"Get whatever you want," Tom told her, pulling a hundred dollar bill from his pocket. "Have a little fun in the gift shop too."

Frank was already five paces ahead, aiming for the pathway that bypassed the lobby. The flash of cash—what a rookie move—to prove he could afford to play with the big boys. Tom caught up, puffing slightly to match Frank's rapid stride.

A Rolls Royce limo sat at the curb. The hotel had several of them for their VIP guests and the driver barely glanced at Frankie's gold room key before he opened the door to the back seat. Unless Tom knew about the perks of the penthouse suites, he would likely assume this was the private car of Woodsworth Coddington IV. Frank was not about to burst that delightful little bubble.

"First Cayman Bank," he told the driver. "As quickly as possible, please." Good, polite Englishmen always said please.

The limo glided down the driveway and onto the island's main road. Frank jabbered on about copper futures and the price of gold and how all those things were such an integral part of the jewelry business. As the airport appeared on their right, he happily spotted several private jets parked near the fencing.

"Ah, they're taking good care of my baby," he said, waving vaguely toward them.

"Is yours the one with the blue tail?" Anderson asked, saving Frank the potential disaster of not knowing the various models. Plus, it was the biggest one.

"Yes, the *Kristina*. I called her after my dear fiancée who was tragically swept away in a riptide on Bali, only days before our wedding." Careful, Frankie, not too many details.

"Oh—so sad," said Tom, averting his eyes from the plane.

Ten minutes later the car pulled up outside a turquoise and white building. "Here we are, sir," said the driver.

"Wait here," Frank told the man. "I shouldn't be long."

Under his breath he said to Tom, "Quickest ten-fold return I'll ever make."

"I'm coming along," Tom said. As they approached the ornate brass-trimmed doors he added, "I really want in on this investment, Woody."

The rope tightened. The man was his.

"All right then. Let's do some paperwork."

Frank strode to the counter for international transfers and explained the need to move funds from his account at this bank to someone in London. The attractive black woman handed him a simple form and he began filling in account numbers. In the space for Amount of Transfer he wrote $1,000,000.

Tom's eyes widened. "I, uh, don't have quite that much to put in. Is a lesser amount okay?"

Frank stiffened. "How much less?"

"Afraid I can only go two-hundred grand."

"I'm sure that's fine," Frank assured him. "I began much smaller as well."

"I'll need those forms too," said Tom to the teller. "I assume with the right routing numbers I can move money from my U.S. account as well?"

She smiled. Accommodating the quirky needs of wealthy people kept her employed. Tom wrote his own bank account number from memory, then copied the "Send To" account number from Frank's form and filled in the amount, $200,000. The teller took their forms and began inputting data into her computer.

"Your receipt, Mr. Anderson," she said with a smile, handing over a slip.

Anderson stared at it a moment, put it in his pocket and let out a long breath.

The woman looked at Frank. "I'm afraid you forgot to sign your form, sir." She pushed it back toward him.

"Oh, that was inattentive of me."

The one place where Anderson could catch on to the whole scheme, if he was watching. Frank stole a glance and saw that his mark had turned toward the door. He dashed off the actual name on the account, his own, and passed it quickly to the woman. If she saw he was transferring money from his Cayman account to an identically registered one in Switzerland she gave no indication.

Five minutes later the two men walked back out to the Rolls.

"All right, old chap," said Frank in his most jubilant Woodsworth voice. "All we have to do now is lounge around our lovely hotel, enjoy the beach and wait for the market to open Monday with news of our coup. I have a feeling your Danielle will be ever so grateful to you."

THIRTY-THREE

BILL CAPLIN SAT in his generic government car a half-block down the street from the house where a robbery suspect lived with his mother. The stupid kid (had they always been this immature at twenty-five?) shot at a convenience store clerk, hit a can of oil on the shelf instead, grabbed the cash from the till but tracked the damn oil out the front door and down the alley. It didn't take rocket science to figure out the prints would lead to the home of this punk who'd been caught on camera robbing the same place two weeks ago. The house was less than a block from the store.

Caplin's purpose in sitting here now, rather than hauling the kid out by the scruff of his neck, was to make sure the perp didn't leave the house before the crime scene folks arrived to bag his shoes. Procedure! It became more ridiculous with each passing year.

Bending over backward to follow cumbersome rules and treat suspects with more respect than the victims got, those were only a couple of the reasons Caplin was more than ready to retire. But every time he thought of retirement, it reopened the festering anger at the fake Dick Stone, anger that always seethed just below the surface.

Sure, he still had his city pension coming but that fifty grand would have bought him the boat he planned on taking down to Mexico, living on it while his skin turned dark brown and he ate shrimp every day. A guy could live like a king on a couple grand a month down there. Without that boat, he'd be paying for housing and it kind of burst the whole bubble of his vision. Now, he'd have to take a second job for a few years and save every scrap before he could do the dream. Dammit, he didn't want to wait for it. His old man and brother had died in their early sixties when the old ticker gave out. Bill had been 'this close' to realizing his vision.

Meanwhile, every passing day made it harder to admit what had happened. Reporting the theft of such a chunk of his retirement money was simply too humiliating. Yeah, yeah, he knew that's what most victims of con men felt and that's why so few of those guys were ever caught or prosecuted. But geez, he was a cop. He should have seen through the guy and arrested him on the spot. His fist tightened around the steering wheel until he heard something crackle. He released it and shook out the tension.

He'd pretty much decided he would keep quiet and just pursue it on his own. He reached into his shirt pocket and pulled out a copy of the mug shot Penelope Fitzpatrick had tentatively chosen, a small-time grifter named Frank Woods. So far, Caplin had only had time in his off hours to learn that Woods was just one of many aliases this guy used. He wished he knew more about computers—some shortcuts would sure help at this point.

His cell phone rang and he took the call without looking at the readout.

"Hey, detective, it's me. Todd Wainwright."

Shit. This guy was becoming a pain in the neck.

"Have you caught up with that Dick Stone guy yet?"

Why did people think police work went the way it did on TV—every crime solved and all the loose ends wrapped up in an hour?

"No, Todd. I've got a lead on his identity but nothing on his whereabouts yet."

He could hear the museum guy grousing at the other end. Too bad.

"Todd, I'll let you know when I have anything. You know, you're free to search for him too."

"Oh, I wouldn't have any idea how."

"Yeah, well, I don't exactly have the complete resources of the department here," Caplin said. "Not unless you want your name brought into it and the whole thing a matter of record."

"No, no. That's okay. I'm sure you're doing all you can." Todd thanked him and ended the call.

"Damn straight," Caplin muttered to the empty car.

THIRTY-FOUR

PENELOPE CHECKED HER email every five minutes for the rest of the afternoon, and something delightful seemed to be waiting for her each time.

From Gracie. To All Heist Ladies: Success! Our man identified by manager at the Grand Cayman Regent. Registered as Woodsworth Coddington IV (seriously!!). He's staying in the penthouse suite and there's a little question about his credit card. They were not aware of a woman staying with him, but if I get in touch with my "aunt" would I please have her visit the front desk?

From Pen. To All: This will be fun! I have four seats booked—everyone in?

From Amber. To All: My passport's at my mother's. No time to get it L Wish I could, but better stay near computer at home in case you need further research.

From Gracie, Sandy and Pen. To Amber: Sorry you can't come but good idea about the research.

From Pen. To Gracie, Sandy: Flight leaves at 11:00 tonight. You have two hours to pack!

From Sandy. To Pen: Yowza! Will I be back for work Monday morning?

From Pen. To Sandy: We can make it happen.

Pen went immediately to the airline site, canceled Amber's ticket and finalized reservations for the other three.

They would arrive Saturday morning and return Sunday afternoon. She could only hope it would provide enough time for the confrontation with Frank Morrell and to retrieve the stolen cash and necklace. If banks there were not open on Saturday, Pen was prepared to extend her own return for an extra day. It had been a long time since she'd made such spur-of-the-moment travel plans and she found herself getting excited.

She called Benton and told him only that she needed to make a quick trip, asking if he would drive her to the airport. At this point, she didn't want to get into explanations or the need to defend her actions. She just wanted to go.

Nine p.m. brought a flurry of excitement as the Ladies met in front of the American Airlines ticket counter. Sandy headed for the check-in kiosks but Pen touched her shoulder.

"Over here," she said, indicating a window at the counter.

"First class?" Gracie squeaked. "You booked us first class?"

"It was a pretty full flight and this was the only way to get seats together." Pen hedged. She'd really wanted to do something nice for the girls in return for the time and effort they were spending to help her. Then she caught Gracie's stricken look. "Oh, my—don't be mistaken. This is completely my treat."

Relief. Then a wave of giddy excitement. They were on their way to the Caribbean.

THIRTY-FIVE

DANIELLE AND I are going to treat you to lunch, Woody." Tom Anderson leaned toward Frank across the seat of the Rolls Royce, on their way from the bank back to the Grand Cayman Regent. "I can't thank you enough for bringing me along today."

"Lunch would be very nice," Frank answered, working to keep up his British reserve, since all he really wanted to do was get out of this man's presence and yelp for joy.

Two hundred grand in his Swiss account after a couple days socializing with this auto parts businessman, the guy who thought he knew so much about investing. He resisted the urge to sneak a glance at his watch. All he had to do was keep the Andersons in the dark and avoid the hotel manager for another sixteen hours.

"Man, Monday morning can't come soon enough for me," Anderson was saying. "I can't wait to take a look at that ten-fold return you promised."

Frank forced his smile to mirror Tom's eagerness. "It will be grand, won't it?"

The car rolled to a quiet stop in front of the hotel's main entrance. Tom got out at the curb. Frank climbed out on the side away from the building.

"Look, I've got a quick stop to make," he said. "Let's meet

at the beach. I heard about a tasty little place for lunch and it's only a short walk."

"Great," said Tom. "Danielle's probably already out working on her tan. I'll tell her to put on some clothes. Fifteen minutes?"

Frank sent him a little salute as he ducked into a narrow pathway beside the building. No way was he going to wreck things now by walking through the lobby. Alone in the shade of a huge tree with flaming red flowers, he let out a long breath and rolled his shoulders a couple of times to release the pent-up energy. He loved to play the con, loved to watch the mark lay down his money, especially loved watching those dollars move along right into his bank account. He didn't love the idea of having to keep up the pretense this many more hours.

How was he going to keep Anderson from checking with his own bank, potentially stopping the funds transfer and botching the deal? At the very least, he had to keep the guy occupied until after banking hours, another four or five hours. The afternoon stretched ahead, much too long.

He patted the money belt where the necklace and cash sat, felt his pockets and found the two cell phones. Damn, he'd meant to get rid of the one from Arizona. The thing was like an anchor around his neck. He pressed a button on it and saw another call from Todd Wainwright. Geez, would that guy never let go?

A glance at the time told him he had a few minutes yet before meeting the Andersons. He ducked between two buildings and headed for a small pier where he'd seen fishing boats dock when they picked up their charters. He wondered how deep that water was, supposed it didn't matter—almost any amount of salt water could ruin a cell phone.

He strode toward the pier and walked to the end of it. No

one was around at the moment. The morning's passengers had left hours ago with their sunscreen and high hopes; they wouldn't return until they were salty and sunburned, with or without fish. He held the Arizona phone discreetly in the palm of his hand, walked to the end of the pier, pretended to enjoy the breakwater a quarter mile away and the horizon well beyond. With the incoming splash of a wave, he slipped the unwanted phone into the water, giving it a little flick to send it beyond the wooden pilings. There. Done.

Lunch went well. Tom was full of himself and his business savvy. Danielle quizzed her husband about the Rolls Royce they'd taken to the bank. Was it nice, honey? Wouldn't we look grand driving around Kansas City in one of those? He practically promised her one as soon as they got home.

Twice, Frank had to steer the conversation away from travel plans. He didn't want to say anything that would cause the Andersons to change their plans or try to track his.

"Say," he said after graciously allowing Tom to pay the lunch check, "I didn't realize this restaurant didn't serve alcohol. Let's all go back to my suite and have a celebratory drink to our success."

He'd picked up, early on, that Danielle was one of those tourists who goes to beach resorts with the idea that while she's on vacation there will be no responsibilities and no schedule. Beach time and drinking were her goals, and from what he'd noticed last night she could really put it away. She quickly latched onto his invitation. The longer he could keep the couple occupied, the less chance they would learn too much before it was too late.

"Oh my god," said Danielle when they walked into the penthouse suite. "Oh. My. God. How big is this place, anyway?"

"Three bedrooms, four baths." He spread his hands to indicate the living room furnished with European style rococo and the latest designer colors. A grand piano sat in one corner, a dining table for twelve beyond. The balcony was above the treetops so the view consisted of acres of undulating green palm fronds with the luminous turquoise water beyond.

"It's a little much just for me," he told them, "but the smaller suites were full." He gave a what-do-you-do shrug.

He'd discovered the fully stocked bar as soon as he arrived and now, with the confidence of a man at home in his surroundings, he offered to pour. Danielle immediately snapped up the 18-year Glenlivet. Tom said he would take one, as well.

Tom knew how to pace himself, it turned out, but his wife didn't. By four o'clock she was snoring in a very unladylike manner from one of the deep armchairs.

"Appears my wife could use a nap," Tom said, not quite meeting his host's eye.

He walked over to Danielle's chair and tried to rouse her.

"Let me give you a hand, old man," offered Woodsworth IV. "No worries. Who among us hasn't needed a nap at some point."

Tom gave an embarrassed smile of gratitude and the two men proceeded to lift Danielle to her feet. She roused enough to stumble along.

"I'd better help you the rest of the way," Woody said. Danielle was the curvaceous sort, not some reed-thin fashion model.

They got to the elevator and, luckily, the ride was only two floors down. Tom managed the key while Frank propped Danielle against his shoulder, hoping she wouldn't topple. He would no doubt yank his back out if he had to catch her. Inside, Tom led the way to their king-sized bed. She mumbled a bit in her sleep. While Tom removed her shoes and jostled to get the duvet over her, Frank turned discreetly away.

Discreetly enough to spot a heavy gold bracelet and decent diamond dinner ring on the dresser. They were in Frank's pocket before Tom looked up.

"All right, then," Woody said, as Tom cleared his throat, still having a hard time looking Frank in the eye. "I'm sure a nice rest and a good dinner will set everything right."

"See you sometime tomorrow, okay?" Tom said, following him to the door.

"Oh, absolutely. Breakfast, perhaps, in the restaurant. Say, ten-ish?" He gave a formal little bow.

Like hell, he thought as he rode the elevator up. The hotel's shift change happened at five a.m. and he planned to be in a taxi on his way to the airport at least an hour before that persistent day manager came to work.

THIRTY-SIX

AN OVERSEAS FLIGHT, first class, was the most luxury Sandy had ever experienced on an airplane and she made sure to thank Penelope for the indulgence. For herself, Pen was glad for the creature comforts but a night-long flight was still a long one and, although she'd been able to stretch out, this was nothing like sleeping in her own bed at home.

"Welcome to Grand Cayman," the flight attendant said over the PA, "where the local time is six a.m."

Pen stood and stretched before reaching for her bag in the overhead bin.

"Let me help you with that," said the senior flight attendant. She easily lifted the wheeled suitcase down. "My, you packed pretty light. You must have more in the hold."

"It's a quick trip," Pen said.

"My kind of traveler," the woman said. "You wouldn't believe the passengers I see in the terminal, struggling with three or four huge bags. Goodness, don't they know a beach resort only requires a couple bathing suits and a cover up or two?"

Gracie and Sandy retrieved equally small suitcases and they stood to wait for the doors to open and a ladder to be wheeled into place.

"Follow the painted yellow lines on the floor inside," the attendant said. "They'll take you right into the customs hall."

The three friends walked side by side through a pathway of red plastic cones on the tarmac. The humid air hit like a wet shroud.

"I feel my hair wilting already," Sandy said. "Thank goodness I'm not here for a beauty contest."

"Even the beauty queens aren't up for a contest at this hour of the morning," Gracie said.

As the hall narrowed inside the building, Pen fell behind the others. The only thing that kept the corridor from feeling oppressively tight was the fact that the walls were mostly of glass, the tarmac with waiting airplanes outside on her left, and the various airline departure gates on her right. All at once, something caught her eye.

Standing in a line at one of those departure gates was the man she'd known as Richard Stone. No, Frank Morrell—she corrected herself.

"It's him!" She nudged Sandy's shoulder. "There he is!"

Sandy and Gracie turned, confused. "Who?"

Impatient shouts came from behind them. "Hey, move it along up there—"

Pen pushed her friends forward, rushing to get out of the passageway. But when they passed through double metal doors, they were not in the same area where she'd spotted Morrell. The immigration hall opened before them, with roped off lanes for returning residents, visitors, and those with certain passports. Pen halted but Gracie pulled her aside, out of the path of brightly clad tourists in foul moods because they were so determined to start having fun.

"It was him—Richard Stone, em, Frank Morrell—back that way, standing in a queue of people about to board a plane. We have to get out there…"

But a customs official was standing at the door through which they'd just come.

"No access this direction," the woman recited in a bored tone.

"No—I—it's just—"

"Forget a bag? Do not worry, they will clear the plane and bring it out for you, madam."

Pen stared longingly. If only she could see which plane he was boarding. But the stout woman in uniform was hearing none of it.

She realized Gracie and Sandy were waiting for her to lead the way. With no other choice they got into one of the long lines to have their passports stamped. By the time they cleared immigration and customs, Pen knew Morrell was surely on his plane and most likely it would have departed. She squeezed her eyes shut.

"Pen, it's not the end of the world. We're all tired. Let's find a hotel and get some rest," Sandy said.

Eyes closed, Pen visualized the scene with Frank Morrell standing in wait for a plane. Gate 14. The sign above his head registered in her brain.

"Before we leave, I need to know," she said.

She walked to an electronic monitor listing arrivals and departures. At Gate 14, it showed Flight 93 had just departed for London and Zurich. Frank Morrell had skipped yet another country.

THIRTY-SEVEN

THE THOUGHT OF more travel, of going all the way to Europe, felt simply overwhelming in their present, jet-lagged state.

"Let's go to his hotel," Gracie suggested. "Maybe we can ask some questions there, find some kind of clue where he was going next, learn whether London is his destination or if it's Switzerland."

Or somewhere beyond, Pen thought. Once a person got to Europe it was a simple matter to use the train system and be in another country within a few hours, and relatively anonymously. She decided not to voice that thought—everyone was discouraged already.

Gracie pulled out her phone, where she'd noted the name and address of Frank Morrell's hotel. At the curb she flagged a taxi.

"The Grand Cayman Regent, please," she told the driver.

"Once we get there, what then?" Sandy whispered, once the cab was rolling.

"I have an idea," Pen said. She leaned back in her seat for the short ride to the hotel.

When the taxi stopped under the hotel's shady portico, Pen turned to the others. "If you ladies will see to the luggage, I will obtain a room key." She raised her eyebrows coquettishly.

"What are you up to?" Sandy said with a little grin.

Pen fluffed her hair and applied fresh lipstick. "Here, take my purse and carry-on bag. I need to appear as if I've been here all along. I'll meet you at the far end of the lobby or near the elevators, somewhere out of sight of the front desk."

She hopped out of the taxi and practically sprinted to the sidewalk, where she adjusted her posture and put a jaunty bounce in her step. With an air of confidence she stepped through the wide entry doors. It still wasn't quite eight in the morning and she hoped the morning desk clerks were not fully alert just yet.

Two clerks stood by, the younger female sipping from a coffee cup. She chose that one.

"Terribly sorry," she said, "I went off for my walk and forgot my room key, and my nephew is out. Would you be able to print me another?"

As hoped, the girl set down her mug a little reluctantly. "Room number?" Her tone was satisfyingly bored.

Luckily, Pen had checked before leaving the cab. "Five-oh-one."

She glanced around the lobby, trying not to appear the least bit concerned as the girl tapped a few keys at her computer terminal.

"Name?"

"Coddington. Woodsworth Coddington."

Two more clicks. A moment later a gold plastic card was handed over.

"Hm, there's some sort of note here about…" the clerk began.

But Pen had already turned away with a thank-you and a brisk step. Gracie and Sandy were standing near the elevators.

"That one," Pen said, indicating the button for the upper floors.

The door slid open without a sound. Inside, they saw

that three penthouse suites occupied the entire fifth floor. When they arrived moments later they found Suite 501 to their right. The new key worked perfectly. A collective sigh as they wheeled their bags inside.

"Whoa!" Gracie said.

They took in the huge living-dining room, grand piano and all. Cushions on the plump chairs and couches were somewhat smashed down, and the coffee table held empty drink glasses. A bowl of mixed nuts was nearly empty. The bar beside the widescreen TV was open, with bottles of Scotch and vodka sitting out.

"There are three bedrooms and four baths!" Sandy exclaimed after a quick foray through the place. "Only the king bed in the master looks as if it was used."

"Are there three beds between the others?" Pen asked. "A few hours sleep is all I'm interested in right now."

"You think we should stay here?"

"I don't see why not. The brute paid for all this with my money, after all."

"Um, I'm not sure he did," Gracie said, reading a sheet of paper she'd picked up from the marble floor. She held it out to Pen.

The bill was for over twenty thousand dollars, including several lavish restaurant meals and items from the hotel gift shops. A handwritten note across the front said, *A little matter with your credit card, sir. Please contact the manager at your earliest convenience.*

"Well, we know that won't happen, now that 'Coddington' is Frank Morrell again and is on his way to Europe," Sandy said.

"I'm certainly not under obligation to pay the man's bill, not after he stole more than a million dollars from me," Pen said, gritting her teeth. "But I'm too tired at the moment to think how to handle it. Put out the Privacy notice, lock the bolts on that door and find beds for yourselves. We'll discuss this when we're fresher."

Sandy pointed the way toward the two unused bedrooms, each furnished with two queen beds. She and Gracie said Pen should take a room to herself and they would share the other.

"Once we have our wits about us again, we'll search the bedroom he used and see what clues we might find."

Pen slept soundly for a few hours. When she looked at the bedside clock it showed 11:49. With the dark curtains closed, she felt momentarily confused whether it was morning or night. But, since she was wide awake, she got up and pulled the hotel's complimentary robe over her nightgown. Opening the drapes revealed it was, indeed, midday. Beyond the sliding glass door lay a small terrace and a grove of palm trees, with the vivid Caribbean sea beyond. But Pen had no time to enjoy the fact that she was in the tropics. Frank Morrell's actions still grated at her and she wanted answers.

THIRTY-EIGHT

PEN'S BEDROOM HAD its own coffee maker and she set it to brew a small pot while she showered and dressed. She carried her mug to the suite's living room. It seemed Morrell had entertained here before he departed. Perhaps the reason he'd come to Grand Cayman was less about an offshore bank account and more about meeting up with someone. She'd like to know who.

She went systematically through the room, opening drawers (nothing of a personal nature), fanning through magazines and observing placement of the used glassware. Three people, she surmised—two of them Scotch drinkers, while the third appeared to be a very watered-down vodka. Near the vodka glass, tucked under the edge of a wooden coaster, she found a business card.

Thomas Anderson, Raceway Auto Parts, Wholesale and Retail. The printed address was in Kansas City. On the back of the card were handwritten notes. A phone number and Room 325.

Most likely it was a room here at the hotel, someone (or two someones) Morrell had invited up for drinks. She wondered what the connection might be. She left the card on the foyer table where she'd set her own key card for the room, then went into the master bedroom Morrell had occupied.

The king size bed was unmade, a messy tangle of sheets,

the duvet lying in a pile on the floor. It appeared the oc-
cupant had a restless night. She hoped so. She hoped the
man's conscience bothered him. A lot.

A tropical-weight suit lay rumpled across an upholstered
chair, with a flowered shirt beside it. A pair of pale tan
dockside shoes were a nice match for the suit and looked
as though he'd just kicked them off. Another tropical shirt
hung in the closet, the tags still on it. No suitcase, no toi-
letries in the adjoining bath.

On the bathroom vanity she spotted a slip of paper, a receipt from one of the hotel's gift shops. It listed the clothing
items she'd found, plus a Rolex watch. Her jaw tightened.
Mr. Morrell was certainly having a fine time at her expense. Or possibly not—she recalled the hotel bill with the
handwritten note about a credit card problem. It looked as
if Morrell liked to take, without giving anything in return.
She took the receipt with her.

She was going through the nightstand drawer when she
heard sounds in the living room.

"Pen? You're up?" Sandy said.

"In here," Pen called out.

"Amber's emailed me," Sandy said, staring at her phone
as she walked into the bedroom. "She wants to know how
it's going. I already told her we arrived safely."

Pen shuffled through the few postcards and envelopes
that she found in the drawer. A battered scrap of paper
floated free. She grabbed it before it hit the floor.

"Hm, what's this?" She turned it in her hand. Without
looking directly at Sandy she said, "Tell Amber about our
seeing Frank Morrell leave the airport here this morning
and ask if she has a way to find out whether he is booked
only to London or if he's going on through to Zurich on
that same flight."

While Sandy thumbed a message on her phone, Pen looked closely at the small paper. It contained only a name and number.

Anton van der Went—31-20-061452

"Oh, and ask her what country and area code this is." She read the digits. "Maybe she could do a search on this name, as well?"

Gracie emerged from the bedroom with rumpled hair and a yawn. She wore her sleep clothes, a light pair of shorts and a tank top.

"That wasn't nearly enough rest," she said, "but if I stay in bed now I'll be up all night."

Sandy had brewed more coffee and now handed Gracie a cup. They plumped the sofa cushions and relaxed into them while Pen filled them in on her search of the suite.

"What do an American—tourist probably—from Kansas and somebody with a Dutch name and foreign dialing code have in common?" she asked the others.

"Other than both their names showing up in our con man's suite? I have no idea," Sandy said.

"Let's start with the American," Gracie suggested, picking up the room's phone.

"We have a room number," said Pen. "How about a visit instead? There's simply nothing like the face-to-face interview."

Gracie raced off to get dressed and ten minutes later they were standing in front of room 325. There was no answer to Sandy's knock at the door.

"Now what?" Pen asked. "We seem to have reached an impasse."

"They have to come back sometime soon," Sandy said

after using a house phone to verify that Mr. and Mrs. Anderson had not checked out.

"Well, it seems unproductive to sit outside this door, waiting them out. They could be on a sightseeing tour or having lunch followed by beach time...what if they don't come back before dinner?"

"Come," said Pen. "I have an idea."

They rode the elevator down in silence and found the hotel's main restaurant, an open-air place with beach views and a well-stocked bar. Pen walked up to the bartender.

"Might I have a hotel guest paged in here?" she asked.

He nodded. When she gave the name, the handsome man smiled. "I'll save you the trouble. That's Mr. and Mrs. Anderson over there, the table by the rock wall."

Pen turned to the others with her hands spread. *See there? Simple.*

THIRTY-NINE

PARDON ME—MR. ANDERSON?" Pen asked as she approached the table. Sandy and Gracie had decided to hang back rather than overwhelm these strangers.

The man wore his polo shirt and tan khaki slacks well; everything about him said 'successful businessman.' The wife was attractive in an overdone way—too-long acrylic nails, too-large bleached hair, too-gaudy diamond on her hand. She might have done better to have gone a cup size smaller on the breast implants, and her lovely complexion would soon be ruined if she kept up the tanning, but none of that was Pen's concern at the moment. She only wanted information about Frank Morrell's plans if she could get it.

"I apologize for intruding on your lunch," she said. So far, lunch only consisted of cocktails. "I'm looking for a man called Woodsworth Coddington. Someone said you might know him?"

Anderson's smile brightened. "Oh, Woody! Yes, of course. Are you related?"

Related? Pen had to pause and think what he meant by that.

"I just thought…your accent being so similar." He gestured toward the third chair at their table and she sat down.

"Oh, right. Well, no. We're more just acquaintances."

It didn't seem to matter to Tom Anderson, and his wife

barely smiled as she shielded her eyes from the sun and took small sips of her drink.

"We met Woody our second day on the island. Great guy. We really hit it off."

"I wonder if he might have mentioned his plans? Where he was traveling after this?"

"Well, no. Danielle and I figured he might be down for lunch soon. Thought we'd treat him to dinner tonight. And then Monday we planned to run into town together, a little business deal we've got going."

Business deal. Pen's alarm bells began clanging furiously.

"Em, what sort of business deal? If you don't mind my asking. It's just that I—"

"Well, I can't tell you the exact nature of it, of course," Tom said.

"It's all on the up-and-up," said his wife, the first time she'd spoken. "Woody's got contacts like you wouldn't believe. He's in the jewelry business, you know."

"Oh yes, I know." Pen felt a sickening flip in her stomach.

"So generous, honest as the day is long…" Tom took another sip from his glass.

"He said he could get us a super deal on some rubies," Danielle said. The sparkle was beginning to come back to her eyes.

"Mr. Anderson, I'm afraid—"

For the first time he looked at her seriously.

"It's just that this man calling himself Coddington… His real name is Frank Morrell and he managed to barely escape the authorities in Arizona." She didn't know if that part was true but it sounded more convincing than 'he stole my necklace.'

"Oh, that can't be right," Anderson said. "This guy, well, he was *English*. So proper, so refined."

Such a great actor. Pen could see she was getting nowhere with them.

"We're going to the bank on Monday where we'll check
our accounts for the returns on this investment we did.
Look, he put five times more into it than I did. He's got a
lot more to lose and there's no way he'd want to do that.
The man is very savvy."

She smiled weakly. Savvy was right.

She pressed on. "But he said nothing to you about his
travel plans after Cayman? Was he going home or was he
going somewhere on business?"

Both Andersons shook their heads.

Pen stood and said goodbye. She'd spotted Gracie and
Sandy walking a pathway toward the beach, and she headed
their direction. A short stroll was all the time it took for her
to relay what she'd learned from the Andersons.

"I feel badly that they also got swindled by him, but
what else could I have done? They refused to believe me."

Sandy patted her arm. "You did what you could. We
have his business card and if we can get Morrell arrested
we can give this information to the police."

"Yes, I suppose that's best."

"I wonder if he has roots in England," Gracie pondered.
"Maybe that explains why he was on that particular flight?
Going home to someone?"

Pen didn't think so. He'd been utterly convincing as an
American, a private investigator in Arizona. They walked
back toward the hotel, discussing what to do next, but no
one had any great ideas.

Feeling a little edgy about the deception they were pulling themselves—staying in a lavish suite they weren't paying for—the ladies decided to hole up there with the Do Not

Disturb sign out. If someone came around and confronted them, Pen would explain and pay for one night.

It was late afternoon when Amber emailed Sandy again: Found an Anton van der Went online. Diamond merchant from Amsterdam. Not a good reputation. Watch out.

Pen immediately placed a call to Phoenix.

"I don't know how it's related," Amber assured her, "but when I came across the guy's name and diamonds in the same sentence I thought you should know. Apparently he runs a storefront in the diamond cutting district, so some of his sales must be legit. But there are complaints about him too. He was accused five years ago of accepting stolen merchandise and re-cutting the stones so they could be sold anonymously."

"Book us on a flight to London," she said. "The first one out of here."

Sandy was waving for her attention. "I can't, Pen. I have to be back at work on Monday."

Gracie nodded at Pen's inquiry whether she wanted to go along. "I'll call Scott and let him know."

Amber had something to add: "Morrell was booked through to Zurich on this morning's flight. I haven't been able to absolutely confirm whether he actually went…"

"Make it Zurich," Pen said, "for myself and Gracie."

"I'll email your confirmation numbers the moment I have them," Amber said.

Pen turned to the others. "Let's get a good night's sleep here. Gracie, I know we packed for the tropics and I'm afraid we'll find this clothing unsuitable for Switzerland in April, but we can purchase a few—"

She stopped herself. It was exactly what Morrell had done, the reason he'd abandoned his local clothing in his room. She felt confident they were making the right decision.

That night, she tossed in bed, still uncomfortable about the large hotel bill. In the dark, she padded to the hall table where the dunning notice lay. At the bottom she wrote down the information she knew—Morrell's real name and what little they knew about him. She enclosed cash for the value of one night, the one they were spending right now. She felt badly about the nights he had not paid for, the expensive meals and the extravagant gift shop purchases—especially since he'd no doubt worn the Rolex out of here—but it was the best she could do to help.

FORTY

DETECTIVE CAPLIN, what's this on your computer?" Captain Remington stood behind Bill's chair, walking up so quietly Bill jumped.

Bill's eyes darted between the captain's face and his screen. It was pretty damning—he was using the department's facial recognition program to look for a match on the mug shot Mrs. Fitzpatrick had identified as the man she knew as Richard Stone. If he stopped in mid-search, he would have to start over, but the program's use was normally restricted to crime lab technicians working on the most urgent cases.

"It's not personal business, is it? You know I warned everyone…"

"No, sir." It grated on him to show deference to this man twenty years his junior. It really was time to retire. "This is a suspect in that robbery at the Philpont Museum last fall. One of the victims identified him but we have reason to believe he uses a number of aliases."

All of that was true but it didn't please Remington.

"Didn't we determine the stolen item only qualified as petty larceny? Why are we wasting department time on a case this old?"

"The suspect identification is a recent development. I just thought I'd—"

Remington picked up two folders from Caplin's desk.

"These newer cases are more urgent. Get on them. You can piddle around with that cold case on your own time."

Caplin held his tongue. "Yes, sir."

He glanced back at his monitor where the comparison photos were ticking by. Remington had walked on, no doubt to nit-pick someone else's work. Maybe he wouldn't notice if Bill left the program running while he worked these other files. He made a show of opening the folder on top and picking up his desk phone to call one of the witnesses in another convenience store robbery.

Pissed him off that a few hundred bucks from a convenience store got priority over a valuable piece of jewelry. Of course he had to suppress thoughts of his own involvement and the fact that the necklace's value had been purposely faked. A whiff of that around the department and he would be out on his ear in disgrace.

He punched in the number for the witness he'd already spoken to twice. He just needed to verify a little discrepancy. While the phone rang, he glanced back at the screen.

A match against his Richard Stone photo had showed up. The name on the other mug shot was Frank Morrell. Then it got interesting—Morrell was aka Frank Martin, Martin Frank, Frank Woods, Stone Martin and some others. He hung up the phone when it went to voicemail.

A rush of relief. Finally, some solid leads. He made sure Remington was nowhere nearby, then hit the key to print out the dossier on Morrell. A stroll to the printer across the room and he snagged the info he needed.

Remington had said to work the museum case on his own time—well, fine. He would do that. He had fourteen vacation days he'd not been able to take last year (because an intense case held him up) so he would use them now. He put in the request, framed more as an emergency, with

HR then gathered the current-case files off his desk and dumped them on another guy's desk before walking out the door.

He'd no sooner made it to his personal car than his cell phone rang. Damn. Was Remington going to disapprove the vacation time, make him come right back? But the readout showed Todd Wainwright's name.

"What?" Caplin knew his tone was rude, but really, he'd basically told Todd he would let him know if there were developments.

"Uh, Detective?"

"Yeah, Todd."

"Just checking to see—"

"Nothing, Todd. I've got one new lead but no time to work on it yet. I know your loans are due. I know your life is going to shit. Mine is too. I just can't help you right now." He clicked off the call and put the ringer on mute. Right now, he didn't want to hear from anyone.

He got in his car and started to back out, belatedly remembering he'd left his list of passwords in his desk. Not that it mattered. He had no access to the department's resources outside the city's intranet system. He was going to have to use old-fashioned police work to do this. He exited the police garage and headed toward the airport.

FORTY-ONE

FRANK WALKED PAST the high-end airport gift shops, contemplating some shopping in Switzerland. It could be a kick. Not that he had much desire for the trappings of the rich—fleecing them out of their stuff was much more fun. Plus, he already had the Rolex he'd picked up on Grand Cayman. But his business cards with the Tiffany logo were still in his briefcase and who knew what interesting doors would open for him?

He bypassed the baggage claim and walked out the front doors.

"Holy crap!" He gasped as black needles of icy rain went straight through his tropical clothing.

He dashed straight back inside. Twenty minutes later he emerged wearing an Armani wool suit and overcoat, fur-lined gloves and a thick scarf around his neck. Better, although everything here was so Euro-stylish he would probably not wear them beyond this trip. He'd feel way too conspicuous back in Indiana. Assuming he went back to Indiana anytime soon. Depended whether the Phoenix police had put it together and learned his real identity by now.

With that in mind, he flagged a taxi.

"Alpen Haus Hotel," he said.

"Zat is a nice one," the driver said. "Good neighborhood."

Frank knew it would be. Aboard the flight he'd chat-

ted up a well-dressed couple and asked where they liked
to stay in Zurich. He casually mentioned the name of his
bank, planting the idea he'd like to be near it.

The driver headed south on the 51, acting as if the wet
highway and reflected oncoming headlights were no problem.

Frank felt exhaustion sweeping over him; he needed a
good night's rest. In the morning he would scope out the
whole situation. First priority was to get to the bank and
transfer Tom Anderson's two hundred grand to another of
his own accounts. It had to be in a different bank, prefera-
bly in another country, definitely under a fresh alias. There
must be no direct way to trace the money. He'd worn out
the good name of Woodsworth Coddington IV, so it needed
to retire for awhile.

His Tiffany business cards said Richard Stone; unfortunately, all the wrong people knew about that one. From the
money belt, he came up with a passport for Richard Frank—
it would work for his hotel registration and he could always
print more cards if needed. For a fraction of a second, he
wondered what he was doing here, why he kept up the game,
carried multiple passports and tried to keep all his names
and backstories straight.

During the long flight he'd felt on edge, the electrical
realization that one small slip-up would reveal him to the
authorities. Since the museum robbery, he'd taken an additional hundred grand from the old lady, two hundred grand
from that bozo on Cayman, and stiffed the hotel there for
around twenty-odd.

His mother's voice lurked in his head, "Frank, when is
it going to be enough?"

She'd been talking to Frank's father. A generation later,
she would say the same thing to her son if she knew.

When *would* it be enough? He gave the question a full minute's thought, then discarded it. No one said it ever had to be 'enough.' The game, the chase—that was what made his heart race and laughter well up within him. He was in it for the fun. Fatigue talking, that's all this was. He leaned back in his seat and half-dozed for the duration of the ride to the city center.

The taxi came to a stop on a quiet street a few blocks off the Bahnhofstrasse; it seemed like a decent neighborhood where Frank could sleep and recoup his strength. He checked into the Alpen Haus, getting a room on the third floor. Once he'd checked the windows and double-locked the door, he stripped and headed for the shower, laying his money belt with the necklace on the vanity in the bathroom. No way he wanted that baby out of his sight until he met with the diamond cutter from Amsterdam. The meeting was still two days away.

FORTY-TWO

An icy clear sky greeted Pen and Gracie when they landed in Zurich. The first class flight attendant had been a cordial young woman who told them a storm had passed through during the night, dropping temperatures to unseasonable lows. They'd already discussed the fact their wardrobes for the Caribbean would need to be augmented in Switzerland. Back in London, while waiting for the connecting flight, they'd each picked up a jacket and pair of warm pants—jeans for Gracie and wool for Pen.

Standing at the baggage carousel, Gracie heard her phone chime with an incoming text message.

"From Amber," she said.

She held out the phone for Pen to see: Your hotel is Swisshotel Parade. Call me once you've checked in.

"Thank goodness for her," Gracie said.

Pen nodded. They retrieved their bags, left the customs area and slipped their coats on before walking out to the sidewalk. A blustery wind told them the storm had not completely passed through. Pen stepped up to the first cab in the taxi line and gave the driver their hotel information.

As they entered District 1 in the heart of old Zurich, Gracie ogled the view.

"I can't believe I'm here. Europe! My god, it's just like all those historical romances I used to read—except for the cars. The buildings are so *old*. Oh, look at that church, how cute!"

Pen smiled. As they crossed the blue-green River Limmat, she remembered her first trip to Europe since her childhood, the sense of history and her own awe at everything. The ancient buildings were reminders of America's youth as a country. They passed a couple of museums and soon she spotted the more modern aspects—shops under all the major designer names, upscale cafés and coffee houses. They would certainly have no problem finding anything they needed in this neighborhood of gray stone buildings and cobblestone streets.

"Scott would love this," Gracie said. "Did I ever mention he's a history buff?"

Her dark hair swung in an arc as she switched views from the right to the left side of the taxi. "Hard to imagine the only thing I ever used my passport for was a couple trips to the beaches in Mexico. I *have* to talk him into a trip here together sometime."

The taxi slowed and Pen noticed a discreet gold-lettered sign showing they had arrived at the Swisshotel Parade. Heavy glass doors opened to a mid-sized lobby of gleaming marble floors, modern groupings of furniture and a dark wood registration desk. Abstract art decorated the walls and Gracie looked a bit disappointed, no doubt expecting something a bit more ancient-looking.

Their room reflected the same modern décor.

"Don't worry," said Pen, "once we've caught our breath we'll surely find time to take in a cathedral or two. Maybe we can find a castle. There are loads of historic places nearby."

She had her phone out and was adding the international dialing code for the U.S. to Amber's number.

"How was your flight?" Amber asked over a connection as clear as if she were in the next room.

"It's all going well," Pen said. "We're in our hotel. Nice

choice, by the way, although Gracie was hoping for something old enough to have a few ghosts."

"Only the décor is new. The building dates way back so maybe she'll see some medieval knight roaming the halls."

"Where do we go from here?" Pen asked. She put the phone on speaker so Gracie could get the information first hand.

"You're gonna love me for this. Our Frank Morrell should be staying nearby. He gave his name as Richard Frank and his hotel as the Alpen Haus. I looked it up and it's not far from where you are. It might only be a tram stop away…or maybe walking distance. I can't tell exactly from my online map, but I can send you a picture of the building."

Seriously? Pen and Gracie exchanged a glance.

"Where did you get this information?" Pen asked. "Or is it better if I don't ask?"

Amber laughed. Her voice changed pitch slightly. "Hello, this is Sara Jones with American Airlines. A passenger from our flight 42 left a valuable item aboard his Cayman to London flight and we need to have it delivered to him…" In her normal voice she added, "He had to list a hotel on his disembarkation form for Immigration."

"So, assuming he was truthful with them?"

"Yeah, could be a big assumption," Amber agreed. "But it was a late night flight. Hopefully, he was too tired to think up a lie. He would have to know Zurich very well to have made up this place. It's a small, boutique hotel near the Paradeplatz."

"We shall check it out."

"Be careful. That gem cutter, Anton van der Went? A little further background check on him shows an arrest in New York a few years ago. He beat up a guy who stiffed him on a fee, got sentenced to thirty days."

"So, if possible, we want to get to Mr. Morrell or Mr. Frank before this diamond cutter shows up," Gracie suggested.

If it's not already too late, thought Pen.

FORTY-THREE

FRANK WOKE UP feeling like a sack of garbage. After sleeping all night and nearly half the next day, his head felt thick and woozy. His throat was scratchy and he remembered some kid behind him on the plane had coughed through most of the flight. Dammit—he couldn't afford to be sick right now.

He stumbled from bed and stared out the window to the street three stories below. The rain had stopped but it was still a miserable gray out there. He needed to get to the bank—should have set his alarm and done it this morning—and really wanted some food but hated the prospect of dressing and walking around a strange city in the wind he could see funneling down the narrow streets, whipping the coats of the few passers-by. Maybe this place had room service.

The good news, he supposed, was Anton van der Went should be here late tomorrow. Frank hoped to get a chunk of cash for the gemstones in the necklace. Once sold, he could stop sleeping with it under his pillow and quit strapping the awkward shape of it around his waist. The high from making a million-dollar score was quickly fading; at this point he just wanted to cash out. He'd be lucky if van der Went offered thirty percent and he successfully countered with fifty. More likely it would come out somewhere around thirty or thirty-five, bottom line.

Still, along with his other successes, the trip to Arizona hadn't been a waste. That chubby guy who worked at the museum would take the fall, if one was to be taken. Last Frank had heard, the cops bought the story about the piece being worth very little and had quit pursuing the case. At least he could rest easy on that score. The old lady was another story.

When he'd returned the fake necklace to her, he got a funny feeling. She wasn't the typical older, easy mark. This one had something—he wasn't sure what. Social connections, almost certainly. But there was more. A cheesy writer might call it 'indomitable spirit.' You know, like when one of those investigative TV reporters interviewed a person on the street and raved about his or her pluck.

Frank didn't personally believe in that "go the extra mile" b.s. To him, spirit was what *he* had—a free-spirited, fun attitude toward life. Make every minute count, rack up all the scores you could, come out the winner! Now, *that* was spirit.

He turned away from the chilly window and rummaged through his few bits of clothing to find something warm to wear. Other than the designer suit he'd purchased at the airport, his choices were cotton slacks and a stupid flowered shirt that fit in nowhere except an island. His stomach rumbled and he searched futilely for a menu. Where did a guy get some food around here?

He ended up putting on a robe he found in the closet and sitting at the little desk to boot up his computer. In under ten minutes, he'd discovered his hotel was only a couple blocks from the biggest pedestrian shopping district in the city. The bank he sought was right there and surely he could find food. With no choice but to buck up, he put on the woolen suit and overcoat and walked down to street level.

While I'm at it, he thought, turning a corner to get out of the bracing wind, I'd better come up with some ordinary clothes. Can't meet this Dutch guy wearing Armani—he'll laugh at my demand for a higher cut. Can't exactly hang out inconspicuously either.

When he spotted Barclays Bank, he headed that direction first. When it came right down to it, money was more important. Completing his last job, getting Tom Anderson's money completely out of sight, took precedence over his growling stomach. He would treat himself to a fantastic lunch once he finished business. See? Mom really would be proud of his work ethic.

At the counter he took several deposit slips and filled them out in various amounts until the total equaled two hundred thousand U.S. dollars. Part of it went to an account in London, part to Nevada, part of it right back to Grand Cayman. At this point, Tom Anderson would have a difficult paper trail to establish to prove all this had once been his money. That is, *if* the man had nerve enough to admit he'd been so stupid. Most of them never did. Most likely, Anderson would go to his grave believing he'd just been unlucky in his investment.

Ah well, what did Frank care? This guy made so much money selling car parts at rip-off prices to people like Frank's mom, in a year's time he'd have it all back. Frank refused to have a scrap of sympathy for the mooch.

He collected his deposit receipts and walked out, taking it as a good sign that the clouds had parted and a good-sized patch of blue sky showed. Some phrase about weathering the storm flitted about in his head. He spotted a sidewalk café where the outdoor tables were all but abandoned; however, inside the place was well lit and inviting. He ordered the biggest sandwich on the menu.

His meal no sooner arrived than his phone chimed with an incoming text message: NOON TOMORROW, IN FRONT OF THE CLOCK MUSEUM. VAN DER WENT.

Clock museum. Where the hell was that? Frank took a bite of his sandwich and reread the message. On a city map where every place seemed to contain gasse, strasse or platz how would he know what a clock museum would be called?

WHERE IS IT? he texted back. People who used all capital letters always seemed pretentious to him, but he could play this game. Plus, he would bet money the gem cutter wouldn't transact a deal out in front of some public place. There would be a secondary place they would go together before Frank would agree to bring out the necklace.

He finished his lunch with one eye on the phone's display at all times but van der Went's lack of response seemed to say, *Don't be a stupid American. Find it.*

Okay, he decided, he could find it.

FORTY-FOUR

DETECTIVE CAPLIN WOKE with a sense of unease, the vague restlessness of having no plan for the day. Then he remembered—he didn't have to go to work. He'd taken vacation days to devote time to finding Richard Stone and getting his cut of the money, to get his retirement fund back. He rolled out of bed and stared at his unshaven face in the bathroom mirror. What if he simply stayed this way? Never went back, gave up the dream of the boat and Mexico?

He could live off his city pension, even these few years short of full retirement he was vested enough in the plan to get most of his monthly amount. Another year and he could claim at least a portion of his Social Security. But then what? He'd sit here in his average little house in his average little suburb, watching sports on TV all day while he drank beer and got fatter and fatter in his recliner chair. He slapped his cheeks to work up the blood, to snap himself into a frame of urgency.

He had two weeks to catch up with Stone—except he had to start thinking of him as Frank Morrell now—to find him and somehow drag the money out of him. Who knew? The weasel could have spent it all by now and Caplin didn't want to take some luxury car or condo in Miami in trade. He wanted his cash. Making himself angry all over again gave him a shot of energy.

He got dressed—no suit today, just jeans and a decent brown button-down shirt. His instinct was to walk out the door but he reminded himself he would get more accomplished with a little groundwork. He set a pot of coffee to brew and sat down at the small desk in the corner of his living room where he'd assembled his information. Cold case files could leave the station so he'd brought this one home, along with the printout from yesterday where he'd identified many of Morrell's aliases.

Problem with a guy like Morrell was they changed names like they changed their socks, sometimes even more often. And Caplin didn't have use of the department's resources for this one. Although he owned a laptop, he had little knowledge of all this new social media stuff. He used his to send emails to his kids and to browse pictures of boats for sale. He shoved the image of his dream retirement boat aside now and picked up the phone. Old fashioned police work—that's what he'd told himself.

He started with what he knew. The last time anyone had direct contact with Frank Morrell was when he'd delivered the fake necklace to Penelope Fitzpatrick. According to her, the investigator 'Richard Stone' had driven away in a plain white sedan. Only about a million of those in this city, Caplin thought.

His own knowledge of Stone/Morrell was practically nil. They'd met when Todd Wainwright at the museum dropped a bombshell during questioning over the robbery. The two, Wainwright and himself, had been alone in the museum director's office where Caplin had called each employee aside.

"I know who did this," Todd had whispered, a knowing look on his face, a certain squint to his eyes. The look of the rat who's about to give up a cohort.

"Tell me."

Wainwright shook his head. "I can do better. I can get you a cut. Especially if this investigation kind of stalls out."

Just that morning, the wife had given her ultimatum. *You brood all the time, your misery is infecting the whole family and I'm sick of it. Drop this dumb idea of a boat and Mexico or I'm out of here.* She'd left for work and he had the feeling she might not come home that night.

"I'm listening," he'd told Wainwright.

"Later. I'll be having a beer tonight after work at The Pelican."

And that's when the whole scam came out, how this thief knew a guy... He would switch the real necklace for a fake, the owner would get back what she thought was her real jewelry, this guy could fence the real one for a whole lot of money and he was willing to do a split. An insider at the museum and a cop who wouldn't pry too hard—each could earn a share.

Caplin was no rookie and he'd seen plenty of stings before. Wainwright didn't look like the type, but you never knew. He'd insisted on meeting Richard Stone face to face and seeing the real necklace. Their one and only encounter had taken place in the men's room at a pancake house, midday, only the two of them, Stone body-blocking the door while Caplin took a close look at the necklace. It was the real deal, he felt sure.

Stone would need a couple months to have the piece copied and he wanted the investigation to fade away during that time. Wainwright would do his part, now Caplin had to do his. The necklace, Caplin knew, was worth over a million dollars. A third of that—yeah, it would set him for retirement nicely. Even more so without the drag of a wife who didn't share his dream. They set up a simple set of coded messages they could use to stay in touch, shook on it, and Stone had pocketed the necklace and walked out.

Caplin's coffee sent out an enticing aroma and he went to the kitchen for a cup. Everything had gone perfectly, including his divorce four months ago, until Stone didn't show last week. An hour sitting under that freeway overpass, watching Todd Wainwright's agitation. Caplin knew they'd both been had within the first fifteen minutes.

He carried his mug to the desk, opened the file and took up where he'd left off with phone calls to the rental car agencies and airlines. It was tedious, hearing 'no' all the time, but he'd done this his entire career. He knew eventually there would come a 'yes.'

FORTY-FIVE

GRACIE PACED THE hotel room, clearly antsy after their call to Amber. "How are we going to get the necklace back from this Frank Morrell or Richard Frank or whatever name he's using, before he meets with the gem cutter?"

"My dear, that is the big question, isn't it?" Pen had insisted upon having a moment to unpack.

"Okay, we know Morrell's hotel. I think we should get over there and just stake out the place. We'll surely catch him coming or going, right?"

"Better yet," Pen said, straightening her spine, appearing taller all at once. "I shall walk in there and knock on his door. I'll demand my necklace back."

"Uh...are you sure that's a good idea?"

"Well, what better? Spotting him on the street might be difficult."

"I worry about your safety if you do this alone. At the very least I should be with you."

Pen considered. That much was true. "The hotel will surely have a security guard or burly bellman we can call upon to join us."

Gracie obviously wasn't keen on the plan, but the idea they might have the necklace in their possession within the hour was definitely appealing.

"Let's do it."

They grabbed their coats, stopping at their hotel's concierge desk for directions, then headed toward Paradeplatz. Their friend's hotel would be just two blocks farther, according to the very polite gentleman. Crisp air greeted them on the street and they started out at a brisk clip.

"I'm nervous about this," Pen admitted as they walked along. "What if he's already met with the gem dealer? My precious treasure could be gone forever."

"Amber got the other man's name, Pen. If she can track his movements we'll have that to fall back on." As long as he hasn't already been here, taken the necklace and left the country again. She didn't voice that thought to Pen.

The Alpen Haus proved to be a quaint little hotel, three stories on a semi-residential street with a pastry shop next door. The small lobby was filled with heavy furniture, a bit oversized for the space, and carved cuckoo clocks in a display on one wall. A young man in his twenties stood behind the desk; Pen swore she saw him tuck a smartphone out of sight as she glanced in his direction. She made a show of rummaging in her purse.

"Oh dear," she muttered.

Gracie merely stood by while Pen approached the desk clerk.

"My nephew is staying here," she said. "Nice looking American with dark hair. I'm afraid I've lost the note telling me his room number. His name is Richard Frank. Please look it up for me."

There was probably some rule against giving out a guest's number but Pen pretended she didn't know of it, hoping the young clerk cared more for getting back to his messages from a girlfriend or someone. He checked the computer and wrote a number on a small slip of paper. Without a word, he pointed toward an elevator in a recessed niche to his left.

Pen and Gracie rode to the third floor, each wondering a little nervously what they would encounter.

"Three fourteen," said Pen, leading the way.

At the door, she stood a little straighter. Gracie held off to one side. A gentle knock brought no response. A slightly firmer knock. No sign of motion, no flicker of light beyond. Pen felt the hope drain out of her. How simple it would have been if she could have talked to him, let him know she would stand no nonsense—she wanted her family heirloom back. Let him understand how important this was to her. Anyone with a shred of empathy would surely not keep it.

But this. No response whatsoever.

"He's not here," Gracie finally said. "Let's go."

"Do you suppose my necklace is in the room? Maybe we can get in somehow?" But in her heart she knew it was too much to hope. An item valued at more than a million dollars wasn't something one left in a hotel room.

"Okay, there have to be other ways to tackle this," Gracie said as they rode the elevator down. "We'll get back in touch with Amber. Maybe she's learned more about the gem dealer and we can do something with that."

"Perhaps we can run a fake-out on them, a way to keep the two men apart so that other man doesn't have the chance to get my gems. Sort of a divide-and-conquer maneuver, although I don't know exactly how we would manage it."

At the street, Gracie looked around for somewhere they might eat lunch. It was a little late, probably the reason they weren't thinking very creatively. They turned toward the Paradeplatz, which seemed a likely place for food at any hour. They'd gone no more than a few yards when, suddenly, Pen stopped.

"It's him!" She whispered urgently. "Richard Stone—I mean, whatever he's called now."

Stone/Morrell had walked right past them, preoccupied with a device in his hand. Pen saw him reach for the hotel's front door, a moment before he looked up and spotted her.

"Hello, Mr. *Stone*. Or is it Morrell?"

His face registered shock, then recognition dawned. His thoughts were clear as a book—how had this woman found him?

The hand with the phone dropped into his pocket and a smile curved his mouth. Then he spun away from the women and ran.

"Quick! After him!" Gracie shouted, looping her purse strap across her body and taking off after the fleeing thief.

Pen gave chase but her flimsy shoes were no match for the cobbled street. In under two blocks she'd fallen far behind. She shouted encouragement to Gracie as Morrell dashed in front of an oncoming car, crossed the street and ducked into another arm of the labyrinth.

FORTY-SIX

FRANK'S MIND RACED faster than his feet. It was the lady from Scottsdale, the one whose necklace right now rested inside the money belt under his shirt. How the hell had she found him almost half a world away? He cut across the cobbled street, barreling in front of a slow-moving car, not daring to look back and see if the women were behind him.

He had no idea how the younger woman fit into all this, but she was quick. Thirty-something with long dark hair and a chin dimple—a quick impression before it occurred to him rather than talk his way out of this one he should simply beat it out of there.

A couple blocks from the hotel a clothing shop came up on the right—could he duck inside? Too chancy. A likely trap. A display of ladies sweaters with sparkly trims sat out front. A scene from a movie flashed at him. Knock it into the path of his pursuer. He grabbed for it with his right hand, aimed wrong and smacked the hand against the metal rack. Pain shot clear to his shoulder, the sweaters swung wildly but the thing didn't tip. The move only slowed him and he could hear the woman's pounding footsteps behind.

"Call the police!" she shouted to a shop clerk who peered out.

Frank pushed for more speed, but his mental prowess outweighed the physical. He couldn't remember the last time he'd had to actually outrun someone. His breath became ragged and his heart pounded alarmingly. He covered three more blocks, making a fresh turn each time, but she was close enough he couldn't lose her.

One more. Surely he must be nearing the train station by now. Crowds would help. He zigzagged to his left. Stopped short. It was a dead-end alley.

He spun. The woman spotted his move and stood at the narrow opening. She halted there, breathing hard, hands on her hips, recovering her strength. She'd called out a couple of times for police—who knew whether anyone responded or how close the cops could be. He had to get out of this cage.

From a trash barrel beside the back door of a business, he spotted a worn-out broom. He grabbed the handle, brandishing it like a lance.

"Back off, lady." He tried for bluster but his voice came out almost wheezy.

She held her ground.

He advanced, swinging the broom handle. A dozen feet from her, he quit moving his weapon.

"Look, I don't know who you think I am…just leave me alone."

Her glare made him think of his mother when he'd eaten all the ice cream right before dinner.

"Lady…"

Her eyes darted over him, a disconcerting feeling. He had to make a move. In a flash, he rushed forward and swung the broomstick toward her head. It made contact with her forearm as she raised it to defend herself. She let out a howl of pain and he leaped past her doubled-over form. He ran until he could hear trains. When he chanced a glance backward, the woman was nowhere to be seen.

FORTY-SEVEN

ZURICH, SWITZERLAND. Now that was a different rub, Caplin thought. Two days on the phone and he'd learned a bunch. How Morrell went to Grand Cayman under another of his aliases, stiffed the hotel for a felony amount. His man was wanted in two countries now—so far. Switzerland, he had a feeling, was where the money would change hands.

Caplin wanted that to happen—he had more use for cash than a piece of antique jewelry, for certain—but he didn't dare let Morrell get far from the transaction. The cop wanted to be on the spot, if possible, to watch the deal go down and then nab his little friend and whoever was helping him. If he chose to go the official route and could extradite them both, he'd wrap up the jewel theft by returning the piece to Mrs. Fitzpatrick, plus have the cash to replenish what he'd lost. It would be a tough sell to his captain, saying he'd advanced money of his own for a sting. There'd probably be disciplinary action. A forced early retirement. Heh-heh…he had *no* problem with that scenario.

Of course, if the punk made trouble, Caplin had pretty well decided he wouldn't be above snatching the cash and heading south. Being a good cop all his life hadn't netted him a whole lot.

He would have a good ten hours to think about his approach while he sat on a plane. It was more money out of pocket, sure, but this time he felt the investment would be worth it. For now, he planned to compile a list of known jewelry fences across the European Union. He wanted to have a decent guess at whom he was dealing with.

FORTY-EIGHT

GRACIE CLUTCHED HER throbbing right arm next to her body as she limped along. She'd lost track of the number of turns Morrell had made and each time she came to an intersection she searched for anything familiar. She spotted the rack of sweaters he'd tried to shove into her. A young shop clerk with purple hair and a lot of piercings was re-hanging the garments that had fallen. The hotel wasn't much farther.

Pen came rushing up to her when she rounded the final turn.

"Oh my gosh, Gracie, he's hurt you!"

"I'll live."

"You are pale as a sheet. We need to get medical attention."

"Don't call an ambulance—that would be over the top. It's really not that bad," Gracie said, pushing up her sleeve and looking. The skin wasn't broken—thank goodness for the padding of her jacket—but it certainly hurt like crazy.

"Let's at least inquire about a doctor." Pen placed a hand at her good elbow and steered her toward the only place they knew nearby, Morrell's hotel.

The desk clerk at the Alpen Haus seemed relieved to learn the accident had not happened on hotel property and was happy to recommend a doctor only one block over.

The two women walked the short distance to a single-doctor office, small and immaculate, with comfortable leather chairs and carved end tables. The magazines were all in German but the receptionist spoke perfect English. After a short wait, the kindly white-haired man was ready to see them. He examined Gracie's arm with the tenderness and care his sixty-some years had taught him.

"Ve shall want an x-ray, *ja*?" He summoned a nurse and they quickly had the machine ready.

Fifteen minutes later he placed the films on a viewer on the wall and announced, "Is good news. No breaks. Zis soft tissue is very, very bruised but it will heal."

He prescribed ice packs, a sling and pain medication, plus an herbal remedy he said to apply at night on a compress. "Keep ze arm elevated whenever you can. It will help."

Pen thought of everything they'd been through in the past few days. She must insist Gracie stay in the room and rest while she dealt with Frank Morrell. The first thing she would do after getting her friend settled would be a visit to the police.

Although it wasn't a long walk back to their hotel, Pen insisted on calling a taxi. Her friend looked a bit peaked around the edges.

"I feel so badly about this," she said to Gracie on the way to the hotel. "If he had been armed, he could have killed you."

Gracie brushed it off. "It wouldn't have come to that. I should have realized. He was cornered in an alley and grabbed the first thing he could find. But I agree—I got lucky. In the future I'll think twice."

Once in their room, Pen saw to it that Gracie took her pain meds and helped her to slip off her shoes and settle against the pillows on her bed. She phoned Amber, calculating belatedly it was rather early in Arizona and they'd already kept their young computer guru up late into the night.

Amber seemed less than pleased when she picked up. "Did you check your messages?" she asked. "I texted you before I went to bed. That gem cutter is coming in tomorrow morning—or is it this morning? I'm totally confused right now. Anyway, that Anton guy is on his way from Amsterdam to Zurich sometime soon. I sent you the flight number and time."

"Thanks, hon. I appreciate all your work. Go back to sleep now." Pen clicked off the call and stared at the screen on her phone. "I really must become more attuned to these things. I heard a little chime earlier and paid no attention."

Gracie gave a woozy smile from her nest of pillows.

"Oh, here it is," Pen said. She read the message, pleased to see the KLM flight would not arrive until tomorrow morning. She already had her hands full today.

"We need to report what we know about Morrell to the local police," she said, more to herself than to Gracie, whose eyes were closed even though she nodded when Pen spoke.

Pen paced the room. They really should go to a police station, she supposed. The authorities would want a statement from Gracie. The attack was one issue, while the stolen necklace was another. She thought of the detective back in Arizona and how he'd eventually become dismissive of her claim. Would she run into the same attitude here?

FORTY-NINE

A PERSON RUNNING through a train station normally doesn't attract much attention, Frank discovered. His haste had nothing to do with catching a departing train at this point. He merely wanted to become lost in a crowd. He spotted a pack of American tourists following the flag of their guide and he dropped in beside them, needing a moment to think.

Penelope Fitzpatrick's appearance here in Switzerland had shocked him to the core. How the hell had she found him? No way it was coincidence. And the woman with her—*chasing* him through the city—where had she come from?

The tourists paused at the entrance to the various platforms, their guide counting heads. Frank peeled off and walked briskly to a kiosk selling postcards and newspapers. What to do... He couldn't go back to the Alpen Haus. By now the woman and her friend had no doubt summoned the authorities and his room was likely being searched. Thank goodness for the money belt around his waist, he thought for the hundredth time.

Frank had walked out several times when a con went wrong, but never with one this lucrative. He had no intention of giving up either the cash or the necklace. All he had to do was lie low until his meeting with Anton van der Went tomorrow at noon. But where?

If those women had found the small, inconspicuous

Alpen Haus they could pretty much find him anywhere in Zurich. But he didn't want to leave the city either; it was where Anton would come. He could get a message to the gem cutter, but it felt too soon to throw in a change of plans. The guy could blow him off and cancel the whole deal.

He needed time to think. He bought a newspaper he couldn't even read—it would help with his disguise if they were looking for an American. In the men's room he used a bit of water to mess up his hair, giving him a more youthful appearance, and he turned his casual jacket inside out. One of his father's old teachings—buy reversible clothing whenever you could. Rather than light tan it was now a deep green.

At the ticket window he bought a ticket for the town two stations south, some place he couldn't pronounce but it was only thirty minutes away. He could stay overnight and ride back in the morning in time to find the clock museum where Anton wanted to meet.

He found a seat facing the departure board and flipped open his newspaper, watching the crowd for cops and the board for his train. Apart from station security men, he didn't see any extra police, certainly none who appeared to be looking for him. When his destination appeared on the board, he meandered his way to the platform. His first class seat came with beverage service and he happily accepted a beer, letting the tepid brew course through and relax him.

When Pfäffikon Station came up, he left the train at a leisurely pace. A person hurrying draws attention and one thing Frank had learned to do was to blend in and remain unnoticed. With his paper tucked under his arm, he was just another guy coming home from work, a worker heading out for a beer, a husband who wasn't especially eager to get home just yet.

He strolled out of the station, down a street with enough traffic that he didn't stand out, past a pharmacy and an internet café, coming to a street with several banks. Geez, they were thick around here. A block over, he came to an area of restaurants (pizza in Switzerland!) and found a picture-postcard hotel, complete with brown shutters at the windows and flower boxes full of purple petunias. No one would see it as the hideout of a man with a stolen million-dollar necklace.

He paid cash for a room on the ground floor. Inside his room, he was happy to find a menu. He would order dinner and settle in. Now, to stay low-key until late tomorrow morning when he would ride the train back into Zurich.

FIFTY

WHEN GRACIE WOKE from her short nap, Pen shared the thoughts which had run through her head for the past hour. "If my necklace is sitting there in his hotel room, I must try to get it back."

Even as she said it, Pen realized Morrell could have easily gone back to his room and cleared it while they'd been at the doctor's office. If only she'd thought to demand to be let into his room immediately after he'd run. Then she had an idea—more than one side could play at this game.

Gracie started to get out of bed but any movement of her injured arm caused her to flinch. Pen helped her to stand, waited while Gracie was in the bathroom, then insisted she get back in bed.

"I have a plan," Pen said. "It shouldn't take more than an hour. You rest some more and take another of your pain pills when the time comes."

"What are you—?"

Pen held up a hand. "Don't worry. Just a little lying and trickery. I'll be right back."

She popped out of the room before Gracie could protest. They both had cell phones and although the international charges were fairly outrageous, it was reassuring to have the means for emergency contact in place. She followed their earlier route and found herself at Alpen Haus.

A peek through the front windows showed a different clerk on duty so she mustered up her bravery and walked in, a worried look on her face.

"Excuse me," she said. "My nephew, Richard Frank, is staying here. He called me awhile ago to say he wasn't feeling well. It worried me and I need to go check on him. It's room 314. Might I get a key so I don't have to wake him if he's asleep? I just want to peep in."

The young female clerk hesitated, then reached for the telephone.

"Do you not understand that I don't want to wake him?" Pen held her hand out, feeling fluttery inside but appearing outwardly confident of getting her way.

A half-minute later, with a key in her hand, she quickly walked to the elevator. At the door to 314 she debated knocking. She didn't want a confrontation, but with warning Morrell would be prepared. She inserted the plastic card into the mechanism and walked in.

The room was dim and hollow-feeling. She knew at once he was not there. As on Cayman, she found a scattering of personal items left behind—disposable shaving gear in the bathroom, a wrinkled shirt on the floor. A nice suit hung in the closet. This time, there was also a suitcase. In it she found a laptop computer and small portable printer. Temptation pulled at her; this computer probably held all sorts of valuable information that could help catch the con man. On the other hand, all she really wanted was her own property. If she could find her necklace, she would be happy never to see or hear of Frank Morrell again. She went through every zippered pocket on the suitcase but found nothing of interest.

Quickly circling the room, she opened each drawer. All were—no surprise—empty. The pillows, linens and under the mattress also yielded nothing. On hands and knees, she examined the undersides of furniture, drawers and the bathroom vanity. She came back to the suitcase, reached for the computer and pulled it from the bag. Even a short peek might give a clue as to his plans.

She raised the lid, staring at the black screen. A sound caught her attention. The door to the hallway rattled, the handle turning. Pen held her breath, thinking frantically for an explanation.

On the other side of the door a cell phone rang some complicated musical tone. The door handle stopped moving and she heard an unfamiliar male voice answer in German. She slowly exhaled, not daring to make a sound while the man stood directly outside. He spoke loudly enough that if she'd known more than a few phrases, she could have followed the conversation. The voice was not Frank Morrell's—for that, she was thankful.

Could it be the police? Just because she and Gracie had not reported the attack, it didn't mean someone else hadn't. The doctor, perhaps. The clerk on duty when it happened might have given out Morrell's room number. He might have also mentioned two women who'd come looking for the guest in 314. If so, she could hardly pull the visiting-aunt excuse.

The conversation lasted an interminable three minutes by Pen's watch. At last, the man began to move away, still talking, his voice becoming fainter. She slipped Morrell's computer back into the suitcase, tiptoed to the door and peered out the peephole. No sign of a person. With a gentle touch she opened the door and glanced both directions into the corridor. He was gone.

She stepped out and closed the door behind her, wanting nothing more than to get out of this hotel. Now.

I'm getting too old for this, she thought as she practically race-walked to the elevator.

FIFTY-ONE

GRACIE'S ARM LOOKED awful the next morning as a big purple bruise now covered her entire forearm and had spread across the elbow. She insisted, however, it felt much better. The throbbing was gone, she said, although Pen noticed she still held it gingerly across her body and was very careful not to touch it to any hard surface.

Pen had glossed over her close call in Morrell's hotel room, supposing that another guest got the wrong room or a hotel employee had come up, although that person would have knocked before trying the door. Police would have announced themselves and probably would not have walked away. It wasn't Frank's voice and as far as they knew he didn't speak fluent German. It was still a mystery.

They'd gone back and forth the previous evening about reporting both the attack and the stolen necklace to the local police.

"Do we really want to get bogged down in another legal system in a foreign country?" Gracie questioned. "I mean, after all, we'd planned on catching this Frank Morrell and stealing the necklace back."

True, taking action themselves was appealing. If police found the jewelry, it would end up in custody somewhere, potentially tied up for months or years as evidence in a criminal case. Still, they had valuable information and should at least report Frank Morrell's information and what they knew about this Anton van der Went who was supposed to meet him.

Pen watched Gracie over their room-service breakfast, wondering if her friend was feeling up to a trip to the police station. She'd come to the conclusion she would simply phone in the report, unless the police insisted they come in person, when she received an incoming text message.

Amber: Don't bother with Anton at airport. He pulled a switch and came in earlier. Will try for more info. Stay tuned.

Pen held up the phone but Gracie had received the same message on hers.

"Now what? I had hoped to meet the KLM flight at eleven and trail Anton van der Went to the meeting place with Frank." Pen's disappointment was palpable.

Gracie spread honey on a toast triangle. "I suppose we do as she said and wait for more info. Unless we can come up with a way to figure out where they might be planning to meet."

Pen thought of the computer in Morrell's room and wished now that she'd simply stolen it. The man had taken far more from her. It wouldn't truly be wrong, would it?

"Well, we could sit outside his hotel and wait for him to leave, track him to the meeting spot," Gracie suggested.

"I doubt he stayed there last night. He knows we know he's in the city. He has to be thinking we would have reported his assault on you. My guess is that he watched the hotel from some distance and once the coast was clear—maybe the middle of the night—went in and took his most important things away. If this Anton came to town earlier this morning, odds are good they've already met."

Gracie's expression mirrored Pen's own discouragement.

"Okay," said Gracie, wiping her fingers on her napkin. "Before this message came we were all set to tell the police what we know about Morrell and report the attack. Let's do that much. If we can't locate him afterward, we'll just have to get ourselves on a flight back home. Although I still want to see at least one castle or something."

Her decisive words and light tone buoyed Pen a bit. They'd donned coats and gathered purses when Pen's phone rang.

"I'll make this quick—I know it's expensive," said Amber.

"If you have new information, it doesn't matter."

"Sandy's with me, helping monitor some...stuff."

Pen smiled at the way Amber tried to minimize the fact she'd hacked into off-limits sources.

"She spotted a text message exchange sent ten minutes ago between that van der Went guy and Frank Morrell. Here, I'm putting her on."

Sandy's voice sounded jubilant. "Pen? So good to hear your voice again! I can't believe it's midnight here, and I'm completely jazzed about being able to help out."

Pen put her phone on speaker for Gracie's benefit.

"Here's what I found," Sandy said. "This comes from Anton: 'Meeting time changed. Be there at ten.' Then Morrell answers back: 'Where the hell is clock museum?' Does that make sense to you?"

"Yes!" Gracie practically shouted. "I saw a clock museum on the map. It's just a few blocks from here, an easy taxi ride, I'm sure."

Pen looked at the time. "It's already a little after nine. We'd better hurry."

"Good luck," came the response from the American side of the line.

Pen took a moment to ring the front desk and asked them to flag down a cab. Five minutes later, they were rolling.

"I'm a little worried about confronting both Morrell and the other man together," Gracie confided as the taxi negotiated the winding streets. "We know Morrell isn't above striking out at a woman, and this other guy could be even more dangerous."

Pen's mind raced. Of course, Gracie was right. An idea came to her and she pulled a small notebook from her purse. She jotted a note the next time the cab halted at a traffic light. Gracie smiled approval when she saw it.

FIFTY-TWO

FRANK WOKE WITH a pounding head and his scratchy throat was worse this morning. He'd slept badly, worrying over the fact that he'd left his computer behind at the other hotel. Everything had a sense of unreality after yesterday's bizarre turn.

From his lavish suite at the Grand Cayman Regent to this small motorway hotel room with bland gray walls, a lumpy mattress and inadequate duvet, his accommodations had decidedly gone downhill. The upside to the uncomfortable room was he had no desire to linger in bed. He needed to get back to Zurich, retrieve his computer and meet with Anton van der Went at noon. Once he sold the necklace he would hop on the next flight back to Vegas and start enjoying the money he'd banked there. In his book, this particular adventure had overstayed its welcome.

He showered and put on the only clothes he had with him. Not wanting to do anything memorable, he quietly checked out and walked the two blocks to Pfäffikon Station. The only thing offered for breakfast was a hard roll and some cheese. He made do with that and a large cup of coffee. Frank finished the snack and kicked back on one of the benches in the waiting area, wanting to catch a crowded train where he would be hard to spot in the rush-hour throng. They ran frequently this time of morning so he wasn't worried about getting to his meeting on time; mainly he wanted to be calm, collected and thinking clearly before facing the diamond cutter.

He didn't need the extra cash, exactly, but pride wouldn't allow him to give the other man the better deal. He decided on a second cup of coffee, taking his mobile phone out to see how his battery was holding up while the purple-haired girl whipped the espresso.

He spotted a new message from Anton. Shit. It must have come through while he was in the shower. Meeting time changed...

His heart raced. A glance at the station's huge overhead clock told him he would barely make it to Zurich by nine-thirty, and he still had to find the damn meeting place. He texted back: Where the hell is clock museum?

Dammit! He'd planned to get there early, stake out the place. He hated not being in control. It was the secret to every great con—the master ran the show. Only the mooches didn't know what was going on.

"Forget the coffee," he called over his shoulder to the barista. She shot him the evil eye.

He snatched a tourist map from a rack beside the coffee place and raced through the station, found the platform where the next train for Zurich was already boarding, walked too quickly through the security screening and had to do it over. Damn the Swiss and their pride of precision timing. He barely made the train before the doors slid shut.

With nothing else to do during the thirty-minute ride, he spread his map and stared at the lengthy Germanic names until his head began to pound. He couldn't spot any word resembling 'clock' or 'museum.' He crumpled the map and threw it on the floor, drawing attention from the otherwise-bored morning commuters.

Okay, Frankie, not smart.

He took a deep breath and talked himself down from his agitated state. He had the necklace. He was in control. No way would he let this Dutchman and his screwy moves dictate to him. He would arrive on time, but certainly not early. He would name his price. Screw the guy. He began to breathe easier, forcing his hands to be still, his expression bland.

He'd planned to walk to the clock museum and leisurely scope out the area, but that was out. He pushed to the front of the line and took the first cab, ignoring muttered comments about the rudeness of Americans. At least the driver knew where this silly museum was. Frank ignored the man's attempts at chit-chat along the way.

When they pulled to a stop in front of yet another tall gray building, this one with white trim, Frank said, "It looks like a jewelry store."

"*Ja*, it is. Museum is on the lower level inside."

Frank paid his fare and got out, blatantly ignoring the shop front as he strolled past a row of benches under some trees along the sidewalk. A coffee shop across the street would have made the perfect lookout spot but he was running late enough now, odds were good van der Went was already inside, watching for his arrival. Damn—he hated when things didn't go his way.

He rounded the corner, pretended to browse the displays of jewelry, turned and strolled back, again taking his time to observe reflections in the glass while he pretended an interest in watches.

A female voice interrupted his thoughts, a young woman in shop girl attire who stood at the open front door. "Excuse me, sir? Are you Mr. Morrell?"

Frank didn't have time to form a response. Who wanted to know, he wondered.

The girl stepped forward with something in her hand. "This note was left for you." She handed it over and turned back to her job before he could ask where she'd gotten this.

The slip of paper was folded in on itself, forming its own little envelope of sorts. His real name was written across the outside. He unfolded the sheet, which was about six inches square.

Museum too crowded with tours this morning. Come to lobby of Carlton Hotel. 10:15. Anton

"What is this shit?" Frank muttered. Was the guy going to play games all day?

He studied the handwriting, not that it would help. He'd never seen anything handwritten by Anton. This was a firm hand, slightly slanted. Well, hell. He had twenty minutes to get to this new place and there wasn't a cab in sight.

He leaned into the jewelry store and caught the attention of the clerk who'd handed him the note.

"Where is the Carlton Hotel?"

"Em, not far." She gave directions—two blocks up this same street and one block to the left. He would see it on the right. "It's not a large place. You'll see a blue awning."

He rushed out, hoping her directions were accurate. There was no time to get lost and do it over.

FIFTY-THREE

WITH AN HOUR to prepare, Pen debated how to handle the meeting. Frank would likely bolt if he recognized either of the ladies before he entered the trap. Anton van der Went had neatly fallen for the note he'd received, making an impatient gesture but heading off toward the Paradeplatz, where "Frank's" note had insisted upon a more open space for their meeting than the confines of the museum where security cameras would record the whole transaction. Pen had no idea if that was true, but it sounded good.

Twenty minutes later, Frank Morrell showed up and followed his set of directions as well. From her seat in the coffee shop, Pen phoned Gracie to let her know their target was on his way. As soon as Frank rounded the corner, Pen pulled on the wide-brimmed hat and large sunglasses she'd purchased this morning and followed him.

Gracie couldn't help favoring her injured arm but she'd taken off the sling. Wearing a very short skirt, low-cut blouse and come-hither high heels, she hoped Frank Morrell would have his eyes elsewhere but her face. She'd pulled her dark hair back into a sleek bun and wore distractingly large earrings.

All she had to do was lure him to the secluded alcove off the main lobby at the Carlton, a spot with four upholstered chairs and a small coffee table, the kind of place colleagues might use for a quiet coffee and to talk business. Pen would be close behind their quarry as he came into the hotel and she would block the alcove opening once Frank took Gracie's enticing bait. Much of the rest of the plan depended upon bluffing and Gracie prayed it worked.

She saw Frank Morrell as he passed the hotel's front windows. A deep breath, a perky set to her shoulders and she was ready.

"Mr. Morrell?" she called out using her best imitation of a Dutch accent. "Mr. Morrell, dis vay please."

She jutted her bosom toward him as she stood, indicating an empty chair. A leather portfolio sat on the table in front of one of the others.

"So sorry, Mr. van der Went, he is in the gentlemen's room. He vill return in a moment, I'm sure." She made a show of crossing her legs as the two of them sat down. "I am Sophie, Mr. van der Went's, em, secretary."

Gracie sent an engaging smile his way, watching the hotel's entrance in her peripheral view. Pen's large hat caught her attention—her cue had arrived.

"Ah, Mr. van der Went—here is your client now," she said loudly enough for Pen to catch it.

When Frank turned around, there stood Penelope blocking the narrow pathway to the rest of the lobby.

"Mr. Stone," she said coldly. "Or should I say Mr. Morrell?"

The shock on his face was priceless. Gracie almost smiled behind his back as he spun to look at Pen.

"I believe you have something of mine. I'd like to collect it now."

"I don't—"

"Don't what? Have it with you? Sorry, that won't fly. You were ready to sell it to Anton van der Went five minutes ago. Don't know what I'm talking about? That's utter bullshit, if you'll pardon the crude language." She stood with arms spread wide. He would have to actually attack her to get through.

"Don't think about trying anything," she bluffed. "Both the local police and Interpol are on alert about this meeting. If I don't walk out of here with my necklace in my possession, the authorities are waiting right outside the door."

Morrell's eyes darted back and forth as he considered her threat. A moment later his shoulders slumped.

"Okay, you got me. You know what? I've done well enough off this trip anyway…sure, you can have the necklace. It's in my money belt. I'll just slip into the men's room to take it off."

"Huh-uh," Gracie said, joining Pen to block him. "Just lift your shirt right here. You've got nothing we haven't seen before."

"Yeah, well, maybe. But I'm also carrying quite a bit of cash and I don't want somebody outside those windows to get a look at it." He spread his arms. "You don't want anyone seeing you receive the necklace either, right? Some thug sees you, that baby's worth knocking a lady over the head to steal it."

Both women gave him hard stares.

"Not me! I don't work that way." He glanced toward the empty lobby, where only one desk clerk was working across the room. "Come on. I do have it—take a look."

He raised his shirt tail, exposing the money belt.

"So? A money belt proves nothing," Pen said.

"Feel it. You'll recognize the shape of your necklace."

He ran his fingertips over the fabric belt, inviting Pen to do the same. Sure enough, she knew the outlines of the necklace. Her hopes soared—at last she would get her beloved piece back.

"Let me just…" he tilted his head toward the sign across the way where the bathrooms were.

"I'm coming with you," Pen said, taking his arm casually as he started to pass. "Gracie? Coming?"

They flanked him as he walked, each woman with an iron grip on one of his arms. At the door to the men's room, he paused.

"Alone, please. A little privacy, ladies." Before they could answer, he'd shaken loose their hands, walked in and pushed the door closed behind him. The lock clicked into place.

Pen and Gracie exchanged a glance.

"Thirty seconds, Mr. Morrell," Pen called out through the door.

"Just a minute, the zipper's stuck," he muttered.

"Twenty seconds."

A shuffling sound.

"Ten seconds, Morrell."

Silence.

"Five seconds."

Gracie grabbed Pen's hand. "Don't announce the time," she whispered. "He's pulling something."

She ran to the front desk and summoned the clerk. "Our friend went into the restroom and seems to be having some sort of attack. Can you unlock the door? Quickly!"

The man fished around in a drawer and came up with a keyring, then followed Gracie back to the closed bathroom door.

"Quick, he may have had a heart attack," Gracie said.

The clerk unlocked the door and pushed it open, stepping in ahead of the ladies.

"Madam, I'm afraid there's no one here."

Pen and Gracie followed. It was true. The restroom was empty.

FIFTY-FOUR

BILL CAPLIN TOOK a cab from his hotel to Zurich's *Kanton-spolizei* station, refreshed after a solid night's sleep. He'd made contact upon arrival with a Detective Manheim, identified himself over the phone and set an appointment for this morning.

Calling in a favor from an old buddy in the major crimes division of the FBI had netted Caplin a list of potential fences who could 1) financially handle a piece as important as the tsarina's necklace, 2) had contacts to either dismantle the piece or sell it privately, and 3) weren't already in prison. Right now he had short-listed six such men and he wanted the opinion of this Manheim as to which might be the most likely to meet with Morrell.

Caplin knew he didn't have much time. Once Morrell made his deal he would likely be on the next plane to Anywhere In The World. And, of course, he had to tread carefully—he was here with no official authorization from his own department, working an old case without any of his superiors' knowledge.

His vague nervousness was alleviated as soon as he met Detective Manheim, a man in a business suit, about his own age, clearly a veteran who'd seen a lot. The man's smile and handshake established an immediate camaraderie.

"Come into my little office," Manheim invited.

The space was actually more of a cubicle but he offered coffee, which Caplin gratefully accepted.

"Let's see this list of names you spoke about."

Caplin handed over a copy. "The piece I'm looking for is worth over a million dollars. It was taken in a single-item robbery at a museum in my city. We ran out of leads so I'm working this on my own time." *Covering my ass in case you decide to discuss this with my boss.* "I tracked the chief suspect to Grand Cayman and learned he had flown here to Zurich two days ago."

"Most certainly, if he wants to fence the necklace, he will try to accomplish it quickly. These sorts do not like to spend a lot of time in one place."

"Exactly. I believe he stayed on Cayman just long enough to make contact with whoever he plans to meet here."

Manheim had a pen in hand and tapped it against the paper in his hand. "This first one—he is most likely not the one. Two days ago we learned he had been detained in London with questions about his travel papers. I think he is not able to move about so freely as your thief would like."

Caplin waited, letting the detective take his time.

"A problem we have here at the moment, there is a major jewel theft ring operating through much of western Europe, especially in the playgrounds of the wealthy. You may have noticed the high-end shops here in Zurich. Two jewelry stores have been targets in recent weeks, with robberies over a hundred-thousand euro each. Total is probably… um…around two-hundred-fifty thousand US dollars. Only from these two shops. When you factor in other robberies in London, Paris, Monaco and along the Côte d'Azur… well, we are into the millions."

"And the names on my list? Are some of these men connected with this ring?"

"*Ja*, I know two of these by reputation. It would certainly be my pleasure to arrest them both."

Caplin felt his smile freeze in place. He really didn't want another department confronting his suspect. The idea was to get his own hands on the cash rightfully due him.

"Is either of them, say, likely to have been in contact with an American in the past few days?" Careful how you phrase this, Caplin reminded himself.

Manheim gazed upward as he considered the question. "If I were to make an educated guess, I would favor the Dutchman, van der Went. All things considered, including his ability to come up with the amount of cash to purchase the piece you describe, he could handle it. *Ja*, he would be my bet. Of course, this Parisian named LeClair—he is a tricky one and he travels widely. I shall run this passport information for you, find out if either has traveled to the places you mention."

"Thank you," Caplin said. "Any information is helpful."

Manheim stood. "It should take only a few minutes. Would you care for another coffee?"

Caplin declined the beverage; he'd had two already this morning. He heard the other detective speak to someone a couple of workspaces away, asking for a computer search of the most recent travel by the two names he'd mentioned.

"Yes, sir," the female officer replied. "There's also…" Her voice dropped and Caplin assumed the two had walked away.

Manheim returned a few minutes later, carrying a steaming coffee for himself. "Ah, you see, now there's another jewel theft reported just now. Apparently a personal loss at one of the local hotels." He gave a what-can-you-do shrug.

"So, these men—the Frenchman and the Dutch—are

they both linked with this international theft ring?" Caplin asked. "I'd like to have their dossiers, if possible."

"Most definitely. I have asked my colleague to print information for you, including photos of identification and what we know about each man's methods. If you are able to take even one of them off the streets, well, much power to you."

Caplin smiled.

Within ten minutes, a female uniformed sergeant appeared. "The files you requested," she said, handing over two neatly labeled manila folders.

The detective took them and flipped open the first one, taking a glance before he turned them over to Caplin.

"Ah, now here is an interesting bit," he said. "Anton van der Went. He flew into Zurich just this morning, an early flight from Amsterdam."

Caplin's alarm bells went off. This had to be the one.

"He listed a private address where he would be staying during his visit. It's all in here." He handed the two folders to Caplin. "Good luck with everything, sir, and do not hesitate to call if you have additional evidence. As I mentioned, I would be very pleased to arrest either of these men."

They shook hands and Caplin said he could find his own way out. He walked the aisle between the half-dozen cubicles that made up the detective unit at the station. Conversations in Swiss German flowed—it was quite a busy department, he realized. He was almost back to the station's main corridor when he caught sight of a dark-haired woman in a very short skirt sitting in one of the cubicles. What had caught his attention was that the officer there was speaking English.

"Yes, Mrs. Fitzpatrick, we shall certainly investigate the loss of your necklace. It's only that we cannot promise a quick result for you."

Caplin froze. Fitzpatrick?

"I know who committed the crime," came a familiar woman's voice. "It's a man named Frank Morrell, an American, and he plans to meet with someone called Anton van der Went to sell my stolen heirloom."

Caplin was now certain. How had she managed to track Morrell to Zurich? And van der Went? She already knew about him?

He wanted to stay and listen to the rest of the interview but didn't dare. If Penelope Fitzpatrick spotted him, she would question his being in the city. He'd been very firm with her—sorry, the case is closed. She clearly was no dummy and she would easily connect the dots and figure out he was somehow involved with the thieves. He needed to get the hell out of there—fast.

FIFTY-FIVE

FRANK LEANED AGAINST a gray stone wall, breathless and dizzy. What had just happened back there? Were the gem cutter and the old woman working together, and how was the dark-haired good-looking one involved? He couldn't believe he hadn't recognized her; he would have beat it out of there right away. If the Fitzpatrick woman was working with Anton van der Went, how did they know each other? Was it pure luck for them or had they pulled one over on him? His thoughts ricocheted like the steel ball in a pinball machine.

He stared at the narrow strip of gray sky above the alley where he'd run, instinct taking over, after he crawled out of the air duct in that restroom and dodged through the hotel's utility rooms and kitchen, finally stumbling through the delivery entrance and running for his life. The women had no doubt called the police, who were probably swarming the place by now.

The more he thought about that scenario, the more convinced he became—the ladies were working on their own. Van der Went was a separate entity. Probably. One way to find out. He pulled his cell phone from his pocket but there was no signal, buried deep as he was in the maze of high buildings. He jogged to the opposite end of the alley from where he'd come and looked around. A small park was across the street, the kind where young mothers brought kids in strollers and a few suited businessmen sat on benches getting a little sun during their lunch hours. He could fit in well enough, he decided.

Enough with text messages and notes, he thought as he saw the bars on the phone's display rise. I'm calling this dude.

A gruff male voice picked up after one ring. "Anton. What the hell?" Frank said.

"You tell me. I don't play these games, Morrell. You send me notes? Come on."

"Don't blame me. How do I know what you're up to?"

"Listen, I could give a shit about your item. *You* need something from *me*. You don't play the game by my rules, I walk."

Frank caught a whiff of a bluff there, but did he dare take the chance? He wanted to leave this city with cash in hand, not a hot piece of jewelry that was becoming more dangerous by the day.

"How do I know you even have the piece you claim? You know, there's much bigger fish out there these days—sure thing deals with people I already know."

This time there was no bluff.

"Okay, okay," Frank said. He looked around and spotted a newspaper at the top of a trash bin. "I'll send you a picture to prove I've got it. Then we meet. You brought cash right?"

Anton chuffed. "Amateur."

"Two minutes. You'll have a picture."

Frank folded the paper on the bench beside him, masthead showing the date at the top. This was a risk, taking the necklace out in broad daylight, but he was tired of the delays. Assuring he had this corner of the park to himself, he reached under his shirt, removed the necklace from the money belt and laid it across the page. Snap, snap—a photo and a Send. He set the phone down and quickly re-stashed the jewels.

Anton called back immediately. "This piece, it is from zat museum job in Arizona, few months ago."

"Yes, that's the one."

"I followed the story. Later, they say the necklace was not worth anything. You trying to fool Anton with a fake?"

Frank went into the explanation about the switch, finding himself losing patience once again. "Look, you'll have to see the piece. Verify it for yourself."

He worked to keep his tone cool, as if the sale meant nothing to him. He could find any number of buyers for the piece. Yeah, in theory. But the reality was he'd become sick of the hassle. The game had been fun for awhile. Now he wanted to dump this thing and get on with something else, something easier.

"I will call you back in ten minutes with a meeting place," Anton said. The line went dead.

FIFTY-SIX

PENELOPE AND GRACIE sat at the desk of the officer who'd taken their story about the encounters with Frank Morrell, aka Richard Frank, their visits to his hotel, the chase through the streets and resulting injury to Gracie, this morning's encounter and the oh-so-close chance to get her necklace back from the thief. The officer was very Swiss-polite and assured her they would look for the necklace, although he advised they could not promise a quick result. She felt her mood plummet, discouraged with police who dutifully took reports but never solved her problem.

"Our lead detective may have some useful information. When he is finished with his current interview—"

"I am finished," said a new voice. A tall man with handsome touches of gray at his temples stood at the opening to the cube. "How may I help you?"

The first officer introduced him as Detective Manheim of the *Kantonspolizei's* robbery division, then went on to recap what the ladies had reported.

"Ah, another jewel theft," Manheim said, leaning against the wall somewhat gingerly. "I'm sorry to report they are happening everywhere. We suspect the notorious Golden Tiger theft ring, although now we are seeing what you would call copy-cat thieves as well. Last weekend two gunmen brazenly raided a very large jewelry show in Cannes, taking more than a hundred million dollars in diamonds."

Pen's astonishment must have shown on her face.

"While your loss is very sad, it is but one piece in a very large puzzle, I'm afraid," Manheim said. "Please be assured we are working with the authorities in France and other countries to track and capture these criminals."

The other officer spoke up. "Many of these thefts have happened in the south of France, you see. Interpol is already setting very tight security measures in place for the Cannes Film Festival next month."

Detective Manheim read Penelope's expression. "Yes, I know, that has nothing to do with your case. All we can say is that we are closely on the trail of these men and when we catch them, all efforts will be made to match the stolen gems with their original owners. Yours is only one of a half-dozen or so where the diamonds came from private owners or historical collections. One case—so sad—an elderly woman's priceless diamond ring, given by her late husband before he died, was taken from her at gunpoint. We do not see these things in Switzerland. We are as shocked by the brazenness of it as anyone."

Not exactly reassuring words, Pen wanted to say. She glanced at Gracie who appeared to be tiring quickly. Her poor friend had endured too much in the last twenty-four hours. She picked up her purse, signed the police report the officer had printed for her, and they left.

Outside, thick clouds had begun to form. The sky seemed to mirror their own discouragement.

"I don't feel much hope about this," Pen confided as they walked toward their hotel.

"I know. I still cannot figure out how Frank Morrell got away this morning."

"The police found an air vent fastened with only one screw. It must have been his hiding place. But how he got out of the room itself...the man is like an eel, slipping away as if the walls can't hold him."

"I think what bothers me most is that the whole thing is so overwhelming. I'm not at all convinced Morrell is part of some international theft ring. Everything about him seems to say he's a lot more local. He's American—the rest of them operate in France. He scammed those people on Grand Cayman with an investment scheme."

"So, even if the international police find and recover the stolen diamonds they're looking for?"

"I don't hold much hope mine will be with them. This chase got you injured, sweetie. The men have managed to stay leaps ahead of us and they've outsmarted the police in at least two countries. How can we handle this? It's too much."

They passed a pastry shop with an enticing window display of cakes and delicate cookies. Their footsteps slowed.

"We missed lunch," Pen said. "Let's see if we can get a sandwich or salad and top it with a nice dessert."

Gracie didn't argue. As they took seats, she pulled her silk scarf from her purse and Pen helped fashion it into the sling for her arm once more.

"Better," Gracie said once her sore arm was elevated.

They ordered salads and felt their energy return. Gracie was first to steer the conversation back to the necklace.

"Knowledge is power, I'm always telling my kids. When they need information, I make them go look it up."

"And...?"

"And we have dear Amber as our walking, talking encyclopedia, the queen of search engines, right? Maybe she'll have some ideas for us. Don't give up yet, Pen. Your grandfather's work was important to him and to your whole family. I don't want to see us quit until we've tried everything we can."

Dessert was a gigantic piece of chocolate cake with frosting that melted in the mouth. Split in half, it was still more than the two of them could handle so they had their leftovers put into a take-out box.

"Okay, the meal helped a lot," Gracie announced as they entered the quiet sanctuary of their hotel room. "I say we call Amber before it gets any later there. Maybe she can set up the call so it includes Sandy and we can all talk out a plan."

Pen nodded, still feeling discouraged.

Bless her, Amber immediately got the discussion going. "Let's see what we can learn about this jewel theft ring," she suggested right away.

"Also, can you track the movements of Anton van der Went and/or Frank Morrell? If one or both of them are working with the big guys, we need to know. And if they aren't, maybe there's something we can do on our own."

Sandy came on. "I've been thinking about what happened to Gracie, the attack when she cornered Morrell. We should take self-defense classes."

"What? Right here and now?" Pen was half joking.

"Well… I suppose that wouldn't be practical. Let's keep it in mind though, for when you get home. I know someone who could instruct us."

Amber turned the topic again. "I've found some articles about the big jewel thefts in Europe. I'm forwarding them to you guys. Read up and see if any ideas come to mind. Meanwhile, I'll dig deeper."

"For now, you both should rest," Sandy said. "It's been a stressful day for you."

In so many ways.

Pen thought of the moment she'd almost had her hands on her missing necklace, the feel of it through the fabric money belt worn by Frank Morrell. If only she'd yanked the belt off him or at least insisted he disrobe right there. How could she have been taken in once again?

She lay in bed that night, a carousel of dark thoughts circling through her head. It frustrated her that there was nothing they could do until they either heard from the police or until Amber came back with new information.

For the first time since leaving home, she felt despair creep over her.

FIFTY-SEVEN

ANTON'S CALL WAS more like thirty minutes in coming, time where Frank's emotions ran the gamut. He was scared the renowned fence had decided to drop the deal; he became angry the guy was jerking him around; he wanted his money out of this thing—now; he wished he'd stuck with stock market scams played on clueless old guys with big egos. Why had he thought the museum job would be a cinch?

He kept his spot on the park bench, pretending to read the German language newspaper, his eyes darting about to see if Anton was out there, checking him out, staying defensive in case someone else had noticed the necklace and was planning a robbery of his own. But the people in the park seemed to fall into two categories: office workers whose lunch hours ended so they meandered away, and mothers with cranky kids who either fell asleep in their prams or got taken home for a real nap. As far as he could tell, the entire crowd had regular turnover. When his phone rang, it startled him.

"Okay, we meet," said Anton. "Where are you now?"

Frank wasn't entirely sure. He read off the impossibly long name of a street sign and described the park.

"You have been there all this time? A park bench showed in your photo."

"Yes, same bench."

"Too long in one place. Police could be watching."

Frank craned his neck to look in all directions and didn't see any but at this point he wasn't going to contradict the gem cutter. "Fine. Tell me where."

"Send me a picture of yourself," Anton said. "It had better match the one I have."

Okay, a wise precaution, Frank thought. But where had Anton gotten a photo of him?

"You do the same," Frank said.

"No—this is my call. You will follow instructions. Send the picture. Then add one red item to your clothing, something I will immediately see."

Frank had hoped to change his appearance a bit more than that, just in case the Fitzpatrick woman was out and happened to spot him.

Anton gave an address on Bahnhofstrasse, which Frank immediately knew would be near the train station. Handy for a quick getaway. A likely spot the police would be surveilling. Again, he wished he could go by his hotel here in the city and retrieve his laptop and suitcase, but it seemed riskier than ever at this point. The women had undoubtedly reported this morning's encounter to the police, complete with his name, local address, and description right down to the clothing.

"Twenty minutes will give you adequate time," Anton said. He hung up.

Frank snapped the required photo, making sure it showed mostly his face. Sent it to Anton then quickly walked out of the park. A shop two blocks away had a rack of casual jackets out on the sidewalk, end-of-winter clearance. He picked up a red one and pretended to examine it until the clerk inside was looking the other direction. Bunching it up, he held it close in front of him until he turned the corner, where he ripped off the tags and slipped it on over the blue suit Penelope would recognize. Adding a pronounced limp to his gait, he went to the next corner and hailed a taxi, giving the address Anton had told him.

The café near the rail station had a low metal fence surrounding outdoor tables that didn't look so inviting today. The clouds overhead had grown thicker and threatened rain, and a stiff breeze fluttered the awning. Frank glanced around, saw no one watching the place, and took a seat as instructed. A steady stream of traffic went by, both taxis and private cars, delivering and picking up passengers from the train station, but no one was interested in food at the moment because the café tables remained empty. When he looked more closely at the building itself, no lights shone through the windows and he saw a small sign which he took to mean the place was closed. He felt a wriggle of concern.

Had Anton deliberately set him up to look suspicious, or was this part of the test? He would give it two more minutes. He glanced at his Rolex and when he looked up saw a stocky man with red-blond hair approaching. He wore a working man's clothing—wrinkled pants and a coarse shirt. Frank purposely looked away, Mr. Casualness himself. At the last possible moment the blond man stepped over the low fence and headed for the restaurant's door.

"Frank. Do not acknowledge me but wait until I walk away and follow. Stay ten or twenty feet behind me." Anton feigned surprise at the dark restaurant, looked at the sign, checked his watch, then walked away.

Seriously? Frank couldn't decide whether to laugh at the drama or grab the man by his sleeve and pull him to a chair at his same table. In the end, he did as instructed, walking casually and pausing now and then to look in a shop window for a moment.

Anton walked four blocks then opened a glass door which opened into a small vestibule. Frank caught up as Anton made a show of checking one of the mailboxes on a wall full of them.

"Lose that stupid red coat," he muttered under his breath. "Check your mail then come upstairs to this one." His finger tapped the front of the box numbered 206.

It grated on Frank to be treated as such a child, given instructions step by step, although he had to admit the extra maneuvers had probably kept them from being noticed. He fiddled with a mailbox, then slipped his coat off. At a moment when no passersby were near, he stuffed the coat into a tall trashcan in the little lobby. The door to apartment 206 stood open about an inch and he tapped before entering. Anton appeared to be alone, although Morrell blatantly snooped into the galley kitchen and tiny bathroom before he took the chair suggested by his host.

"Let's see the merchandise," Anton said, hand extended, fingers wiggling.

Frank didn't see any point in dallying. He reached into his shirt and worked the money belt zipper, pulling the necklace out. It had been awhile since he'd looked closely at it and, as always, its intricacy and sparkle quickened his breath.

"Beautiful piece," Anton said, pulling a loupe from his shirt pocket and starting at one end to examine the stones. "Very fine work."

"Supposed to date back to the early 1900s or something. Museum had it displayed as something once worn by some Russian royalty."

"The tsarina, Alexandra," Anton said without missing a beat.

Like Frank gave a shit about fancy European titles. To him, the piece was jewelry that was worth cash. A lot of it.

"I can move the piece," Anton said. "Something like this, a private collector will want. No need to recut the stones. Of course, unless things become too hot. There is a lot going on right now."

"I don't care about that. How much can you give me for it today?"

"So impatient, Americans. Everything is right now, right away. What do they call—immediate gratification?"

"So? *Yeah*, I'd like to move it today."

Anton took his eye away from the necklace. "I will show it to some people—colleagues. We shall see what we can offer." He started to place the necklace in his pocket.

"Oh, no, no, no. The necklace stays with me until cash changes hands."

"Typically, a wire transfer to your account," Anton said.

"Nuh-uh. You think I was born yesterday? Nothing I can't carry away in my hands."

The Dutchman's look said that's exactly what he thought of Frank—this was a rube with no sophistication in the diamond trade. Well, fine. He could think whatever he wanted but Frank was not letting that piece out of his sight. He held out his hand and Anton handed the jewels back to him.

"This thing is bigger than you think, American. Bigger than Interpol. And the reason it stays that way is we check everything. And we double-check it."

"Fine with me. But I'm going to be closer than your twin in the womb until we make a fair exchange. You get the jewels, I get cash money. One million U.S. dollars."

This time Anton actually laughed out loud. He stood up. "Get out of here. You seem inexperienced but you aren't stupid. The very most you'll get is a third of that."

Frank debated walking out. He hated the Dutchman's haughty manner. He wanted the cash from this job—the whole thing had become a giant pain in the ass. But he'd pulled too many cons over too many years to ever let the prize out of his sight.

"Five hundred thousand," he said.

"Three-fifty. If you want it, we leave in an hour."

FIFTY-EIGHT

CAPLIN LEFT THE police station as quickly as possible, using a side exit and hailing a cab almost immediately. Two blocks away he stopped looking over his shoulder. It was worrisome the Fitzpatrick woman was here and she knew almost as much about the case as he did. He'd always been the kind of cop who wanted to understand the details, the one who worked the jigsaw puzzle of each case with an eye toward the finished picture. It bothered him that she'd turned up with so many of the pieces already in place. Had she actually seen Frank Morrell with the necklace? He wasn't sure, based on the fraction of the conversation he'd overheard just now.

He gave the cab driver the address of his hotel and clutched the police files closely to his chest until they arrived. In this comedy of errors and coincidences, it occurred to him that he might have another potential disaster on his hands if it turned out Mrs. Fitzpatrick happened to be staying in the same hotel. As far as he knew, her not knowing he was in the city was his one advantage over her.

He paid the driver and went inside, stopping at the front desk. No, he was told, there was no one named Fitzpatrick registered. He started to walk away when he remembered the younger woman at the police station, the one wearing the short skirt which had first attracted his attention. He turned back to the clerk and described her, but the clerk could only say she didn't remember anyone specifically like this woman he was looking for.

Settled once again in his small room, Caplin brewed a cup of coffee in the tiny carafe provided and settled with the files, leaning back against the headboard of his bed. He liked to start at the end of the file, the beginning of the case, and watch how it had unfolded for the local police. He opened the first file and flipped to the back.

The dossier included background information on Interpol's lead suspect, Andrej Lubnic, who had escaped from a Swiss prison six months earlier. The forty-five-year-old man was found guilty in 2010 of several jewel thefts, sentenced to ten years in prison and apparently escaped with inside help and another prisoner for company. Like the famous Pink Panther theft network, this one had pulled off dozens of robberies in watch and jewelry stores throughout Europe and the Middle East, oftentimes with one lone gunman walking into a store, smashing display cases, scooping up bags full of treasure.

Caplin's eyelids were drooping by the time he caught up with Lubnic's current movements. The chase appeared headed for Nice, France where, according to notes Manheim had made for him this morning, the city would be packed during the coming two weeks. With a renaissance festival, a sailing regatta, Le Mans car race and art festival all taking place at the same time as the year's largest jewelry show, there would be plenty of ways for thieves to target the jewels. Costumes and getaway measures would abound, and even security on high alert would be hard-pressed to watch everything at once.

It was a good news/bad news situation. If Caplin could get to Frank Morrell in the midst of the melee, he would have as good a chance as anyone of getting away once he'd collected his money from the con man. On the other hand, catching one thief in a city full of them—with international police forces watching their every move—that would be the challenge.

He closed the folders and picked up the phone. Twenty minutes later, he had a seat booked on the first flight to Nice in the morning.

FIFTY-NINE

THE MOMENT THE train rolled out of the Zurich *bahnhof*, Frank felt his mood rise. No way would some women put the fear in him! This was *his* game—*he* called the plays. The joy of the con was always in the act of walking away, cutting out, getting away with it. The necklace rested safely against his belly and the guy who would pay big money for it was sitting three rows ahead of him.

Van der Went insisted they travel separately, but that didn't mean Frank wouldn't have his eye on the Dutchman during the trip. He studied the man, as much for his style as for the deal they were about to complete. Anton looked like a mill worker on his way home, blending seamlessly with others in the commuting crowd in his wrinkled pants and coarse shirt, a flat cap on his head, a small knapsack near his feet. At the next stop, a lot of the working types got off. Anton draped his casual jacket over his seat and visited the lavatory. Frank tensed, wondering if Anton was pulling a sneaky way of getting off the train. But the man came back wearing a neat white shirt and tie, and the pants had lost a lot of their slouchy appearance. His hair was combed and he stowed the cap and rough shirt in the knapsack.

Frank was impressed. Most people would never realize they were looking at the same man. At the next stop, the casual jacket got turned inside out changing its color from blue to gray. The knapsack went from cloth to leather, and the man now wore a pair of wire-rimmed glasses and spent the rest of the ride consulting his smart phone.

Frank realized he would need to implement similar changes in his own appearance before he finalized the deal with Anton and these colleagues. By the time he boarded a flight for America, he'd better be someone that no one in Europe would remember.

SIXTY

GRACIE NOTICED THE display on Penelope's ringing mobile phone. Amber. Pen was in the shower so Gracie picked it up.

"We're coming to join you!" Amber said. "Sandy and I."

"Oh, thank you! She's been really low… But, are you sure? I mean, it's expensive and you shouldn't miss work…"

"We've both taken vacation days. Four of us can accomplish more, plus we felt so bad that you got hurt. All I need to know is what's the best way to get from the airport to your hotel?"

"Well, slight change of plans. Pen overheard the police detective in Zurich talking about a gang of active jewel thieves in France. We think Frank Morrell is heading for Nice, on the south coast. We're leaving today to go there. Does that mess up your plans?"

"Easy change. I'll get it done now."

"There are a ton of events going on down there," Gracie said. "I'd better reserve rooms."

"Rooms?" Pen said, stepping from the bathroom with her hair turbaned in a towel.

Gracie held up Pen's phone. "Amber called. She and Sandy are flying into Nice to join us. Sorry—I saw who it was and just reached for it."

"That's wonderful," Pen said. She took off the towel and began running a comb through her chin-length blond hair.

"I'd begun to feel a little overwhelmed with all this. It will be nice to have their help."

A *little* overwhelmed? Gracie felt a rush of relief at the smile on Pen's face. Ever since Morrell's brazen getaway and their visit to the Zurich police, the two women had been on the go. Finding out Morrell had sneaked back to his Zurich hotel and cleared out his room, learning the clerk had overheard bits of his conversation with someone, a mention of Nice. She was proud of their detective work, nervous about what would happen if they'd drawn the wrong conclusions.

Gracie began to look for hotels with available rooms. "Looks like we'll have to settle for something very cheap or something very pricey. The mid-range places seem to be full."

"Go for the nicer place. If Frank Morrell keeps up his habit from Cayman, that's where he will go. Plus, I'm always skeptical of small and cheap."

Gracie found a suite at the Palais de la Mediterranee, cringed a little at the rate but gratefully accepted Pen's credit card to cover it. The three bedrooms would work fine for the women and, if things went well, they might even get to spend a little time on the beach.

Pen emerged a few minutes later, perfectly turned out as usual, and they finished packing. A quick cab ride to the airport and five hours later they were landing in Nice, surprised to find it wasn't a lot warmer than springtime Zurich.

Pen switched on her phone while they waited for baggage. "A message from Amber," she said. "Have a feeling your guys will be staking out the biggest jewelry show of the year. It starts tomorrow. We are at PHX. See you in a few hours!"

Pen thought about that. Although Morrell probably

wanted to sell her necklace and get himself off to another part of the world as quickly as possible, the lure of such a show would likely attract every jewel thief on the continent. She relaxed slightly. At least she and Gracie could take a few hours to orient themselves to the city and work out a plan. When she mentioned it to Gracie, her friend simply laughed.

"You don't think Amber will have the whole thing mapped and plotted by the time we see her?"

True. The Heist Ladies' youngest member most definitely seemed a master of logistics.

Their taxi cruised a wide boulevard with stately hotels on the left and the shoreline on their right. The driver was a chatty sort.

"The mademoiselles are visiting our city for the jewelry show? *Oui*, it will be held at the *Nice Acropolis*. For myself, I am more interested in the regatta or perhaps the Le Mans race next weekend." On the water they could see dozens of sleek sailboats, moored now, with crews working on the decks. "My wife, however…she would be at that jewelry show in a moment if only she could afford to purchase something."

They passed a modern building, vaguely pyramid-like with a flat top. The driver pointed toward it.

"*Oui*, they say there will be four-hundred million euro worth of jewels in that place."

What else would the world's most audacious jewel thieves be watching this week?

SIXTY-ONE

As BEFORE, Frank followed at a short distance behind Anton as they made their way from the train station. He hoped for a brief glimpse of the Mediterranean but the area where they walked was packed with unimaginative blocky buildings, mostly white with red-tile roofs. After walking about fifteen minutes, they came to a three-story apartment building. Anton held the outer door for Frank, as any polite neighbor would do, and Frank preceded him into an empty vestibule. Once Anton was satisfied no one would overhear, he spoke. "Number 301."

Frank pretended to consult the mailboxes on the wall while Anton started up a narrow flight of stairs.

"Is this your place?" Frank asked once the two of them were inside with the door closed.

Anton gave one of his customary down-the-nose looks. "Something like that."

Geez, Frank thought, a little friendliness wouldn't kill you. The apartment was furnished minimally with modern chrome and leather furniture, a black furry-looking rug over the scuffed wood floor, a kitchen with downsized, basic appliances.

As if Anton had read his mind, he relented slightly. "Sorry. It's only that I have bigger things on my mind right now."

*Bigger than a million dollar piece of jewelry? Hmm...
Now* that *might be worth knowing.*

"The gem show?"

"You know of it?" Anton almost covered his surprise but not quite.

Frank prided himself on being observant, and the headline on the business page of a newspaper he'd seen someone reading on the train had not escaped his attention. "Everyone knows about it," he answered with his own hint of haughty one-upmanship.

"Then you know it will be the most closely guarded exhibition of the year. Police and electronic surveillance will be at an all-time high alert status."

"Naturally." Frank wasn't sure where this was going. All he wanted was to sell the piece that was increasingly making his belly itch.

"The Pink Panthers plan to rob the place blind."

What? Frank turned toward a chrome-and-glass shelf that held a few books with French titles, magazines about architecture and a few cheap vases and knick-knacks. Gave himself a moment to consider Anton's statement. He'd heard of the Pink Panthers, of course. Most thought of either a cartoon character or a Peter Sellers film. So, there truly was a jewel theft gang by that name. By the time he turned where Anton could see his face again, his sophisticated expression was back in place.

"How will they get away with it?" he asked.

"They won't. The Golden Tigers will be there first."

All these gangs with their pretentious names. Frank's mind flitted through the possibilities. What could he get for himself here? With the Russian piece as his ticket, he might persuade the big guys to take him seriously, let him in on the deal, turn the present three-fifty into multi-millions. He felt his pulse quicken.

"You cannot be seen with me, you know," Anton was saying. "If the Tigers see you, it's quite possible you and the necklace you carry will become a target."

Frank considered this while Anton went to the kitchen and turned on a burner under a kettle, offering coffee. His necklace making him a target with one of the jewel theft rings? It didn't quite add up. Then again, a niggling feeling told him he was out of his league with these guys and anything could happen.

Always dream big, Frankie. His father's voice came back to him.

"Sure, coffee would be great," he said, settling into character. If he could be an inside stock trader on Grand Cayman, he could just as easily become a sophisticated international jewel thief here on the Côte d'Azur.

SIXTY-TWO

GRACIE TURNED IN a circle, staring at the lavish furnishings in their suite at the Palais de la Mediterranee. "Pen, I can't thank you enough for sharing this experience with me. With all of us. Sandy and Amber probably wouldn't ever be able to do this on their own either. This place is exquisite."

Pen waved off the compliment. "You've all pitched in so selflessly to help me with something I could never have managed alone. It's a fair trade."

"So, now what? We need to come up with a plan."

"My first thought is that you and I need disguises. Frank Morrell has seen us and we need to make him believe we lost track of him when he left Zurich."

"Agreed."

"I wish I had a better feel for this jewelry show, what types of people will be there, what methods we might use to blend in."

"I worked a few trade shows before my kids were born," Gracie said. "I could pretend to be an exhibitor, walk around the show floor with a badge of some sort."

"It's a thought. Let's ask Amber if she can figure out how to make something like that."

"But it's not quite enough. He'll know our faces...we need more."

They discussed it over a three-course seafood dinner and

decided a good night's sleep would help clarify their thinking. The other team members would arrive in the morning.

AMBER ARRIVED PREPARED to work, Pen was pleased to see.
The youngest member carried a computer and wireless
printer in her luggage and in no time at all had set up a little office on the desk in the suite. While Sandy napped to
recover from the long flight, Gracie took a shopping list
provided by Amber and headed to an office supply store
for specialized paper.

"The problem with posing as exhibitors is that those
badges will no doubt contain a magnetic strip, hologram
or some other type of encryption," Amber said. "They're
not going to allow anyone behind the scenes who poses a
risk to the whole show. You can bet security will be tight."

Pen had to admit she was correct.

"What about if we attend as potential buyers, wealthy
ladies who are on a huge shopping spree?"

Amber looked up from her screen and nodded. "That
could work. Now how do we disguise ourselves?"

She scrolled through a few pages on her browser then
her face lit up. "Pen! What about this?"

Pen had just chosen a plum from the complimentary
fruit basket and she walked back to the desk to see what
Amber was looking at.

"Perfect. Absolutely perfect!"

SIXTY-THREE

WILLIAM CAPLIN CONSIDERED himself a good cop, one of the best at his job, honest to the core. He told himself this each of the past three mornings after sleepless nights peppered with nightmares about his role in the museum robbery cover-up. He'd arrived in Nice on a late flight, immediately gone to a low-price hole in the wall hotel because it was the only thing available, and thought nothing in the world would wake him.

So, why am I standing here at four in the morning? He stared into the mirror above the rickety washstand in his room, hating the dark bags below his eyes, the droop of the jowls he'd never much noticed before this month.

It's an attack of conscience, his better half replied. *You've never done anything like this in your life.*

But you're in it now. Your retirement fund is gone if you don't do something to get it back.

The thing about justifying bad behavior was that after awhile the arguments in favor began to nag at him, began to sound weak, like the whiny words from those crooks he'd prided himself on putting away. Those guys always had a million excuses—they had their reasons, they needed the money, their victims could afford the losses, it was nothing to them, Mama always needed an operation. Something. Something decent human beings didn't do. Something a good cop would never do.

He should go to the local department head, meet the Interpol men, tell them everything he knew and let Frank Morrell suffer the consequences.

Retirement fund.

Justice.

Do the right thing.

Do the profitable thing.

Then there was the Fitzpatrick woman—what had she been doing in Zurich? At the police station. It couldn't be coincidence she was there at the same time as Frank Morrell. Did the foolish woman think she could actually catch the con man herself? And now that an international police force knew about her stolen necklace, what chance did Caplin have of getting to Morrell first?

He drew back his fist, wanted to punch the mirror. A stupid move, a thing one of those two-bit punks he'd sent to prison would do. Injuring himself and waking the rest of the hotel wouldn't be smart, no matter his emotional state. He dumped two aspirin into his palm from the bottle in his ditty bag, swallowing them with a swig of bottled water. The toilet was down the hall and he made it there and back without making much noise.

He flopped back on his bed, cursing the sagging mattress and lumpy pillow. What the hell was he doing in Europe anyway?

When dim light began to show through the thin curtain at his window, he got up and dressed. Surely a beachside resort town would be stirring at this hour. Coffee might help put his dilemma into perspective.

SIXTY-FOUR

SANDY EMERGED FROM her bedroom, a little fuzzy around the edges, yawning but awake.

"I figured I'd better get up or I would sleep all day and be awake all night," she said.

"Hungry?" Pen asked. "I was thinking of some lunch."

Amber spoke, not taking her eyes from her computer screen. "I'll wait for Gracie."

"It's probably best if we don't all four go out together anyway," Sandy said.

"True. We don't want to draw notice as a group," Pen said. "I can bring back something for everyone, or just order room service if you'd like."

In the end it was decided that Pen and Sandy would take a walk and check out the area, while Amber did more research on the gem show and waited for Gracie, who'd been sent on a second errand after returning from the office supply store.

Pen put on her large hat and big sunglasses, making certain to wear slacks and a jacket Frank Morrell had never seen before. The last thing they wanted was for him to spot her before she spotted him, and they had to take into account that he could have already arrived here and be somewhere in the vicinity of the gem show venue.

According to Amber's research, the big event opened tonight with a champagne gala for the wealthiest buyers and she was doing her best to get Pen onto the invitation list. The goal of attending wasn't so much to take in the fabulous displays of jewelry on offer, although that part of it would be an enticing sidelight—they wanted to scope out the layout, entries and exits, and the likely ways robbers might target the place.

"Of course, I need all of you to keep an eye out for my necklace," Pen told Sandy as they left the hotel, walking alongside the lengthy Promenade des Anglais which stretched for miles along the beach front. "There is always the chance Frank Morrell sold it quickly and it may turn up."

"Surely no one would be so foolish as to put a recently stolen item on display," Sandy ventured.

"Yes, that's probably true. We shall most certainly need to keep our ears as well as our eyes open."

They kept up a brisk pace—the rocky beach and sea on their right hand and ornate buildings backed by green hills to their left. They passed a tourism office and a large park with some kind of monument and a sign indicating a theater nearby. Beachside restaurants dotted the way but they put a mile or more behind them before they reached the end of the walking path, turned around and began earnestly looking for a lunch spot. The *Beau Rivage* offered beachside dining, views through floor-to-ceiling windows, linen tablecloths, and a French menu featuring delectable crepes, for which Pen had suddenly developed a craving.

"For once, I don't care about the extra butter," she told Sandy, dipping into her pasta. "This is delicious."

She was about to take a second bite when a man walking laboriously across the rocky beach caught her attention. Wearing a business suit and overcoat with dress shoes that must have proven extremely painful on the rock surface, he plodded along with his eyes directed toward his next potential misstep.

Pen's fork dropped to her plate. "Oh, my god," she said barely above a whisper.

"Pen? What is it?" Sandy looked up from her plate.

"Out there on the beach, that man." Pen had begun to rise from her chair.

Sandy saw the only person within view who wasn't wearing beach attire.

"I know him. It's the police detective who tried to find my necklace back in Phoenix. What the heck is he doing here?"

SIXTY-FIVE

DETECTIVE CAPLIN TOSSED the paper coffee cup he'd been carrying. With a good breakfast in his stomach, two cups of strong coffee with the meal and this one he'd requested to go, his attitude had improved. He would do the right thing and go to the police. If the French police could catch Frank Morrell here, at least the man would do time for his crime. Serve him right for screwing his partners and heading out on this international chase. Damn the crook and damn the whole situation!

Todd Wainwright's face came to him briefly. The pudgy museum employee who'd gotten himself deeply in debt and talked Caplin into looking the other way. He wanted to judge the guy, but hadn't he done the same thing? Let money become an excuse for breaking his own personal code of conduct?

Caplin would face disciplinary action—that was a certainty. He might lose his pension. But he could once again feel good about himself. And, with luck, Mrs. Fitzpatrick might get her family heirloom back.

He walked onto the rocky beach and stared out at the rolling sea, calm and blue, dotted with white sails as the regatta competitors moved into position. He'd always liked the sea. Maybe he could still find a way to spend his final years in Mexico, even though his dream life aboard his own boat seemed unlikely at this point. A shack near the beach in some little town like Punta Lobos would suit him. Hell, he could still improve his Spanish in a place like that.

"Detective Caplin."

The voice sounded very nearby and he turned, startled. Penelope Fitzpatrick stood no more than ten feet away at the edge of the concrete promenade. He felt his plan crumble.

SIXTY-SIX

PEN PULLED HER shoulders back, standing tall as she watched Caplin's face register a range of emotions. He was startled to hear his name called out but didn't seem especially shocked to see her.

"What are you doing here?" Pen demanded, her face hard as granite.

Behind her, Pen sensed Sandy watching from the restaurant. She'd dropped her fork and rushed out so quickly, no doubt her friend wondered what was happening. Caplin picked his way through the rocks and came to face Penelope.

"The same thing as you, I imagine," he said.

She drew herself up, hiding the thousand thoughts coursing through her right now.

"I am here to recover my stolen property," she said. "I've tracked the thief this far and I won't give up."

He nodded agreement.

"But…but you closed the case! You're here tracking a nine-hundred-fifty dollar necklace?" It made no sense.

Caplin hung his head. "I was wrong about that."

"You most certainly were! I tried to make you see—" Her emotions welled to the surface and she turned away for a moment. "Detective, what ever was going through your mind?"

He attempted a half-smile and a little shrug, but she sensed he was still hiding a great deal from her.

"At this point I want to help you," he said.

Skepticism registered on her face.

"Really, I do. I trailed Frank Morrell and a man who is probably his buyer. I'm going to contact the local police this morning and report what I know."

"No!" A hundred thoughts went through Pen's head.

Caplin gave her a puzzled look. "Why not?"

She took a breath, looking around to see if Sandy had come outside. She hadn't. "I have a plan—actually, *we*, some friends and I, have a plan. We're going to locate Mr. Morrell's contacts and steal back my necklace. We heard of a few other heirloom pieces and we want to get those back to their rightful owners, as well."

The detective's face registered mild humor and a dash of patience. "My dear lady, you don't have a clue, do you? There is a major international theft ring behind these losses. You are—"

"Oh, I know," she replied. "I've heard all about them."

His face registered surprise.

Actually, Amber was at this moment doing the research but Pen refused to let Caplin have the upper hand.

"And how do you plan to stage this big theft of yours?" he asked.

"You've heard about the gem show this week?"

He nodded.

"Tonight is a gala event to kick off the festivities. I still have a few connections in this world." Never would she admit her connection this time was a twenty-one-year-old computer hacker.

"That might be a good start," he said. "But you won't find the Golden Tigers attending a swanky party. One of their leaders escaped prison two weeks ago and there's no doubt he'll be lying low for a while. Interpol is combing most of southern Europe looking for this guy."

Pen thought about that. If the police charged in, captured these thieves and confiscated all the stolen items it would be months, if not years, before she saw her necklace again once it was held as evidence in such a major case.

"Let me help you," Caplin said, surprising Pen.

"What—assist us in stealing my necklace back?"

"Yes."

"But the local police…"

"I'll use them to learn what I can but my information will come directly to you."

She pondered this. No doubt Caplin had inroads she and the Ladies could not hope to break, but could she trust him? What could possibly be his motive in offering assistance?

SIXTY-SEVEN

THERE'S SOMETHING SO fine about a really good con man,
Frank thought. No one observing a great player ever knew
what was going on in his head, what his real goal might be.
Not the case with the men in this room. One look at these
dudes and you knew—they were thugs.

Thugs bothered Frank. They didn't talk their way out of
a jam, they used force. They thought nothing of pulling a
gun, leaving you for dead in an alley. They did prison time
without missing a beat—although, granted, the slammer
was better than college for an education. Frank just didn't
want to take the extra time away from the game.

The guy over there in the corner, for instance, jabbering
away in nasal French. He had the look. He'd been sent up
and now he was out. Body language said it all. The dude
hadn't earned his release—he'd broken out somehow. Didn't
matter the details, Frank had seen a million of 'em, guys
like this.

When they arrived at this small house on a winding back
street in Nice, Anton had addressed the thug as Lub. Frank
absorbed details like a sponge: heavy features, coarse dark
hair, thick fingers, a plain blue shirt Lub had slept in for
three days. French most likely wasn't his native language but
he'd learned it young or was simply a natural. At the beginning of the meeting, when he'd greeted Anton in English, he

used heavy consonants with stretched-out vowels. Eastern Europe somewhere.

The two men accompanying this Lub were equally disreputable-looking and conversed rapidly with him in whatever native language they shared. Another one was obviously French and it was at his insistence—and most likely to exclude Frank—they all spoke French.

Frank had never studied a language, including his own, but he had a natural flair for words and had been around long enough to have picked up a few basics. For instance, he knew the central topic of this conversation was jewels, and by the number of times someone's glance slid toward him he knew Anton was telling them about the piece Frank wanted to sell. He also knew none of these men trusted him. Fair enough—he didn't trust them either.

What he didn't understand was why all the hoopla. He'd brought the piece, Anton had studied it through his loupe and nodded approval. So...why didn't they just agree on a price, hand over the money, and he'd be on his merry way? He already had that part of it planned out—a train to Cannes, switching directions a couple of times, ending up in Italy where he would catch the first flight could get back to the good old U.S. of A. He was sick of historical (meaning cold) old buildings and skinny little streets where you couldn't tell east from north.

If it wasn't for the dangerous gleam in Lub's eye, Frank would have demanded the answers to his questions. As it was, he had no logical choice but to bide his time and so he sat quietly in one of the chairs at the dining table in this place, some kind of safe house, where they'd been summoned this afternoon to meet. He feigned interest in a brochure he'd found, about some kind of wild animal park, while the rest of them chatted. He never took his eye off his necklace, though.

SIXTY-EIGHT

How do I look?" Amber asked, twirling so the black garment flared slightly.

"Like a true Arab princess," Gracie said with a laugh. "And *moi*? Was my choice of fabric a good one?"

"Perfect. And excellent that you came up with a seamstress to make them for us on short notice," Pen said, fitting the second of her dark contact lenses in place. Blue-green eyes would not do for this assignment, so she and Sandy had to go a little further with their disguises.

The doorbell rang and Sandy rushed to answer, unclipping the face piece, the *niqab*, from her *chador* as she ran.

"Ah, you must be Marcel," she said.

"I am." The handsome forty-year-old man with an impeccable haircut and traditional tuxedo stepped forward. "But tonight, you may call me Farouk."

"Ooh-la-la, Farouk," Amber teased. She turned to the other ladies. "Told you I was lucky to find an actor on such short notice. How's your Arabic?"

He waggled his hand. "Passable enough as long as the subject is a simple one. I know my accent is spot-on. I've done a number of Arab language commercials."

"We'll make it as easy as possible for you," Pen said, stepping forward and introducing herself. "The subject will be jewelry and we may have you pose a question or two, depending on what we see at this party. You must be our voice, since none of us speaks a word of the language. Mainly, you can pretend to be an interpreter and escort. Four Arab women would never be allowed to attend such a gala unaccompanied by a male relative. You are my nephew."

Marcel nodded and offered his arm to Pen. "Are we ready then?"

Outside the hotel, a stretch limo waited and the agency had added the elegant touch of placing small flags at the front.

Pen whispered through the cloth covering her face. "Remove those," she told Marcel. "It would be rotten luck if a real Saudi prince is there and knows those flags do not belong to any country he's ever heard of. We may be breezing through the place in very noticeable costume but we do need to play our roles and be as inconspicuous as possible."

The four women climbed into the back of the limo and Marcel discreetly pulled off the small flags as he circled to get into the driver's seat. On the way to the *Nice Acropolis* they reviewed their plan. If something should go awry, they could flee without fear that anyone had recognized them. All carried their cell phones and a meeting place had been chosen two blocks away, a coffee shop where everyone would report in case they became separated.

Fairy lights decorated the trees outside the convention hall and Marcel pulled to the curb to discharge his four princesses. He had to hand over the limo keys to a valet, something Pen had not anticipated and did not like. But from this point forward the women could not speak except very quietly, only when absolutely alone with each other.

She exchanged a glance with Gracie, then a slight nod toward Sandy and Amber. Inhaling deeply, she took Marcel's arm and proceeded toward the front door where two uniformed security officers were checking invitations. It was show time.

SIXTY-NINE

FRANK KEPT SNEAKING looks at Anton, wondering how long this frigging deal was supposed to take. He'd picked up on the fact that the Dutchman had other business with the men—yeah, he got that. But, geez, couldn't they just get the money for the necklace and be out of there? Now!

They'd been in the house a good forty-five minutes before Lubnic got up and went to the tiny kitchen, coming back to the table with a bottle of vodka and some plastic cups. The atmosphere relaxed quite a bit—a sign to Frank that the most important topics had been discussed—and conversations flowed in several languages. Frank caught what he could in English.

"The Salem Diamond is to be on display," said the Frenchman. "I would love to get my hands on that beauty."

Lubnic shrugged, replying in English. "Forty-five carats, it could be cut down…but I do not like handling the famous stones. Everyone's looking for them, the honest dealers will recognize even a fragment of one like that."

Anton nodded. "I do not touch them myself."

What he was really saying, Frank realized, was the Fitzpatrick necklace interested him only because it had not been seen by as many in the world of gems. Those stones would not set off international alarm bells.

"Ah, but the rest of the show," the Frenchman said, "it

is to be glorious. We will sweep in, we take away bags and bags…"

Frank's interest sharpened, but a stare from Lubnic hushed the man. Frenchie abandoned the plastic cup of vodka and brought a half-full bottle of wine from the kitchen. He pulled the cork and poured a generous amount into a clean glass.

Anton finally began making restless movements. "We should go."

The Frenchman took a slow, appreciative sip of his wine, set the glass on the countertop and walked out of the room.

Anton and Lub spoke quickly in the language they'd used earlier in the meeting. Frank listened intently but only caught a few words, a name—Leblanc—and something that sounded like mausoleum.

The Frenchman returned from what Frank assumed was a bedroom, approached Anton and handed over a large, thick envelope. Anton flipped through the euro notes inside, pulled out a large hunk of them and placed the envelope on the table.

"The necklace, please."

Frank had placed the valuable piece in a cloth bag and carried it here in an attaché case he'd purchased this morning. Now he was glad he had. He didn't want this bunch seeing his money belt, not that his few thousand in cash would be of interest to a gang that played in the millions of dollars. He carefully laid the bag on the table and pulled the necklace out. He heard a collective intake of breath. The emeralds were impressive, even to this group. He pushed the handsome piece toward Lubnic.

"We're done, then?" he said, scooping up the envelope. As a show of trust, he merely thumbed through the cash before placing it in his case. "It was a pleasure doing business with you, gentlemen."

Although it really hadn't been—more like a pain in the neck, all their wrangling and trailing Anton all over the place. He walked out of the house, turned a corner and waited in a recessed doorway to watch. When ten minutes passed with no one emerging from the meeting, he felt sure they wouldn't try to follow. Once more he wondered how much money these guys had made through all their jewel heists. Enough that a quarter-million euros wasn't worth their time to chase him down and steal.

A little wave of admiration—he knew plenty of con men who wanted to have the cake and eat it too, who would have taken the necklace and found a way to keep the cash as well. He wondered when he might feel that way.

Frankie, when is enough really enough? came his mother's voice. He hailed a taxi, smiling to himself and thinking: *Not yet, Mom.*

"Nice Acropolis," he said to the cabbie.

Although the theft and sale of the necklace had been a pain, now that he had contacts in the jewel trade over here, the idea of a large-haul job held more appeal. Hell, it was worth it, obviously, since these Panther dudes did it all the time. He'd always been a fan of the short con, quickly in and out, take some mooch for the cash in his wallet or some old lady for a social security check or two, but it took a long time to amass this kind of money with those jobs. The long cons paid better but took forever to complete. He found himself warming to the idea of getting into the smash-and-grab thrill of scooping up handfuls of jewels and then trading it quickly for a briefcase of cash like the one he carried now.

The Acropolis convention center was lit up like a Christmas tree when his cab pulled up at the curb. Guys in tuxedoes manned the door, and well-dressed people got out of nice cars which pulled around a circular drive and deposited them at the front steps. He paid for the ride and stepped aside to scope out the situation. He was wearing a decent suit. From the briefcase's side pocket, he withdrew a silk tie he'd lifted from a hotel gift shop in Zurich, draped it around his neck and knotted it in place. With his standby Tiffany business cards, he might just be able to pull this off.

All he wanted at this point was a good look-see. He might be impulsive, but he would never dash into a place like this, with this kind of security, not knowing what he would find inside.

SEVENTY

ABOUT FORTY ACRES of jewelry filled the massive exhibit hall—or so it seemed to Sandy. Despite the restrictive black frame around her view, she had to admit she was in awe of the show. Glamorous women in the latest fashions browsed, and the men with them insisted they try on anything their little hearts desired. Hard to imagine there was this much wealth in one city at one time.

Watching the crowd also made Sandy glad for the cover of the *chador*. Actual, wealthy Arab women would be dressed to the nines under their black, but at least Sandy and the rest of the team didn't have to keep up that pretense.

Pen edged closer and spoke quietly. "Remember to browse thoroughly but don't spend too much time or we'll never get through the whole place."

All four women had spent time studying photographs of Pen's missing necklace, memorizing details—not that there would be many pieces in the world to compare with it.

"We can't split up too greatly or it will look suspicious. We only have the one male escort," she told her team.

They devised a sort of system where the four would approach one of the glittering glass cases, keeping to the section featuring emeralds. No point in spending time over sapphires or rubies or mere diamonds, Pen reminded them. The search became easier as they automatically weeded out rings and bracelets, focusing only on necklaces.

Pen took a bit more time, scanning any piece with a single stone to rival any of hers. Although she knew the necklace had been intact three days ago in Zurich, there was always the chance Frank Morrell had moved it quickly and the stones were now dispersed.

With each seller, Marcel the actor put on his best accent and inquired whether the vendor carried other things that were not on display, especially any antique pieces?

Twice, they were shown tiaras purported to have belonged to European royalty but nothing compared to the necklace they sought. They had covered no more than a third of the offerings when Pen caught Sandy's attention.

"This outfit is making me claustrophobic, I'm afraid. I must get some air." Pen walked toward a sign indicating the women's toilets.

Inside a stall, she latched the door and removed the cumbersome black fabric from her head. The cooler air on her face felt good but a restroom wasn't the best place to breathe deeply of fresh air. Removing the garment entirely, she folded it to resemble a cloak and draped it over her shoulders.

An exit door at the end of the short corridor seemed unattended. It would surely lock behind her and not allow her back inside but if she didn't get away from the hot lights and stifling crowd for at least a few minutes, she felt she would scream. Not for the first time, she yearned for the wide-open spaces of her home in Arizona, wished this entire adventure was behind her.

She pushed the door open, praying no alarm would sound, and stepped out into the cool evening air. The scent of flowers overlaid the sea air which was always noticeable in this city. She breathed deeply of it and let her eyes adjust to the relative darkness, pathways lit only by small lights and decorative strands on the trees. Almost at once a figure appeared, a man striding toward her.

Oh, dear, she thought. Am I in trouble already?

But as the man came closer she recognized him. Detective Caplin.

"Still looking for the missing property, Mrs. Fitzpatrick?" he said. His voice was not unkind and she accepted the question for what it was.

"Yes, I'm afraid so. Trying to cover all the bases, I suppose you would say."

"Me too. I've been tracking Morrell all day. He's made contact with those thieves and spent some time with them. Frankly, I think he's probably already sold the necklace. The only discrepancy in that theory is that I trailed him here. He tried walking up to the front door but was turned away. In the half-second I looked away he disappeared. I'm not sure what he's up to."

The detective cleared his throat softly, his eyes scanning the area constantly. "You're better off to stay in disguise, Mrs. Fitzpatrick. Go back inside and when it's time, leave with your escort. I'll contact you when I have anything new to report."

"Are you certain? You will tell me where my necklace is, not hand over this Morrell character to the police?"

"I'll contact you," he repeated. He vanished into a shadow.

Pen felt the weight of discouragement once again. Caplin thought Morrell had sold the necklace already. She turned toward the door where she'd left the building but it had no outside handle. She would have to reenter through the front. She slid the black cloak over her clothes and walked back, showing the gold-toned identification bracelet she'd been issued when they arrived the first time.

SEVENTY-ONE

FRANK CURSED THE doorman under his breath. Stupid rule about black tie attire, he thought as he walked away. Although the bigger obstacle had been that his Tiffany credentials carried no weight here. Everyone on the premises was in the jewelry business, the man had said. What mattered were the names on the invitation list. If your name wasn't there, you weren't getting in.

He stalked away, trying not to let his body language reveal his disgust. There was always more than one way to skin a cat, his dad used to say. Out of the doorman's sight, Frank found a pathway leading to other entrances to the building. The west side one was locked down tight, draperies over the glass doors obscuring all signs of the activity inside. Circling to the north, the rear of the building, he saw a plain steel door swing open.

Out stepped a woman in a white dress with a dark wrap of some kind around her shoulders. Her blond chin-length hair caught his attention. Penelope Fitzpatrick. He felt sure of it. Her presence at the gem show could not be a coincidence. And Frank Morrell didn't believe in coincidences anyway. He shrank back into the leafy folds of a giant oleander bush and watched her stroll in the opposite direction. A man approached her but they were now too far away to identify Frank, so he casually walked away.

His mind raced—stay here and try to gain access to the building, or get a taxi and leave this city as soon as possible? He couldn't keep lugging around this briefcase full of cash without taking a big chance on losing it, but the pull of that building full of riches still tugged at him. He'd give anything to know what the Golden Tigers had planned, how they would manage to rob a big place like this with such tight security. The more these thoughts ran through his mind the more he realized he was tired. Between dodging the Fitzpatrick woman and keeping up with Anton, he'd not had a decent night's sleep in ages. He wasn't thinking clearly and that was always dangerous. He spotted a stone bench a little farther down the pathway and he sat, just for a moment, to sort things out.

Not even the success of his recent con would ever be enough for him, Frank knew. The lure of the massive haul inside tugged at him. Anton and Lubnic had seen that Frank operated in good faith. With a robbery this big, the more hands, the better, he reasoned. They would surely let him join the gang for this one.

He glanced over his shoulder and saw that Penelope Fitzpatrick was gone. The man she'd been talking to was heading toward Frank so quickly he would have to jog to outpace him, and that would most certainly look suspicious. The guy had the look of law enforcement and the last thing Frank wanted was to answer questions about the briefcase and its contents. He tucked it out of sight beside the solid legs of the bench, rose and walked with his back to the man, keeping a leisurely pace. With luck, the guy would rush past him and Frank would switch directions, grab his case, and get the hell out of there.

His first clue that the plan wouldn't work was when he felt a yank at the back of his collar. He spun around.

"Well, well, if it isn't Frank Morrell. Or should I say Richard Stone?"

Frank turned to find himself face to face with the cop from Phoenix.

SEVENTY-TWO

CAPLIN ALMOST LAUGHED at the look of pure shock on Frank Morrell's face when the con man spun to face him.

"Surprised? Yeah, even American cops can have a passport these days." He loosened his grip on Morrell's collar when the man turned to him with a smile.

"Bill! How good to see you here!"

Caplin felt his eyebrows rise. "Let me guess—you were just looking for me because you have that necklace with you?"

"Well, no. I don't have the necklace anymore."

Caplin sensed he was telling the truth.

"So, then you've got my share of the money," he said. "You were about to bring it to me, huh?"

"As a matter of fact, yes. Well, I should say I was going to head home and bring it to you in Phoenix tomorrow. The cash is in the safe at my hotel right now."

Caplin watched the man's face. Frank kept his eyes locked with Caplin's and there wasn't a trace of a stammer in his voice. Yet something was off.

"Who'd you sell the piece to?"

"Some guys."

"Come on, just any old guys? Was it somebody connected with this show?" Caplin gave a nod toward the building. "Or you just happened to be walking by and decided to hang out here awhile?"

"Actually, yeah. I saw there was a gem show in town, wanted a look. Guess my name didn't make it to the invitation list. Couldn't get in." Frank's gaze dropped, first to his shoes then slid to a spot somewhere on the ground behind Caplin. "What about you? Been inside? Bet it's quite the deal in there."

Caplin sprang while the con man's guard was down, reaching out and grasping his throat, shoving him hard, driving him up against the building ten feet away.

"Listen, punk. I'm not impressed with your good-old-boy manner and your breezy friendliness. You and I are not pals. You've taken something of value from an unsuspecting woman and then proceeded to screw your partners. That behavior makes me want to choke the shit out of you." He tightened his grip on Morrell's throat, enjoying the surge of power he felt as the man's eyes bulged.

Morrell tried to speak but only guttural crackles came from him.

"What's that? I can't hear you too well." Caplin let up slightly on the pressure.

"Golden Tigers," Morrell gasped. "They have…the necklace."

"The international jewel thieves? How'd you get in with them? Never mind. Where are they keeping the stolen jewels?"

Morrell's eyes darted side to side as he dreamed up a story. Caplin shoved his head against the stone wall again. "Don't make up some bullshit story, man. Nothing says I have to let you walk out of here. Tell me where they are."

Morrell tried to clear his throat, but his words came out with a rasp. "I don't know. They talked some…some foreign language."

"So tell me the parts you did catch. I see it in your eyes, dude. You know more than you're telling me."

"A house on *Rue Trois*, like a safe house. Anton took me there."

"Give me the street address. Now!"

"One twenty-two."

"What else?" Caplin again tightened his grip for a moment.

"I caught…mausoleum."

"Hey, you there!" Down the walkway a uniformed officer was running toward them. *"Qu'est-ce que tu fais?"*

Caplin's attention focused on the man who came toward him, nightstick drawn.

"I'm a police detec—"

But in the moment of inattention, Morrell wriggled free and ran. He grabbed something from the ground near a park bench and headed east. By the time the gendarme reached Caplin, Morrell was out of sight.

SEVENTY-THREE

PEN FELT DEAD on her feet by the time the ladies had covered the entire show and arrived back at their hotel. With comfortable clothing and glasses of wine they sprawled over the couches and chairs in the suite's living room. They'd already discussed the disappointing results of the jewelry search: no sign of Pen's heirloom necklace or any of the stones.

"So, what next?" Sandy asked.

"Well, I do have a bit of news," Pen said, "something I was saving until we had a bit of privacy. The detective from Phoenix is here in the city. I spoke with him."

Wide eyes and incredulous stares all around.

"The same man who told you his department was dropping the case because your necklace wasn't worth it?" Gracie asked.

"He acknowledges that was not true. Apparently someone working at the museum switched the documents so it would look as though my necklace was a reproduction."

"And then proceeded to help the thief get in to steal it." Sandy's voice was firm.

"He didn't go so far as to admit that. There is still quite a lot I don't fully understand," Pen said. "The good news is that he's here in Nice because of a strong lead and he thinks he can recover my property."

"But we can do that," Amber pointed out. "We found those same leads and we got here first."

"I know. I know, my dear, but it's not a matter of who was here first. It's a matter of getting the necklace. He has contact with the local police and many more resources than we do."

"So you're saying we give up? Quit and let the police handle it?" Gracie seemed a little indignant at the idea.

"No way," said Amber. She had picked up her laptop from the table and was already tapping away at the keys. "We can finish this thing on our own. I don't trust that detective. I mean, do you? Really?"

Pen saw the logic of Amber's argument, truly. Suddenly she wasn't quite sure what to do.

"Let's do both," Sandy suggested. "I mean, it can't hurt to let this policeman keep working on it. But we can do the same."

"And we'll get there first," Amber declared. "The Heist Ladies will not be outdone!"

SEVENTY-FOUR

THE SAFE HOUSE was dark when Bill Caplin approached. He'd parked his rental car down the block, both because of the need for stealth and because parking spots on these narrow streets were hard to come by. The French officer who'd questioned him outside the *Nice Acropolis* seemed reluctant to become involved with an American cop tracking an American suspect.

"Ze judges are, how do you say, hesitating to issue warrants for such cases," he'd said when Caplin told him about the safe house and the deal that apparently went down there this afternoon. "We can file the paperwork. It will take some time for approval."

Fine, thought Caplin, *I'm not waiting for the thieves to get completely away with the necklace while you dick around with paperwork*. So what if he broke into their house and had a look around? What would they do, report him?

One thing his police training had taught— how to search a place thoroughly. He first used the simplest ploy, walked up to the front door and knocked. Listened for the slightest hint of a sound or light from within. A second knock was met with complete silence as well. He walked around to the back, keeping an eye on neighboring houses which seemed in the midst of standard evening routines—people at dining tables, others with television sets on.

Caplin kept to the shadows, blending in with surrounding shrubbery until he came to a back door that faced a small garden full of weeds with one struggling palm tree that would have been beautiful with only a little care. The place had the air of a rental or temporary owner; clearly, no one cared about maintaining the small stone structure or its grounds.

He stood at the dark back door listening to the surrounding sounds. It had four glass panes above a solid panel at the bottom. Some kind of curtain covered the glass. A window faced the yard and he stretched to peer into a small kitchen, but there wasn't sufficient light to tell what lay beyond. Beside the sink sat a whiskey bottle—he assumed whiskey— he couldn't read the label. A moment later he heard a large vehicle coming up the street, most likely a bus.

At the exact second it passed the house, Caplin used the heel of his shoe to break the glass in the back door. No one reacted; he'd barely heard the sound of it himself. He stepped back into his shoe, reached inside and twisted the doorknob. He was in.

It took less than two minutes using his pocket flashlight to get the layout of the small house. Living room with a dining L, small galley kitchen, one bedroom, one bath. Furnishings looked like rentals, not the kind of stuff a person bought for himself. One picture of the bargain store variety in the living room. No TV, no personal effects. Yeah, Morrell had been right. This was temporary digs for somebody.

He thought back to the conversation with Morrell, the scraps of information the con man shared. Some kind of estate, a mausoleum—clearly not in this neighborhood. He began his systematic search with the bedroom, the most common place people hid valuables. Nothing taped beneath the dresser drawers, nothing between mattress and box springs on the double bed, nothing in any of the garment pockets or in the shoes. The wardrobe was something of a joke; the few masculine garments were the sort one packed for a quick trip, not a man's entire wardrobe.

He moved through bathroom and living room to the kitchen, searching quickly and quietly along the way. In the freezer compartment of the fridge, a small packet of cash was wrapped in foil and labeled "Poulet" which Caplin thought meant chicken. Rather an old ploy if these guys were pros. Someone would be back, but this was another reason he believed the safe house was used sparingly and very short-term. He picked up the telephone receiver and found it dead. No surprise—everyone used cell phones these days. The telephone directory next to it was dated 2010, so someone had subscribed to a land line here a few years ago. He carried the directory with him.

One last glance back toward the dining table, where empty glasses smelling of alcohol made rings on the cheap wood surface. Five chairs sat at odd angles, as if the occupants had risen and left quickly. The meeting Morrell mentioned? Most likely.

A small white square on the floor caught his attention and he aimed the light in that direction. A graphic design and some printed words covered it. He walked over and picked it up. A matchbook. How many years since he'd seen one of these? The logo was of a palm tree and the words said *Restaurant Jardin Palm*.

"No idea you would come in handy so quickly," he muttered to the telephone directory, setting it on the table and opening it.

The Palm Garden Restaurant had an ad in the business pages stating its premier location near the Palais de Forestiere. Something to do with a palace and a forest, he thought, although he had no idea for sure. But it was a lead. And a lead could always be followed. He took the matchbook and the directory with him and locked the back door when he left.

SEVENTY-FIVE

THE HEIST LADIES were tired but too wound up over the evening's events to immediately fall asleep. Gracie brought out a bottle of wine, which she poured into four glasses as Pen paced the suite's large living room.

"I keep thinking about Detective Caplin," Pen said when she paused to pick up her glass. "He's on the trail of Frank Morrell but I got the feeling there's more to this than he's telling me. Despite what he said, I have a deep-down feeling if he gets to Morrell first I'll not see my necklace again."

"So, we need to get there first," Amber said.

"Quite simple on the face of it, but how?"

"The detective promised to keep you in the loop, right?" Sandy asked. "So, call him and ask if he's learned anything new."

"This late at night?"

"It's only a little after ten. Surely he'll be awake."

Amber was right, Pen realized. She needed to let go of her idea that everyone worked nine-to-five. She had no idea if his mobile phone worked in this country but it was worth a try. She tapped his number and put the phone on speaker so the others could hear.

There were traffic sounds in the background when he picked up. "Mrs. Fitzpatrick. I hope you enjoyed the gem show and are safely tucked in at your hotel again." A car door slammed and the surrounding noises abated.

"I'm just fine, thanks for your concern." Pen rolled her eyes and Amber held back a snicker. "I'm calling to see what you've learned. French police were talking as I left the show, something about an American cop roughing up a suspicious American man outside the venue."

He made a little denial sound but Pen interrupted.

"It's too much of a coincidence, detective. You were there. There's every reason to believe Frank Morrell was there. I'd simply like to know what happened."

"Like they said, I roughed him up a little."

Amber pulled a *Yes!* with her fist.

"And during this I supposed he talked a bit?" Pen asked.

"Not much. He told me he'd been to a safe house today and sold the necklace."

"Oh, no. Where—?"

"Doesn't matter. I've already been there and no one's around. I'm leaving now to follow up one small lead. Somebody in the group frequents the Palm Garden restaurant. Places around here stay open late so I'm heading there now."

"That's all he told you?" Pen pressed, her voice wavering.

"Well, as I was doing my best to choke the little prick, he squawked out something about a mausoleum. I guess that'll be next on my list to track down."

Pen saw Amber madly typing on her laptop keyboard.

"Please keep me posted, detective. I'm very upset that my necklace is now in other hands."

"I know. The authorities are on the trail of this theft ring and I'm doing my best to follow the guy Morrell was dealing with."

Amber's face lit up and she pointed rapidly at her com-

puter. Pen ended the call with Caplin and stepped behind
Amber's chair to see what the excitement was about.

"To hell with the restaurant," Amber said. "I've found the
mausoleum."

SEVENTY-SIX

IF YOU THINK about it, it's the perfect spot for those guys to have hidden the jewelry." Gracie backed away to let Sandy have a peek.

Amber had brought up a map on her screen, one that showed topographical details. A little balloon-shaped icon pointed to Restaurant Jardin Palm. The cursor wiggled a bit in their little computer guru's control.

"Now, here, just across the road and down less than a half-mile, is a big estate. On the grounds of the estate, a private mausoleum."

"How did you figure this out?" Pen asked.

"Well, as soon as he said the word I could picture a seldom-used place with all sorts of nooks and crannies where things could be hidden. I mean, some kind of stone coffin thingy—what could be better as a treasure chest no one would ever touch?" Amber's eyes glittered. "So I went to the map, searched mausoleum and came up with a variety of them, some at public cemeteries, some private. A public place wouldn't work for them—too many people with access. With the location of that restaurant plugged in, well, there are only a couple private mausoleums very close and this one makes the most sense."

She zoomed the photo in for a better look. The hilltop estate had a winding road leading to it and was set well above the city. Fortress-like walls surrounded the property, and from them the occupants would be able to see anyone approaching by car or from the sea. Amber pointed out the main house, an elegant Mediterranean mansion with white walls and red-tile roofs over its central section and two wings. Pathways led through formal gardens and to a swimming pool. On the east side sat a small structure of marble with a domed roof. When she turned the photo to view it straight-on they could make out the word *Mausolée* on one line and *du Leblanc* below.

"How high are those walls?" Sandy asked.

"Hard to say, and I don't see many gates," Gracie said.

Pen studied the photo. "How do you suppose we will ever get inside?"

SEVENTY-SEVEN

CAPLIN CURSED THE fact he hadn't gotten a GPS with the rental car. It hadn't seemed important at the time—he really needed to move into the modern age or retire. That simple beach house in Mexico was looking better and better. He studied his map once more, meandered several blocks out of the way, finally found the Restaurant Jardin Palm. He walked in at ten minutes to closing, hoping he'd find a comforting drink and someone who spoke English. He got lucky on both counts.

"The kitchen is closing," said the bartender who wore a name tag saying he was Henri.

"That's okay. A whiskey, neat, will do me just fine."

Henri served it in a heavy glass. "You are not a tourist, I think," he said, eyes traveling over Caplin's suit and tan overcoat.

"I'm not. I'm looking for another American friend who's traveling in the area. He said something about staying with some buddies in this part of town. One of them recommended this restaurant."

Henri wiped a glass with a spotless white towel. "Could be. Especially if your friend is rich. This coastline brings the wealthy from many places."

Caplin thought of Morrell's many targets. "That sounds like the sort of people this guy likes to hang out with. You probably know all the locals around here?"

"Locals? Oh, the residents. *Oui*, many are my customers."

"Any of them entertaining a lot of guests this week?" It was a guess, based on what Frank had said about the group at the safe house.

Henri's eyes narrowed. "Who is asking?"

Caplin pulled out his wallet and extracted one of his business cards. "Police. I'm actually after a suspect I followed here from the States. He's tied with some men here and I'd like to catch up with him."

Henri dried another glass and added it to the stack of clean ones on the shelf behind him, clearly giving himself a minute before answering. Caplin studied the man's body language, reading him as an honest businessman torn between helping the law and staying out of a situation that might cost him business.

The cop sipped his drink while the bartender walked to the front door, locked it and turned out the neon Open sign.

"There is one place. The owner of this estate is a good man. He fought in the war and never used his family's position to dodge his responsibilities. They made a fortune in olive oil and Monsieur LeBlanc has been very kind to this city, always helpful to those less fortunate."

Caplin waited as Henri took his time.

"It is now, I fear, the old man may have become too trusting. Some men are staying at his home while he is away in Spain, some men I do not like the looks of. Etienne LeBlanc told me it was the nephew of his oldest, dearest friend." He shrugged. "I do not know. One of them could be his friend's relative, but the rest…these do not seem of the same—how do you say?—the same caliber?"

"Where is Mr. LeBlanc's home, the place these men are staying?"

Henri tipped his head to the right. "Just up the mountain

there. It is a large estate and the main house sits at the very top. A most spectacular view. When I began the restaurant twenty years ago, Etienne entertained more frequently. We catered many lovely parties there, *tres belle*."

Caplin swallowed the last of his whiskey. "Thanks. I appreciate the information." He left a generous tip and Henri let him out.

Okay, he thought as the cool night breeze hit him. Breaking out a back window in a small house on my own, I'm not opposed to, but storming an estate with who knows how many master thieves…especially if this really is the lair of the Golden Tiger ring… Interpol needs to know about this.

SEVENTY-EIGHT

THE BEDSIDE CLOCK read 2:10 when Pen finally switched off the light and closed her eyes. After Amber's discovery of the LeBlanc estate, excitement had roared through the room like a tsunami. Ideas coalesced into plans, plans required supplies, shopping lists were made.

While Gracie and Sandy wrote lists covering every foreseen eventuality, Amber browsed for more information on the Golden Tigers. Their technique, it seemed, involved storming large jewelry stores and high-end boutiques and sweeping up as much as they could in a quick haul. But there were a few individual victims as well. A woman, whose diamond ring had been in the family five generations, had been held at gunpoint and the ring taken when she happened to be standing in one of the targeted shops; a Fabergé egg from a private collection was suspected to be in the hands of the notorious thieves after being taken in a home burglary. The case sounded suspiciously like the situation with Penelope's necklace.

"If we get in there and find your necklace," Amber told Pen, "I want to look for these other things too. What these guys are doing—hurting old people—it's just wrong." She looked up at Pen. "Sorry, not saying *you're* old or anything."

Pen chuckled. "I suppose I am, to your generation. But

that's okay. We seniors know a few things too." She flexed a muscle to show she wasn't exactly decrepit.

As research for one of her books, she'd met with a lock-smith and learned the fine art of picking a variety of locks. Assuming the thieves would not leave a fortune alone in a building without such measures, she'd surprised the group by describing exactly what types of lock picks she would need. Now, she smiled to herself and rolled over to sleep a few hours.

By noon they'd begun their quest. First, a rental car as it became apparent public transportation had its limits. As Amber pointed out, there was no cool way to make a hasty escape on a bus.

Gracie drove the little four-seat Peugeot, first on a drive-by around the property where they discovered the perimeter walls to be much more formidable than shown from the aerial map. They casually cruised up the wind-ing road, just a group of ladies out for the day, until they came to a heavy steel gate. A thuggish man wearing a pis-tol stepped out of the guardhouse and scowled.

"Oh, like, wow. Sorry! We thought this was, like, the way to the beach," Amber called out in her best ditzy-girl imitation.

She stuck her head back inside and Gracie did a quick turn-around.

"So, no approaching from the front, I suppose," Sandy said in a shaky voice.

"At least we learned that they've got a guy on duty there," Amber said, staring at her laptop.

"I assume an armed guard isn't the norm," Pen said be-side her. "Did you notice the keypad and intercom? And the guard house was not well maintained. I don't think someone is normally there. Drivers come up, state their name, or enter a code."

"So maybe the estate's owner is away and these thieves have commandeered use of the place?"

"Or they know someone. I suppose we can't very well go back and ask."

"Right," said Amber. "We have to go with what we can learn. Right now, our clues have to come from this photo."

SEVENTY-NINE

BILL CAPLIN EXPLAINED it once again. Most of the day had passed while the local gendarmes got organized and coordinated with the newly arrived men from Interpol. Apparently, a joint operation was tricky to plan. He stifled his frustration. As a detective, he usually showed up at a crime scene after the action was done, the crime committed, the suspects gone and the victims left behind. It was not his usual forte to participate in a raid, so he had no choice but to bow to the others. Plus, he was so far out of his jurisdiction it wasn't even funny.

Here it was, nine p.m., and the teams had just been mustered and now the commanding officer was laboriously going through the facts, including what Caplin learned from the bartender the night before.

"Etienne LeBlanc, owner of the estate, has apparently allowed the nephew of an old friend to use his home while he is away on a business trip. Our surveillance team has identified two known members of the Golden Tigers and we believe their leader, Andrej Lubnic, is holed up there as well. Lubnic is considered armed and dangerous. He escaped *Fresnes Prison* a month ago and vanished, which coincides with the timing when we believe he may have arrived here. Another two members of the gang were seen lurking around the gem show two nights ago, along with an

American, identified by Detective Caplin here," a nod in Bill's direction, "as a suspect he followed from Arizona."

An Interpol man stepped up. "Our raid must take place when they least expect it. We must act quickly, as it's believed their plan is to rob the gem show tomorrow and if their methodology remains the same, they will scatter and become impossible to track for months, if not years to come."

A second Interpol officer took the lead, using a pointer to draw attention to a chart he had affixed to an easel. The drawing showed a diagram of the property.

"Here—" he said with a tap, "is the entry gate. It is heavy steel, mounted on stone columns and a stone wall surrounds the entire twenty acres owned by LeBlanc. At the gate is a guard house which is manned twenty-four hours a day by armed guards. These must be gang members, as LeBlanc does not use guards when he is in residence.

"Our plan, therefore, is to simultaneously take out the guard or guards and bash down the gate with a ramming vehicle."

"Won't that create a lot of noise?" asked one of the men in dark clothing.

"It will. At that point, we must move with utmost speed toward the house."

Privately, Caplin thought they would be better off to quietly disable the guard and find the automatic switch that surely existed to open the gate. But this was not his baby. He sat through the rest of the briefing and followed along when the commander assigned him a vehicle.

As he had explained from the beginning, his job was to take the American suspect into custody and recover an item belonging to a victim in his home jurisdiction. He only hoped Frank Morrell didn't start yapping away about Caplin's own involvement in the crime. He really needed to get the sleazy con man alone.

EIGHTY

BLACK SKY DOTTED with stars, no sliver of moonlight to guide them, the Heist Ladies parked at a turnout on the curving road to the mansion. Pen carried her set of lock picks. Gracie hefted the emergency evacuation rope ladder they'd purchased earlier. Each of the four carried a small flashlight. It was nearly three a.m.

"Here's the path," Amber whispered, taking the lead, relying on her memory of the aerial photo she'd studied until it was imprinted on her brain.

The other three followed the beam of her tiny light as she shined it on the ground. The 'path' was actually a game trail, most likely made by the small deer that roamed the hillsides. It was no more than eight inches wide, frequently bisected by exposed roots and jutting rocks. They had less than two hours until daylight would expose them. Two hours to climb the six-hundred foot hill, scale the wall, break in, retrace every step and get back to their car. Although they'd endlessly discussed the pros and cons of choosing the correct hour, every step of the plan had taken longer than anticipated and now here they were. *It is what it is*, as Sandy said.

From the photo, she knew they would have to leave the path after about two hundred yards and make their way through underbrush. She hoped the wall would be in view by then. Meanwhile, she kept a close eye on her wristband step monitor to calculate the distance. At one-hundred-eighty yards she shined her flashlight ahead.

There it was, the wall.

Next in line, Gracie spotted it and nodded. Passed the word back to Pen, then to Sandy. They headed off the trail trying, not too successfully, to be careful of dry twigs and other noisemakers. Pen cringed at every sound, certain their rustle through the woods was being heard by everyone in the big house. At last they came to the wall. Smiles all around—from the car it had taken only twenty minutes so far.

It stood about ten feet high, and their spirits lagged. It had been impossible to tell the height from the aerial photo and they had held out hope that it would be no more than a garden wall, something they could easily hop over, but that was why they'd purchased the ladder—just in case.

The ladder was one of those sold for emergency home fire evacuation, with two sturdy metal arms to hook over a windowsill and wooden rungs held in place by ropes knotted at intervals. The big question now—how thick was the wall? If it was some medieval thing three feet wide, they were screwed.

"Let me scope it out," Amber said. "Give me a boost."

Gracie stepped up, twined her fingers for the smallest member of the group to step on and gave a heave to get Amber to the top of the wall. Amber gripped the stone and hefted herself up.

"Good news," she whispered, straddling the top, "it's not too wide."

It wasn't exactly flat on top either and she found herself constantly rebalancing. In the distance she could see outdoor lighting around the mansion, but the house was a good hundred-fifty yards away. She saw no interior lights.

"Toss me the ladder."

Gracie gripped the top of the piece, making sure to send the hooking device first. Her first toss missed but Amber caught it on the second throw. She hooked the metal arms over the wall and tested it by climbing down. She issued instructions in a whisper.

"It's secure enough, I think. Once you get to the top you'll have to drop to the ground. There are shrubs—I have no idea what kind—hopefully not thorny ones. I'll sit at the top to help. Once we're all over the top, I'll position the ladder the other way so we can get back out."

Good thing Amber had considered that part of it, Pen thought.

Amber climbed to the top, testing the rungs to set them firmly in place. Once again, she straddled the wall and then motioned for Gracie to follow.

"Ow!" Gracie let out when she hit the large bush below. "Well, at least it was softer than the ground," she stage-whispered to Amber.

Sandy followed, then Pen. The others waited to assist with the landing. Amber repositioned the ladder, cringing at the thunk of wooden rungs hitting stone wall.

"The mausoleum is right over there," she said when she joined the group.

Keeping their lights pointed directly at the ground, they approached the fifteen-foot-square stone building from the back. They knew the opening faced toward the mansion and they kept to the soft patch of trimmed grass that grew around the small edifice.

Now, Gracie took the lead, edging around the building until she could see the mansion and the pathway lights leading from it to the mausoleum. All seemed quiet until she heard a voice not ten feet away.

EIGHTY-ONE

CAPLIN BEGAN TO feel faintly carsick as the Interpol van wound its way up the mountain road. The van was the last of four vehicles; ahead were a car with the commander and Interpol chief, a Humvee with a special metal ramming grid on the front, and another van with eight armed SWAT members. His place was merely to watch the action for now; he and the French gendarmes would come in to make arrests once the location was secure and any live fire was finished.

Ahead, the lead car had stopped. He pressed forward to get to a window and some fresh air. The van driver and another officer were conversing rapidly in French and he saw the man outside gesture toward a car sitting in a turn-out. Apparently they decided not to worry about it; the other guy got back into the lead car and the little procession began to move.

"Tourist rental car," the driver said. "Probably out of gas. They do it all the time."

About a mile from the end of the curving road, the four vehicles rolled to a stop and switched off their lights. Any closer, they risked being seen or heard well in advance. The guard would surely alert the entire household to anyone approaching at three in the morning.

Four men in black clothing and bulletproof vests jumped from the van ahead and quickly moved up the road toward the speck of light coming from the guard house. The Humvee had moved to center-of-road, ready to coast forward as soon as the radio call cleared it.

Caplin tensed. Any moment now all hell could break loose.

EIGHTY-TWO

GRACIE FROZE AT the sound of the male voice. She held out a hand behind her, signaling the others to halt. A guard, right at the door to the mausoleum. They hadn't expected one although the thought flashed through her mind that it made perfect sense. This had to be where the treasure was kept. When she heard a lengthy yawn, she ventured a peek around the corner.

One man with a rifle. He sat on the stone step with his back to the heavy wooden door, his weapon lying on the ground but within easy reach. She whipped out of sight when he turned his head. He didn't look terribly alert.

The other three ladies stood in place, barely breathing. Gracie gathered them close, breathed the words: "One man, gun, sleepy. What shall we do?"

"Lure him out, seduce him," Amber suggested.

"Not me—*you* seduce him," Gracie whispered back.

Pen cupped her flashlight to diminish the light, aiming it at the ground. Staying to the soft grass, she backed away.

A groan came from the guard as he shifted position on the hard stone surface. Gracie risked another peek.

From the other side of the building, Pen emerged with a hefty tree limb in hand. The man blinked, noticing Gracie for the first time. Pen raised the branch and, without a second's hesitation, gave the guard a quick whack to the head. His body went limp.

"Wow," Pen said. "I've written that scene a bunch of times but never knew what it would feel like to do it. Kind of icky."

"Considering he was reaching for the rifle, kind of good you did it. Go, Pen," Gracie said.

"Come on," Sandy said. "He didn't have time to alert anyone but that doesn't mean they don't check on him."

"She's right. Throw his weapon into the bushes and get him out of the way," Pen said. She tossed the tree branch aside and pulled her lock picks from her pocket.

The ancient lock on the heavy door posed no problem at all, but the modern deadbolt above it took an excruciating amount of time to open. Pen worked patiently with the tiny torsion wrench and hook pick while Sandy held a light for her. Amber and Gracie watched their unconscious guard while keeping alert for any lights or movement at the house.

It was the longest three minutes of their lives.

EIGHTY-THREE

CAPLIN HAD TO get out of the stuffy van or risk losing the dinner he'd eaten hours ago. He watched the vague shadows of the black-clad men quickly disappear against the backdrop of trees that lined the road as he stretched his legs and breathed deeply of the clean air. Radio chatter fed into ear buds but in the van the commander monitored their progress via a receiver unit Caplin could overhear. Minutes ticked by. Reports were deliberately kept minimal.

"Approaching gate. Two guards," came a rasping whisper.

Everyone around the commander tensed. Alert was what you did as a police officer.

Caplin thought of the house at the top of this hill. Police attention was wholly focused on the Golden Tigers, the hope they could break up the gang with full-scale arrests and recovery of a haul of stolen loot. His concentration remained on his American quarry, Frank Morrell.

He thought of what he'd said to Penelope Fitzpatrick, how he wanted to return her necklace to her and get the chance to send Morrell to prison. Standing here now, however, he wondered at the possibility of getting Morrell off to himself and retrieving the cash he knew the con man had collected by selling the million-dollar piece. There might still be a nice retirement in this for himself. He was savoring that thought when gunfire broke out.

EIGHTY-FOUR

THE DEADBOLT SLID back with a laborious click. Pen pushed the door open and flashed her light around the interior.

Three stone vaults, large rectangular boxes made to contain human remains. Aside from some carved stone plaques on the walls, the small room held nothing else. The Heist Ladies stared. No one had thought what it would mean to get the lid off one of these things, to possibly encounter a corpse.

"Where do we start?" Sandy asked.

Pen noticed the lid of one box sat less straight than the others. "This one's been moved."

Each woman took a corner and shoved with all her might. The stone lid might have moved a quarter inch.

"This could take forever," Gracie said.

"It could break our backs," Pen added, feeling a twinge already.

"Okay." Amber paced to the doorway and back. "We need to be smart about this. We don't have to remove it completely, right? Sliding one end of it aside just enough for a peek inside would be good enough."

They gathered at one end and concentrated their effort. The lid moved three inches.

"Again!"

Six more inches.

Amber aimed her light into the dark space. "Well, it's not a skeleton."

A noise from outside caught their attention. Gracie crept toward the door, her flashlight in her fist in case the guard needed another sedative.

Two more bursts.

"Oh my god, I think it's gunfire!" Gracie said.

EIGHTY-FIVE

FOUR SHOTS. An impossibly long twenty seconds of silence. Static on the radio. The Humvee moved into the lead position as the commander demanded a report from the eight SWAT men. Two more shots, then the radio crackled.

"The guards are down. Repeat—guards are down! We're opening the gate for you!"

The Humvee began to roll, followed quickly by the commander and the two vans. As the vehicles passed through the open gate, four of the SWAT team gripped handholds on their van and leaped to the back bumper for the ride. The other four had, presumably, run ahead on foot.

Caplin barely regained his seat before his van moved up the road. His nerves felt stretched taut, his stomach aflutter—not from the ride now. He tried to imagine what they would encounter when they reached the mansion.

EIGHTY-SIX

Now!" Sandy ordered, taking a surprisingly strong hand. "We have no time to dawdle here, ladies. Let's get this thing moved!"

No one questioned her authority. The bank manager in her had stepped to the forefront. With all four of them shoving, the vault lid swung aside. They stopped pushing when the large container was half open.

"Suitcases?" Tiny Amber had to stand on tiptoe to see into the depths. "Why would the vault have—?"

"It makes perfect sense," Pen said, reaching over the edge and tugging at the handle of the nearest one. "Bags like these would hold a lot of jewelry, plus the men could grab them and leave at a moment's notice."

A roar sounded in the distance, some type of large vehicle coming on fast.

"No time for explanations, girls. We've got to get out!" Sandy again spurring them on.

"I'm not leaving without my necklace if there's a chance it's here," Pen declared.

"Quickly then!"

They began digging with a vengeance. Two airline carry-on bags, three duffles. Pen unzipped a duffle bag which was filled with small pouches and boxes. Through the cloth of a gray velveteen bag she felt a familiar shape. She tore at the drawstring top and reached in.

"Oh, my." Gracie's breath caught.

"It's my piece," Pen said, her eyes glowing. As she touched the stones a vivid memory of her mother flashed forward, telling Pen about her grandfather's heroic efforts to get the family out of Russia at the most dangerous time, their trek through miles of wasteland until they reached the sea and stowed away aboard a freighter, all the while carrying the final remains of his once-thriving business.

"Pen, we need to—"

"Yes, you're right," she said.

"Wait," Amber said. "Look at these."

In one hand she held an exquisite enameled egg encrusted with sparkling gems. A small box revealed a diamond ring.

"I think these are the pieces we read about, things taken from individual owners. I want to return them."

"We can't possibly man—"

The roar of vehicles grew louder. Sandy stood at the doorway. "Men are surrounding the house. If we don't get out now we never will."

That settled it. Pen zipped the velveteen bag inside her coat pocket. Amber pocketed the egg and the ring. The rest of it would have to be sorted out by the police. Pen left with a backward glance, hoping the rightful owners would all get their things back.

EIGHTY-SEVEN

CAPLIN WAITED PATIENTLY—partly at the French commander's orders, partly because he really didn't want to be caught up in a gunfight. He needed to arrive at that beach in Mexico unscathed.

"All right, detective," the commander's lieutenant said, signaling him toward the front door of the white stone mansion.

Caplin entered a splendid wide hall, where the plush oriental carpet was somewhat askew and an expensive-looking vase lay in shards where it had hit the marble floor. On their stomachs, lying in a row were nine handcuffed men—some clothed only in their undershorts, some wearing nothing, all with sleep-rumpled hair.

"A couple of them woke in time to take shots at us," one of the SWAT team said to the commander. "Most were in their beds when we pulled them out."

"Sir, I'm afraid one of them got away," said another officer as he came down the staircase to Caplin's right. "I've got men searching the grounds."

The American detective looked closely at the faces but none was Frank Morrell. A wave of disappointment rose in him. Was Morrell right now running through the forest below? Or had he never been with the Tigers in the first place?

EIGHTY-EIGHT

PEN COULD HARDLY catch her breath by the time they reached the car. Abandoning the rope ladder, practically flying over the wall and down the trail—all to loud shouts and the flashing lights of police vehicles. It crossed her mind that someone—probably Caplin—might have reported that the women intended to get the necklace back. Had he set the local police on their trail?

Surely not. He had seemed so sincere when they spoke. On the other hand, Richard Stone, aka Frank Morrell, had been very sincere as well. Con men always were.

She felt an adrenaline crash by the time they arrived at their hotel. She fell into bed immediately, the velveteen bag clutched in her hand.

Surprisingly, Pen awoke at seven amazingly refreshed. She sat up in bed, taking a few minutes for herself, admiring her grandfather's handiwork once again. If only he'd lived long enough for her to have known him. The family faces came back to her, dear Mum and Dad. How they had struggled through the years and yet held firm to their resolve not to let Grandfather's masterpiece out of their hands. She felt a flush of mortification as she realized she would have been responsible for its loss.

Out in the suite's living room she heard voices. She donned a robe and joined the group.

"Late breaking story," Sandy read from a newspaper someone had brought in. "Nine members of the notorious Golden Tiger jewel theft ring arrested in a raid on the home of billionaire magnate Etienne LeBlanc."

"That accounts for the gunshots," Amber said, barely looking up from her laptop. "It says here that one man got away but police do not believe he was a member of the gang."

For some reason a picture of Frank Morrell flashed through Pen's mind. Oh, never mind, she thought.

"Just curious..." Gracie said. "Does that story mention anything about the jewels being recovered? I mean, specifically whether any items were *not* found?" She gave a pointed stare toward the Fabergé egg on the coffee table.

Amber smiled up at them all. "Nope. Not a word."

EIGHTY-NINE

FRANK MORRELL SMILED at himself in the mirror.

"Frankie, you still got it," he said to his reflection, giving one last dab at the scratch above his eyebrow with a wet paper towel. He tossed the towel into the trash bin, hoisting his new knapsack onto his shoulder. It was five a.m. and the train for Cannes would leave in twelve minutes.

One final glance to check his appearance. His image blurred a little as this morning's events replayed in his mind. Pandemonium when a bunch of cops raided the mansion on the hill. Frank's plan all along had been to sneak away; he'd been lifting useful items for the two days he'd been there. A couple shirts here, toiletry items there, the small backpack from a closet in what was probably the owner's son's room. His payoff from the necklace, of course, stacked neatly in banded packets at the bottom.

At three a.m. he'd been lying on the bed in the room they'd given him, watching the numbers tick by on a digital clock, unable to sleep but waiting for the perfect moment. The gang had spent most of the night talking quietly in a room with the door shut. He knew they were plotting their robbery of the gem show. Lub had ordered Frank to mind his own business; he would get his orders when they headed for the Acropolis the next day.

That didn't interest Frank anymore, not since he'd figured out about the mausoleum. His idea was to wait until they all fell asleep, either talk his way past or overpower the guard at the mausoleum, and help himself to a nice chunk of the loot. He knew they were keeping it there; why else would they station a guard where supposedly there were only dead old bones? Seriously. How stupid did they think he was?

Frankie's too smart—he don't fall for that shit, he said to himself.

About an hour after the mansion had gone quiet, conversations ending, bedroom doors closing, that's when all hell broke loose. And the moment the front door burst inward and he heard cops treading through the halls—that's when ol' Frankie bailed. Out his bedroom window and down a drainpipe. He'd glanced wistfully at the path to the mausoleum but screw it—no way was he hanging around for this deal. He ran through the woods and leaped over the wall, skirting the hubbub at the guard gate and made his way to the highway, where he'd given a late-night cabbie a sob story about being in a car accident and how his wife had been waiting for him at the train station for hours… the usual drill. It got him a lot of sympathy and a free cab ride to the station.

Now, all he had to do was make that train. He wouldn't hang around Cannes—it was too nearby and the situation was too hot. Before the end of the day, he planned to be in Spain or Italy—no plan was firm until he scoped out the situation—and by that night he'd somehow be on a plane for America. No one had any reason to associate him with the Golden Tigers, so the big robbery at the gem show would have them all scrambling for a bunch of Eastern European thugs, not some happy-go-lucky American who, they would be told, had won big in Monte Carlo and was heading home.

He left the men's room and walked toward the platform where his train should be rolling in just about now. He'd just passed through the archway and cleared security when he heard a familiar voice.

"Well, well, well, if it isn't Richard Stone. Er, I should say Frank Morrell." Detective Bill Caplin stepped out from behind a concrete pillar and blocked Frank's path.

"Do I know you?" Frank put on his most winsome look.

"Okay, play it that way," said Caplin. "I know you've got a pile of cash on you, and you know that you owe Todd Wainwright and me our shares. All I have to do is yell 'bomb' and there'll be a dozen men down your throat in a second."

"And down yours a minute later when they discover I don't have a bomb."

"But the cash will be of interest to them. And my police ID trumps whatever fake story you've got cooked up."

Frank glanced around. His train was filling up—he probably had thirty seconds to get aboard.

"How is young Todd anyway? Did he get canned? I never figured him for one who could keep up a story very well." Frank kept his eyes on Caplin but his attention was acutely focused on that train.

"Todd isn't my problem right now. You won't be either, if you pay me what you promised. Otherwise, my problem is getting you back to Arizona for prosecution."

Frank only caught half of that last sentence. At a moment when the crowd thinned, he bolted, dashing aboard the train a split-second before the doors closed.

NINETY

BILL CAPLIN SMILED as the train pulled away. "Right where I want you, jerk face."

He tapped a contact name on his phone. "The five-twelve train from Nice to Cannes," he said to the gendarme at the other end.

He fumbled to upload the photo he'd taken of Frank before his quarry noticed him, knowing the French police were at the ready to capture the American who'd eluded them at the raid on the LeBlanc mansion in the early hours of the morning. A passing teen smiled at the old man's dilemma and pointed to the correct icon—the photo was on its way.

No doubt Frank Morrell had left enough of his fingerprints and DNA around the house—a few stray hairs in the bathroom, a used toothbrush, prints on a drinking glass. Too bad there was no one to testify that he wasn't really a member of the gang.

Caplin had heard French prisons were unbearable. Dark, dank stone cells a man couldn't stand up in, where they threw you in naked with a bucket for your waste and twice-a-day bread and water to eat. Old Frankie would be begging for extradition to the United States within a day or two.

And if he somehow *didn't* get convicted by association with the Golden Tigers, Caplin had an extradition order ready and waiting; it could be filed on a moment's notice.

Too bad for Frankie Morrell.

He sighed deeply. *Too bad for me, too.* With the case in the hands of international police, Caplin knew he and Todd Wainwright would never receive their shares from the Philpont robbery. His vision of the boat in Mexico dimmed.

Just as well, he thought. The shadow of the stolen money would hang over him, and he couldn't imagine living out his retirement years looking over his shoulder.

NINETY-ONE

PENELOPE'S TELEPHONE RANG as she was setting out a wedge of excellent aged English cheddar along with wine glasses and a Cabernet she'd been saving for a special occasion. It had been all she could do not to break it out when Benton picked her up at the airport three days ago. Her jubilation over retrieving her heirloom had buoyed her mood throughout the long transatlantic flight. But tonight was an even more special occasion.

"Mrs. Fitzpatrick, how are you? Bill Caplin here."

"I recognized your voice, detective. Or have you retired already?"

"Paperwork's in the pipeline. I'll be out of here at the end of the month."

"I hope it will be everything you've been wanting."

There was a pause before he spoke. "It's been a positive month. I wanted to let you know Frank Morrell was arrested in the south of France and immediately agreed to extradition."

Pen felt a cloud pass over her jubilant mood. "Will I need to testify?"

"The evidence alone will probably be enough. I will most likely be called back and I'll let you know if you're needed. I'm sorry to say your necklace was not recovered among the pile of jewelry found at the estate where most of the gang was arrested." He paused for a long beat. "I have a feeling you already knew that, though."

Pen quickly changed the subject. "What about the couple on Grand Cayman? Will he face charges for that crime as well?"

"Hard to say. So far, I gather Tom and Danielle Anderson haven't pressed charges. The man seems to have a blind spot about admitting his gullibility and the extent of the loss. If he doesn't report the crime and sign a statement, well, there's not much the police can do. Whether they follow up or not, it will take a long time to figure out all of Morrell's various bank accounts and find a paper trail showing where their money went."

Pen heard a vehicle in her driveway.

"I have guests," she said, wishing him well, both in sorting out Morrell's crimes and in his upcoming retirement.

A second car arrived before she got to the door. The Heist Ladies had arrived and it was time to open that special bottle.

NINETY-TWO

SANDY WAITED A moment for Gracie and Amber to step out of Gracie's car, and the three approached Pen's front door together.

"Welcome! Welcome," said Pen, spreading her arms wide to embrace each of them in turn. "Is everyone doing well after the long journey?"

There were a few groans about jetlag but also smiles all around. Pen ushered them into her living room where the wine and cheese waited on the coffee table.

"I'd love to hear about the return of the other items we recovered," she said as she poured wine into four glasses. "Reports?"

Amber went first. She had wanted to stop in New York on her way home to check in with relatives, especially her aging grandmother. The diamond ring's owner in Manhattan was an easy addition to her trip.

"The lady reminded me of you, Pen. Classy," Amber said. "She lived in this most fantastic apartment and you could tell the place was sort of a shrine to her husband who had died twenty-five years ago. Mrs. Rubenstein, her name is—she was so happy to get the ring back. She told me it was her engagement ring. Can you imagine? A young couple with the money to have something like that? She actually cried when I handed it to her. She said she'd given up hope of ever seeing it again—that's when she really cried." Amber took a deep breath. "Anyway, she made a point of saying there's a reward in it for each of us and she will be eternally grateful."

Sandy had volunteered to carry the priceless Fabergé egg to its owner in Virginia, as the stopover had also given her a chance for a quick visit with an old friend.

"Congressman Williams wasn't nearly as emotional as your Mrs. Rubenstein, but he was clearly very thankful. Over tea, his wife confided that he'd invested a great deal in the egg hoping it would grow in value. It represents a large portion of their estate. Even though he was sort of brusque about it, I could tell the wife was very relieved. I'm really glad we were able to help."

Nods and smiles all around. "Those stories really made it all worthwhile," Gracie said.

Pen raised her glass. "You don't know what this means to me," she told them. "I, too, would like each of you to have a reward for helping me. In my entire life, I've not had friends who would dream of going to such lengths. Each of you is a treasure I will always value."

They all nodded a little self-consciously. "I don't know about the rest of you," said Sandy, "but this is the most fun I've had in ages."

"I don't want a reward," Gracie said. "I agree, this has been huge fun. The adventure and the friendship is reward enough for me."

"To us—the Heist Ladies!" Amber said, raising her glass. "It was great knowing all of you and pulling off such a successful job. I'm kind of sad it's ending."

As the glasses clinked, a loud sniff came from Sandy. There were a few moist eyes in the room.

"You know what I'd like," said Gracie, her expression

sober. "I'd like to stay together and do this again. Think about it. We could really help people who have lost something of value—it doesn't have to be jewels or wealth. There are a lot of ordinary people out there who have been taken in by someone, people who can't afford the losses they've suffered. When the law doesn't help them, maybe we can."

"I like that idea," said Pen with a catch in her throat.

Amber's eyes sparkled. "I love it!"

The doorbell rang. Pen set her glass down and went to answer. A delivery man held out a flat, rectangular package, for which she signed. When she glanced at the label she saw it was from her publisher.

"My goodness," she said, ripping at the tape as she walked back into the room with the other ladies. "With our recent excitement, I'd forgotten all about this. The edits were done months ago—it's my newest book."

The others crowded around to take a look at the glossy cover.

"Well, this means I need to start writing a new story." Pen's smile glowed as she looked around at her friends. "And now I have an idea what it will be about."

* * * * *

CONNIE SHELTON is the author of more than 30 novels and three non-fiction books. She is the creator of the Novel In A Weekend™ writing course, and was a contributor to *Chicken Soup For the Writer's Soul*. She and her husband live in northern New Mexico with their two dogs.

Get a free Connie Shelton e-book when you sign up for Connie's mystery newsletter at connieshelton.com.

Plus, receive advance information on new books, along with a chance at prizes, discounts and other mystery news!

Contact by email: connie@connieshelton.com
Follow Connie Shelton on Twitter, Pinterest and Facebook